The Fire Arrow

BY RICHARD S. WHEELER
FROM TOM DOHERTY ASSOCIATES

The Fire Arrow

A BARNABY SKYE NOVEL

RICHARD S. WHEELER

A TOM DOHERTY ASSOCIATES BOOK / NEW YORK

This is a work of fiction. All the characters and events portrayed in this book are either products of the author's imagination or are used fictitiously.

THE FIRE ARROW

Copyright © 2006 by Richard S. Wheeler

Excerpt from *Canyon of Bones* © 2007 by Richard S. Wheeler

Edited by Dale Walker

A Forge Book
Published by Tom Doherty Associates, LLC
175 Fifth Avenue
New York, NY 10010

www.tor.com

Forge® is a registered trademark of Tom Doherty Associates, LLC.

ISBN-13: 978-0-765-35172-2
ISBN-10: 0-765-35172-2

First Edition: May 2006
First Mass Market Edition: February 2007

Printed in the United States of America

0 9 8 7 6 5 4 3 2 1

For John Fryer, my friend and counselor

The Fire Arrow

one

Death rose out of the night. A rush of hooves on frosted ground. A chilling howl. Whickering horses. A faint rip, thud, gasp, and sigh. The earth trembled.

Barnaby Skye struggled awake. Violence had struck the camp. There was only the thin leather of his lodge protecting him, and that was no protection at all. Victoria gasped.

He sat up, threw the thick buffalo robe aside, jamming away the sleep. Dead ash, embers gone, only blackness inside his lodge. He peered through the smoke hole. Bright moonlit night. Stars scattering through the October skies. The Judith River country, aglow in the moon, full of buffalo; full of death.

He knew then. A raid. Blackfeet, who else? The horses already gone but now a worse evil, the enemy in the midst of the Crow hunting camp, every man for himself, death stalking the camp.

He felt about for his Hawken, didn't find it, but found his belaying pin, that weapon of choice for generations of British seamen. A polished hickory club, thick, heavy, and flared to protect the hand or stop its passage through a ship's fitting. He grasped it just in time. The flap burst open and a dark force smashed in, swinging savagely. A battle-axe slashed the lodge cover, bedded itself in the robes inches from Skye. A knife glinted. Skye jabbed first, felt the belaying pin connect, then smashed hard just as a knife whipped by. Caught the warrior at the base of the neck. Skye jammed the stick into his face, heard teeth snap. The warrior retreated, howling, staggering out into the moonlight.

Skye sprang up, pushed outside. The last of the Blackfeet were retreating north. The moonlight caught shadowy forms retreating into the gloom. A few half-naked Crows, kin of Skye's wife Victoria, chased on foot, carrying lances, only to fall back as arrows fell among them. One gasped and tumbled to the frosted grass.

Skye was barefoot but he scarcely noticed. He did not see a horse anywhere. His own two buffalo runners, picketed beside his lodge, had vanished. In the distance, the thrumming of two hundred hooves diminished and died. Nine lodges of Crows, and not a horse among them, unless a few escaped the herding of the Blackfeet. Crow warriors armed themselves, but it was too late.

It had happened so fast. The Blackfeet had overwhelmed or tricked or killed the night herders, the village youths not yet old enough for battle, and made off with the prized horses. But their triumph would not be complete without visiting some death or injury on the hated Crows. So they had raided the camp on Louse Creek after driving off the ponies, entering lodges, counting coup, killing if they could, making a great victory out of it. Death in the night.

The hush suddenly returned, and it was as if there had been no violence, no death, no injury. Several Crow warriors hunted for horses, trotting here and there. Women, along for the skinning and hide-scraping and preserving, peered fearfully from lodge doors. Silvery moonlight flooded the encampment, making the lodges almost as visible as in bright day. And now they wailed, for there were bodies sprawled grotesquely on the frosty hardpan.

Skye studied the murk from whence a last hurrah of arrows might come, but he saw only the silvered limbs of autumn-bare trees and brush along the creek. It had been a poor place to camp. He trotted toward a knot of people gathered around one of the fallen.

It was the boy, Knot-on-Top, and he was dead, pierced by a Blackfoot arrow. His lifeless eyes studied the moon. Hardly a dozen years had this man-child lived. Three women knelt beside him, including his mother, Wolf Dreams. She did not wail. She sat mutely, cradling her son's arm in her lap.

Grim warriors guarded the perimeter, but it was too late. Grief had come to this buffalo-hunting camp. The fletching and the dyed rings on the arrow protruding from the chest of Knot-on-Top told the story to anyone who knew of these things: Piegan. The most numerous and sometimes most pacific of the Blackfeet bands, and all the more dangerous for that.

"Aieaa," muttered Otter, the headman who had led this hunting party to this desolate end.

Skye sorrowed, and trotted toward another downed Crow, fearing the worst. He was not mistaken. Sees Dawn, the other boy guarding the herd, lay facedown, his head cleaved by a war axe, perhaps the very one that nearly chopped Skye's head in two. He would never see another dawn. He was Victoria's nephew and clan-brother. She would weep and in her own way vow death and disgrace upon whatever Blackfoot had slaughtered one of her own. Where was she? Skye didn't see her, and wondered about it.

Off in the murk, several Crow men returned leading a few horses. So some had escaped the Blackfeet net after all, slipped into brush in the night. Skye studied the small band, looking for his two dun buffalo runners and not seeing them. He owned only three horses including one for Victoria, and was poor by Crow standards, for a man's worth was measured in horses. Skye had neither the skills to capture any nor the means to buy any.

He wondered where Victoria was. She must have been deep asleep. He would check on her. There was little he could do here in the frost, as the moon bathed the fallen. He had some small reputation among the Crows as a valued warrior and hunter, but he could not speak their tongue enough to make friends or take part in the village life. It was time to check on Victoria, whose silence worried him.

He hastened to his small lodge, a place shared only by his woman, and crawled in. Instantly he knew something was wrong. He dropped to his knees beside her, shocked by her long silences, and her brief desperate gasps for air, and the strange twist of her body, her head cocked backward, mouth open to suck life into her lungs.

Too dark! He could see nothing.

"Victoria!"

She gasped.

"Victoria! What?"

She spasmed, some sort of shudder rolling down her small, lithe body. He tugged the buffalo robe aside, and then he couldn't pull it free. The robe was pinned to her. Then he discovered the thin, cruel wand of wood rising out of the robes, the feathered end of an arrow, the same arrow that had awakened him with its soft rip through the lodge cover.

"Victoria!" The sight of her, so dim in blackness, seared him. He needed fire!

He scrambled for wood, found some just outside the lodge door that she had gathered in the evening, grabbed some handfuls, set them upon the cold firepit in the center of the lodge, found his powder horn lying next to his Hawken, dribbled some over the kindling, hunted blindly through his possibles until he found his flint and steel, fitted the steel through his ham-thick fingers, and struck sparks savagely. The loose powder flared, blinding him.

She trembled and gasped.

One small stick caught, and then another, small blue light, and then welcome yellow. He could see. She wasn't looking at him; she stared straight up, a death rictus twisting her lips, her eyes sightless.

"Oh, no . . ."

Fire at last, tender flickering light casting its gloomy rays upon the small household of Barnaby Skye. The arrow had pierced the robe, and pierced Victoria under the robe. He could not see where and was afraid to touch her or it. She gasped again. Her lungs weren't working. Swiftly he clasped his great trembling hands over her chest, pushed air out, and let her suck air in. Something was stopping her lungs from drawing air in and out. Her face was blue. The fire wavered and started to die. He thrust more brush over the dwindling flame until it flared again.

She wasn't breathing. He squeezed her chest and she gasped. He pushed and pulled her ribs, making air move.

He needed help, but where could he turn?

He summoned words and yelled.

"Come!" he cried into the moonlight.

Someone did come, a woman whose face he couldn't see. Then he heard talk, and two women crawled into his lodge and took it all in with swift glances. He knew the women: old Makes Rain and her sister, Lifts the Doe. Makes Rain was a blessing; she was reputed to have great powers of healing. But she was also no friend of Victoria. For Makes Rain didn't believe that a woman of the Crow people should marry someone else.

She glanced sharply at Skye, and then produced a small, worn paring knife that had seen much work at this buffalo camp. Slowly she inserted the knife into the robe at the place where the arrow had punctured it, and sawed through the robe, little by little, while Victoria gasped, until at last the robe was freed and she and Lifts the Doe could peel it away from Victoria, ever so carefully.

Victoria was gasping again, and Skye slowly squeezed and released her ribs until she was breathing, if the slow suck of air into her lungs might be called breath. The Blackfeet arrow protruded from her abdomen, just under the ribs, lit by the dying flame. Blood had collected around the wide slit of a wound, staining her trade-cloth chemise. Gently, the old woman sliced away the cloth until the wound lay exposed. The arrow had pierced upward two or three inches from the abdomen, no doubt cutting into those muscles that operated her lungs. A broad steel point, probably a Hudson's Bay trade item, had buried itself in her, and there was no way to remove it without starting a rush of red, red blood.

They stared, helpless, at that fatal shaft. An inch more would have killed her but the lodge wall and robe had slowed the thrust. Victoria lay gasping, doomed unless she could breathe, and breathe soon.

two

Victoria gazed up at Skye, helpless and desolate and in pain. Skye compressed her chest again, and again she sucked air; a moment's life. But she was sinking. And he could do so little for this woman he loved so much.

Tears had gathered in her eyes; he could see the wetness in the flickering light. She was struggling for life but her lungs had quit her.

"Victoria. I must pull that arrow."

She nodded.

"More fire," he said to Makes Rain, in her own tongue. She stared, not liking the commands from a young man not of her people. But then she nodded, slipped outside, brought in wood, laid it carefully on the flames, fed it until the fire rose hot.

Skye squeezed Victoria's chest again, and again, and again, making breath with his hands. Then he withdrew his thick-bladed buffalo skinning knife and laid the blade on the flame.

Long ago, aboard the ships of the Royal Navy, he had assisted the ship's surgeon a few times. Perhaps he was chosen because he could read; most seamen couldn't. He had watched awful things, limbs sawed off, the trepanning of a skull, and the cauterization of wounds.

A red-hot knife blade was all that would stop the bleeding once he wrestled the arrow from her body. He had no curved surgical needle, no gut or string or thread to close her wound.

He waited for the knife to heat. The women stared, uncertain of his intent, waiting for death. Lifts the Doe began a low death song, certain she was witnessing the last moments of Victoria's flickering life.

The flame was slow to heat the knife, cold and smoky. Skye pumped her lungs, forcing her to suck in air, hating the pain he was causing, hating the worse pain to come, the blood, the desperation. He had only the knife. If it failed to cauterize, she would perish.

Then he took hold of the arrow.

"Victoria, this will hurt, and I can't help it."

She could not speak. She stared up at him, her desperation stamped across her features.

He tugged. The arrow didn't budge. She screamed. The women held her down. That was good. He tugged harder, twisting the arrowhead slightly, fearful of losing the point. If the shaft came free without the point, Victoria was dead.

He rocked it back and forth, trying to increase the angle each time, while she shuddered and convulsed. It did no good; the tip was buried deep in her flesh.

He wept. She convulsed now, and no grip of the women could stay her from writhing in fearsome pain.

Skye was sweating; the lodge had turned unbearably hot.

He pulled upward, fearful of losing the tip. Blood gouted from the wound. Every time he moved the shaft, blood welled up, a grim red warning of what would come.

Victoria never spoke. She didn't have air enough to speak. He remembered to compress her chest again, and felt her suck air as it expanded. She was in utter torment. He was sickened by what he was inflicting on her.

Nothing was working. Time was dwindling. He slumped over her, pressing his big stubby hands over her abdomen, quieting himself, drawing his own failing strength from some place beyond his merely mortal powers.

He lifted the arrow gently, trying to draw it out by exactly the same path it entered. It gave ground. He had not lost the arrowhead. He tried again, pulling along the trajectory of its entry as best he could tell. The arrow resisted one long dreadful moment, and then slid steadily outward. Then, at last, it came free. The tip was thick with gore. Now bright blood hemorrhaged from her, pooling outward, spreading over her abdomen, draining into the brown robes.

But she gulped for air.

He grabbed the knife, feeling the fierce heat around the bone handle. It was not cherry-hot but it would have to do. He wiped her wound free with one hand and then swiftly brought the broad tip down over the wound, or at least what he could see of it, because blood obscured it. The heated tip pressed into her flesh, spitting steam and blood and frying her skin.

She screamed, a scream so heartrending he loathed himself, yet within that scream was breath. He held the fiery tip to the puncture, feeling flesh sear under it, feeling his own sweat roll down his face. The women held her, kept her from writhing free.

He lifted the tip. The blood had stopped. The wound was a mass of bubbling, seared flesh. The cauterization had taken hold. If she didn't die from internal bleeding, and if her lungs were no longer paralyzed, she might live.

She still writhed. He put the blade back into the fire, fearful that he might need it again. But no more blood oozed from that angry patch of Victoria's side.

He fought back tears. But there was no time for tears. This camp was still in mortal peril. The Piegans might return anytime to finish what they had started.

Makes Rain stared dourly at Skye. Her face told him that this was a thing she had never seen, something sinister, something not known to the People. He didn't care. He watched Victoria's chest, watched the erratic working of her lungs, the long, alarming pauses, followed by sudden spasms of breathing. It would get better. The arrow point was gone. He picked up the bloody arrow, memorizing the thin bands of paint that circled it, the sure mark of its owner. He would remember that paint, that signature, that fletching, this very arrow. And someday when he found its owner, there would be a reckoning.

The cauterization held. Lifts the Doe was wiping away the blood. Victoria writhed, unable to cope with the pain. Gently he wiped her brow and placed his thick hand over her forehead, offering what little he had, which was only love.

The lodge was hot. But he would not step into the icy night. Not until she was quiet, not until the worst had passed, not until she could speak to him, for she had not spoken a single word from the time the arrow struck until now. He held that sinister stick in his hand, not wanting to set it aside.

He had saved her, maybe. For all these years they had walked the paths together. He was a Londoner who could never go home; she had befriended him, loved him, and also taught him to live as the Crow people lived, hunting and gathering, fending off hostile tribes but sometimes raiding other people, gathering furs and robes to trade at the posts run by white men.

He had not been a good provider. How little he knew of hunting and war when he first fled from the Royal Navy and made his way inland to this remote fastness of North America. Much of what he now knew, she had taught him. His trapping friends had taught him more about surviving in the wilds, but there was always the day of reckoning, when the pelts or hides that were the fruits of a year's hard toil were placed on a trader's counter and exchanged for a pitiful few things, powder and shot, a few knives, and trinkets for her. Trapping hadn't been much of a living.

But his free-roaming life had been immeasurably sweeter than the one from which he fled, and each day he rejoiced in his liberty, for he was a sovereign of the wilds and she was his queen, and somehow their love, which stretched across vast barriers of understanding, had deepened and matured.

Now she hovered between life and death, her very soul afloat over her, ready to wing away into the awful void. She breathed, if raggedly. The old women sat stoically, watching Victoria wrestle with death, even as the rest of the night slipped away. Skye heard occasional voices. Several times a Crow man or woman had spoken to Makes Rain, talking so swiftly he could not catch their words. But he knew she was giving them reports on Victoria and in turn receiving word about the condition, and defenses, of the Crow hunting camp.

And so the night passed. He lay down beside her and placed a hand again on her forehead, hoping somehow to convey to her that he was watching over her and that if she had the will to live, she would live, and there would be many more sweet days and sweeter nights.

He had taken her east once, and she had seen the cities and habitats of the Americans, and that had given her understandings that eluded others of her people. She didn't like it there even though she had marveled at the wonders of the Europeans who had settled the United States. And she wasn't herself until she was back in the home country of her people, mistakenly called the Crows by English-speaking explorers and mountain men and traders.

He slipped the cooled knife back into its sheath at his belt, and sat quietly through the quickening dawn. When light poured through the smoke hole, the old women stirred, for they too had kept a vigil all through that night. Makes Rain said something softly that Skye didn't understand, but then she took one of his hands and clasped it between hers, and rubbed her cheek with it, and Skye understood.

The fire dwindled. Sun caught the lodgepoles. Outside, the hunting party was salvaging what it could of the disaster, which wasn't very much. They would not have horses to haul away the tons of pemmican, hides, and jerky as well as the households of the Crow people.

Skye continued to sit cross-legged beside Victoria, never abandoning her. But soon after dawn, her breathing changed, grew less labored, more steady, less desperate, and he sensed she had weathered the ordeal. If somehow he could keep her quiet for a while she would heal.

But how could he do that? He and she would be alone in their lodge, on the edge of Blackfeet country, while the Crow people journeyed back to their own ground, most of them without horses. And Skye had none, not even one for a travois that might haul her away to safety. The trouble had barely begun.

three

Victoria had not spoken since the Piegan arrow had pierced her side, but some ineffable change had come with daylight, some slight progress. Skye quietly jammed his stovepipe hat on his long locks and stepped into the morning, which came late this time of year, and surveyed the camp on Louse Creek.

He counted seven horses, all that had escaped the Blackfeet herders. Nine lodges, including his own. His horses, two buffalo runners and Victoria's mare, were gone. Several young warriors stood vigil on the surrounding hilltops but this Crow camp could offer only a pathetic defense against the Blackfeet if they should return.

Skye had the only good rifle in the camp, though its headman had an old trade musket and another warrior had an ancient Northwest smoothbore. They were defenseless and the Crows knew it. Perhaps the lurking Blackfeet knew it too.

Around him, the Crows were preparing to abandon this place of bad medicine. They would walk. All seven remaining horses were being fitted with travois. These would carry the precious lodge covers, but not the poles, and what few possessions each family had brought along, including some of the abundant buffalo meat from the successful hunt.

But much would be left behind, including vast stores of fresh pemmican, some jerked meat, and scores of fleshed buffalo hides. These would be cached but no one knew whether there would be anything left when the Crows returned. Animals were skilled at breaking into caches, as were other peoples. In hours after the Crows left, this place of slaughter would be overrun by wolves that would devour gut piles, discarded bone and meat. Anything left by the wolves would be dinner for coyotes, or eagles and hawks, or a dozen other raptors and predators. All night, every night, the mournful howl of wolves had circumscribed the camp on Louse Creek.

Skye would stay. He would keep his vigil, he would sit beside the woman he loved, and if it was their fate to be overwhelmed alone, far from help, then he would die beside her. Not that he wished that result, but it was the measure of his iron-hard commitment to her. He and Victoria would walk through fortune and misfortune together.

This was a place of death. The families of the two dead youths were preparing them for their spirit journeys in deep silence. The women would wail their grief later, but now they were wrapping the poor young men, Sees Dawn and Knot-on-Top, in blankets and tying the bundles in thong. Two others were injured, sitting mutely, wrapped in bloody trade cloth, their faces maps of pain. The surviving men were lashing lodgepoles to the limbs of nearby cottonwoods, preparing a place where these young men would be given to the sun.

Grief lay heavy upon this Crow camp, but so perilous was their condition that it was boxed into the souls of the people as they struggled with death, loss, abandonment of wealth and food, hides, tallow, lodges, and horses. Bad medicine here. Something felt in their bones. The headman, Otter, lived under a cloud; he who organized this hunt had offended the powers that animated the world.

Skye said nothing. He had not fully mastered the difficult Crow tongue, though he could communicate well enough and was fluent in sign language, filling in with his hands when his tongue failed him.

He found Otter, the headman who had told them all that his medicine was good; there would be a fine hunt, much meat, many hides, from the buffalo brothers. There had been all of that and more. Otter stared dourly as Skye approached, a small curt nod acknowledging the presence of the alien Englishman in this Crow camp.

"You are leaving?" Skye asked.

Otter stared and finally nodded.

"We must stay."

"You will be alone. I cannot spare anyone to stay with you."

"I know that."

"After she dies, cache what you can. We will return for it."

"She will not die."

"I am told she will."

Skye sensed the thing that always puzzled him about the Crows, a fatalism. Once the future was mysteriously foreseen, all one could do was surrender to it.

"I will bring her when I can."

"You stopped the blood with fire, so I am told. This is a strange thing."

Skye wanted to tell this headman of ship's surgeons and what few things he had learned in the Royal Navy, but he knew that would tax his ability to convey thoughts in the

Crow tongue so he let it pass. Let the Crows think he possessed medicine.

"I have seen it done," was all Skye said.

"We will leave soon. But first there is the thing that must be
done," Otter said. He was alluding to the rites of passage for
the dead, the surrendering of the fallen to the spirit land, the
long trail to the stars. They had died in battle, bravely, with
great honor, and their path would be strewn with petals.

Skye studied the anonymous ridges of the Judith country,
half expecting a howling war party to crest one and bring
death to the wounded Crows. But this cloudless and windless
day was as silent as nature ever got. The Blackfeet were content
with their victory, a great one. Upward of fifty horses, many
coups, and who knows what else? The Blackfeet were a proud
and dangerous people, noble in bearing, and Skye admired
them. But he was a Crow by adoption and marriage and now
his heart was given to these who had taken him in and welcomed him in their lodges. The Crow were a proud people too.

The men had finished making the palls for the dead. These
were lodgepoles tied across the limbs of the cottonwoods
along Louse Creek. A silence befell the camp. There was no
medicine man among them, so Otter led the way down to the
creek, through a quick silence, as the people collected behind
him. Then, Pretty Weasel, the father of Knot-on-Top, lifted the
blanketed form of his son to the scaffold and gently settled it
there. Within the blanket was his boy, and also his son's
amulets, his medicine things, and offerings from his kinfolk.

None of Sees Dawn's kin were present this hunting trip, so
Otter and Pretty Weasel lifted his heavy form upward until it
rested beside his friend and clan-brother Knot-on-Top. Now
the women wept while the rest stood gravely around.

These two would be mourned in the Crow winter camp on

the Musselshell River. But now there was no time; the buffalo hunters must walk away from the lost, whose names would never again be spoken. Walk away, three days and then some, walk away to their lodges and then mourn.

Hastily the small congregation loaded lodge covers onto the travois and hoisted parfleches to their backs, and hid what they could under a caved-in cutbank. The cache wouldn't fool any animal, and probably not any foe either, but there wasn't any choice.

Otter approached Skye, who watched them load, cradling his Hawken in his arms.

"If you are not back before the moon is full, we will know, and grieve," he said.

"We'll be back."

"We'll send help."

"We need horses. A travois for Many Quill Woman," he said, alluding to Victoria's Crow name.

"What are you going to do?"

"Make this camp disappear. Hang the meat as far away as I can drag it. Scatter ashes."

"And our clan-sister?"

"I will be with her night and day, and when I can move her a little, I will."

Otter nodded. Skye liked the man, who now bore a heavy burden, for nothing worse than bad medicine could life's fortunes inflict on a Crow headman.

He watched them flee, an unseemly haste in them as they staggered away, carrying too much, the horses straining under the loads of the travois. The poles bent under the overload and plowed furrows even in the thawed ground. Skye wondered how long it would be before travois poles snapped or horses broke down.

Then they disappeared over the ridge to the south and he stood alone in a ruined camp. Tonight the wolves would come.

He had heavy work ahead, but he would see to Victoria first. He studied the horizons for movement, saw only a circling of ravens, and then ducked into his small dark lodge. The fire had died and it was cold.

She lay on her back, awake, staring up at him, her body twisted slightly as if to shelter the wound in her side.

"Dammit, Skye, you hurt me," she said softly.

"I was afraid you would never speak again."

"I hurt."

"You're alive."

"Sonofabitch!" she said. She used white men's expletives promiscuously, usually to vent anger.

He settled on his knees beside her. "I had to stop the blood."

"I couldn't breathe."

He lifted the wicked arrow with its red-stained iron tip, and showed it to her.

"This far in," he said, showing how far the blood had soaked it. "We will keep this arrow."

She stared, and he saw a wetness gather at the corner of her eyes.

"Now that you saved my life, Skye, I am your slave. That is how such a debt must be paid."

"You're my slave forever," he said. "And I am yours. How many times have you saved mine?"

"I am tired," she said, closing her eyes.

four

Skye checked her wound, fearing most of all fresh bleeding. He pulled the robe back, baring her tawny flesh. It was a small wound, barely an inch across, but blistered and angry all around where the heat of his knife had scorched her. The ugly wound itself suppurated, and the flesh in all directions was red and dark. But she didn't bleed; her lifeblood was not leaking into the brown buffalo robes.

He could do no more. She lay with closed eyes enduring unimaginable pain. He slipped outside into a quiet November afternoon. There was much to do. The ribs of the abandoned lodges poked the sky, and he intended to dismantle them. His safety depended on concealment. The creek-side encampment had a haunted quality, with the cones of lodgepoles mute testimony to flight and trouble.

Louse Creek was a good place to hide because it was notched in the floor of the basin, but a bad place to be caught in an ambush for there was no way to escape the valley of death. Hide and be safe; be discovered and die. It was that simple.

Both the Blackfeet and Crows used four-pole lodge frames;

that is, four poles were tied together and spread into a pyramid, and other poles laid in afterward. But there were subtle differences even in the small hunting lodges, and Skye knew that any Blackfoot warrior would see in a glance that this was a Crow camp. Skye would remedy that swiftly by dismantling the ghost village and piling brush around his own lodge. The lodgepoles would make firewood.

There was household debris abandoned in flight, and he marveled at the number of good robes left behind, simply lying in the grass. He salvaged several and took them into his own small lodge. In all the years of living in the wilderness as a mountain man and as a squaw man, he had never slept comfortably on hard ground, especially cold ground. He thought of it as a failing. The Yank mountain men seemed to adapt to such hardship, but the hammocks on the ships of the Royal Navy were far more comfortable. Now he and Victoria would sleep on several thick warm robes and have even more to pull over them when he could not build a fire.

The Judith country was rife with buffalo this year, and other parties would be hunting here. Blackfeet most of all, but also Gros Ventres and Flatheads, perhaps Kootenai, or even Shoshones or Bannocks. This time of year the buffalo broke into smaller bands so they could forage better; in the summer they collected into giant herds. Hunters from all the tribes relished this time of year when they could surround and slaughter the smaller bands. The Crows had thought to make meat, collect hides, produce pemmican and jerky, and fill leather pouches with valuable tallow. They knew the risks of coming this far north but knew the risks were worth the reward. This time they were wrong.

Skye studied the horizons, seeing nothing. But he kept his percussion-lock Hawken close, and did not neglect his powder horn. He was a stocky man, usually clean-shaven, whose hair hung loose about his head, and whose blue eyes had a way of squinting at distant things and making out shapes and forms not visible to others.

Quickly he dismantled the ghost lodges, pulling the poles away, and then dropping and untying the four-pole pyramids that formed the core of the structures. These had been erected by Absaroka women who were very good at setting up a lodge and making it comfortable.

It took only a half hour to drop the skeletons. He dragged the scattered lodgepoles into nearby brush, hidden from casual sight. He hid debris, kicked dirt over the ash of cookfires, buried wastes, filled two canteens with the water of Louse Creek, and saw to his meat. The Crows had abandoned two forequarters of buffalo, now hanging from a cottonwood tree, well above the reach of any animal except a bear. They were heavy, and bent the limb and threatened to break the braided elkskin ropes suspending them. He and Victoria would have ample food if these were not disturbed. But even smaller creatures, including ravens and magpies and eagles, could demolish the meat, as could a sustained chinook, or warm period. Except for some pemmican that was what would have to sustain him, for he could not risk a rifle shot.

This campsite didn't feel right. He swore a dozen eyes were studying him from the hills guarding the valley. He ached to move his own lodge deep into brush, but not yet, not until he could be sure that Victoria could be carried without breaking open that arrow wound. For the moment, he would stay where he was, keep vigil, and hope no hunting party found him during this time of healing.

His gaze lifted constantly to the ridges, knowing how many hunters were flocking through the Judith country this time of year when hides were prime and buffalo were fat. But all he saw was anonymous blue sky, an occasional crow or hawk, and all he heard was the occasional whisper of wind eddying down the shallow valley of Louse Creek, wind with snow on its breath, wind that had only recently flowed over the white-covered Moccasin Mountains as the trappers called them, or the Big Belts, or the Highwoods, not far from the great falls of the Missouri.

A flock of noisy magpies, iridescent black and white, settled on the abandoned camp, making dinner out of scraps of meat, bits of flesh scraped from fresh hides, and a thousand bugs shaken from the fresh hides as the women worked them. One magpie stood apart on a low branch, and then flew to a perch close to Skye's lodge and sat quietly. Skye understood and rejoiced.

He slipped into his lodge and found Victoria staring at him from pain-filled eyes.

"The magpies are here, and one waits outside," he said.

She nodded, and her response disappointed him. The magpie was her spirit helper, her counselor and guardian.

"The magpies, dozens of them," he said, but she simply stared in the dusk of the lodge.

He felt a certain foreboding and placed a hand on her forehead. She was burning up. Fever, not unexpected after such a wounding.

Now the magpie outside seemed more ominous; as if this one were beginning a vigil. Skye felt a desolation crawl through him. He found a small cook pot, headed for the creek, filled it with icy water, and returned. The magpie was gone. He slipped inside, soaked an old shirt in the cold, and laid it across her forehead. She moaned, not liking the cruel chill, but he persisted. Runaway fever could kill.

Rhythmically, he soaked the rag, applied it, and soaked it again as daylight waned, early at this time of year, and settled into utter blackness. But he did not pause. She was restless, burning up, and had fallen into that profound silence once again.

"Live," he whispered.

As the northern evening fell, he thought of the lithe woman who had become his mate. How he had met her. How they had loved, in spite of all the barriers of language and culture. How she had plunged bravely into his life as a brigade leader for the American Fur Company. How he had struggled to find a home among her Crow people. How she had picked up trapper language and had become fluently profane, occasionally startling the Yanks who ventured into these wilds, the missionary, the Indian agent, the fur company owner. He smiled then. And smiled as he thought of the thousand times she had drawn him into her golden arms and held him in the sweetness of the night, or in a sunny bower on a breathtaking spring day, the two of them alone. He remembered the moments of terror and war and separation, the times white men were their enemies, the times she had cleansed and dressed his wounds, not only of the body but also of the heart, for he was a man without a country and his only home was at her hearth.

Now she was burning up. A wind rattled the lodge cover, and he felt cold tendrils pry up the leather and slide inside the black interior. He continued his vigil, applying cold compresses on her forehead one after another, hour after hour.

She muttered, and he understood. He helped her sit up, and pawed around in the darkness for the canteen, found it, opened it, and helped her drink. She drank, and again, and again, and he regretted not giving her water earlier. Then she settled back and was quiet again.

Her breathing was better but she was lost to him, deep in her own world. The stars had vanished from the smoke hole, and he wondered whether it would snow. Maybe that would be good. It would bury this desperate camp in a white blanket, and hide it from danger.

A howl lifted him to his feet. It was an eerie wail followed by short barks. A wolf was close, only yards away, summoning the pack, for the smell of meat hung in the night air here. Skye listened closely and heard an answering howl, a lonely call from some distant hill. He had heard wolves often in his long and lonely life in the wilds, but rarely so close. He settled down again beside Victoria, felt about for his belaying pin. It was a strange weapon in the wilds of North America, but a familiar one to him. A belaying pin was used to anchor ship's rigging but was a handy weapon well known to any seaman. The pin was shaped to drop partway through the fife rail on the main deck, making an anchor for the running rigging.

Now the polished pin, a relic of his days as a pressed seaman serving the king and then the young queen, Victoria, felt good in his hand.

The wolves were in camp now, just outside the thin leather walls of his lodge, talking in soft yips and growls to one another. He felt one probe the lodge, but it went away. There was meat enough for them if they dug it up: guts from buffalo, hide scrapings, offal.

"The wolves are our brothers," Victoria said suddenly.

He slipped his big stubby hand over her forehead, and found it raging hot, and felt the deepest dread he had ever known.

five

A numbing cold drifted out of the north, chilling the lodge. The small fire had long since glowed out. Victoria lay inert, and only an occasional ragged breath told Skye she lived. Once she began to shiver, and Skye tucked the robes tighter about her. But fever still gripped her body.

For a while, he heard the wolves outside, pawing up buried offal, driven by the lingering smell of meat. Sometime in the night he heard a loud thud, and another, and wondered what had caused it.

But for most of the night, time barely moved, and he fought sleep. It had been a long time since he slept, and would be a long time before he slept again. If he surrendered and stretched into that pile of warm robes, he would be dead to the world. And he could not permit that. He would watch over her, guard her, protect her with his every breath.

And so by iron will he kept himself awake, alive to the smallest change in her rhythms. She awoke once and asked for water. He held a canteen to her lips. She sipped only a little and fell back.

Dawn came late so far north. At first light he shook off his weariness, settled his black stovepipe hat on his long locks, and stepped outside into bitter air. He would soon start a fire, warm his own numb limbs and bring his lodge to life. He would saw frozen meat from his hanging cache, and roast it over a small flame. A quick meal, but one full of nourishment.

But now he consecrated himself to the day. This would be a difficult and dangerous one. He was glad to be alive, glad to have a home in this wild interior of North America, glad to call the Crow people his own. But his gladness this morning was mixed with darkness too, a loneliness that never left him, something that would never heal because he was the outsider. He had no country but he would make of his life as much as he could.

He studied the murky ridges, knowing this was always the most dangerous time, the moment when enemies struck, when their quarry lay in their lodges at peace and unaware of trouble. But he could see nothing. He headed for the hanging forequarters, and found both haunches lying on the frost-whitened ground. The wolves had gnawed hard at frozen flesh and given up; the effort wasn't worth the meal. He lifted the end of the braided leather rope and found that it had been gnawed in two.

The meat would have to stay on the ground. One man could not lift a quarter of buffalo. It had taken several, and maybe some horsepower too, to lift that meat out of harm's way. But Skye had no horse to help him. He set down his be-laying pin and sawed at the thick haunch. It was slow going, cutting through the icy meat bit by bit, but at last he had a small pile of it, enough to feed them both—if Victoria wanted any, which he doubted.

He built a tiny fire in the lodge, waited for it to burn bright and bed the ground with coals, and then began to roast the stiff and icy meat over open flame, a green willow skewer holding it off the fire. For the first time in half a day, he felt warm. The buffalo meat sizzled and burned, but it was soon cooked, and its savory aroma filled the lodge.

She was watching him. She seemed the same, except a great darkness filled her face.

"Meat?" he asked.

She shook her head slowly.

"Are you feeling better?"

She stared, not replying. It was not in her to complain.

He pulled his buffalo meat away from the fire and let it cool.

"You go to the People. Leave me. It is the way of the People," she said.

She was referring to a thing the Crows and other tribes did when they were forced to: abandonment. The ill and ailing were left to die if they jeopardized the safety of the young and healthy. And now she was telling him to leave her; she would die.

He shook his head.

"Dammit, Skye, go."

He grinned at her. "It's Mister Skye, mate."

He hoped she would laugh. He had always insisted on being called Mister Skye. Here in the New World he was as good as any mister in Europe, and Mister Skye he would be. He had bloodied a few trapper noses making it stick.

But she didn't smile, and he understood that her thoughts hovered upon the end of life, and walking the spirit path.

"We will walk together," he said.

She swallowed hard. "Sonofabitch," she muttered, and closed her eyes.

He stared sadly at her. There were many things he could deal with, dangers he was ready to face if he must, but illness simply left him helpless. He could think of nothing that might heal her, not a chant or a prayer or a shout or a medicine or a magical remedy. Not an herb or a potent tea.

Then, oddly, she took the thoughts from his mind, something she often did.

"Willow bark tea," she said.

"Yes!"

He jammed his hat down and headed out, barely remembering to carry his Hawken with him, and discovered enough light to make out the trees; the majestic naked limbs of cottonwoods, irregular and rough, and the orderly, drooping limbs of creek-side willows. There were so many varieties, and he didn't know one from another, but with his skinning knife he peeled tender green bark from small branches, working savagely, as if this act alone, done swiftly, might work the miracle he ached for.

He rushed back to the lodge, built up the dying fire, splashed water into his cook pot, and while it heated he stripped the bark into small lengths until he was sure the boiling water would extract whatever powers lay within the bark. It took a long time for the water to boil, for the bark to steep, for color to appear in the water, and then for it to cool enough for her to sip.

She watched, saying nothing, and he saw the fever burning in her and thought that time was short. He finally fed her a little with his horn spoon. She swallowed, and again, and finally shook her head. It had been so little, not more than half a cup. She lay back upon her robes and closed her eyes. He could see the pain and exhaustion etching her face.

He waited awhile and then stepped out again, feeling an icy breeze threaten to topple his beaver top hat from his head. But it stayed put. All these years it had miraculously stayed put in anything short of a gale. It was time to hike to the ridge to the east and survey the countryside. This land was alive with hunters; this was the prime season for prime hides and prime meat from fall-fattened buffalo.

It was time to check the nearby world for trouble. He didn't want to think about the odds if trouble came. He wrapped a robe tight about him to ward off the icy blast, and struggled up a steep grade that ended abruptly on a plain. The empty land greeted him, its grasses brown and sere, the mountains on the horizons in all directions thick with white. A gloomy gray overcast stole the sun from the world. He let his eyes adjust, began his careful focus on distant prospects, alert to movement, but this dark October day he saw nothing but an empty world. The buffalo were elsewhere and so were the hunters. It was a blessing, but also a curse because he smelled snow in the air and knew what would be whirling out of the north soon.

There would be time enough to gather wood, bring some meat inside the lodge, and then hunker down. Wearily he retreated to the creek bottom, filled with foreboding, for his enemies were not just humans, but cold and drifts and starvation. It would be weeks before she could walk, and walking was the only way they might escape to the land of her people, far south. And if they had to toil through snow, or wade icy streams, her fragile strength would desert her.

He slid down to the bottoms, energized by fear, and hurried to the lodge. He headed for the heap of abandoned lodgepoles and began dragging them close to his own shelter, working at it until he had collected every pole in the camp. They were dry and straight and would burn well and make heat. He filled his canteens with water from Louse Creek. He heaped brush about his lodge to slow the wind. He collected more abandoned robes, which he would turn into an inner liner hanging from the lodgepoles within. He dragged the frozen forequarter to a place close to the shelter, worried about leaving it there, realized he had little choice, and then dragged the second one to the same place. The meat was close enough so he might scare off wolves.

He remembered one more thing: at the willow tree he peeled more of the soft green bark from twigs, and peeled bark from a chokecherry growing beside the creek, and bark from several other shrubs. If there was medicine to be found in this trench across the prairie, he would have it in his grasp, no matter how heavily it might snow.

He turned at last to his forlorn lodge as the brooding overcast seemed to lower itself to the very floor of the plain. And there on a limb beside the lodge, watching him carefully, was a single magpie, her spirit animal, her own totem and fount of wisdom and hope and help.

He slipped through the door flap, settled his black top hat in its place next to the exit, and found her staring upward.

"The magpie is outside," he said.

"Tell the magpie you will bring it meat every day of the storm," she said.

He did. Outside, in the cutting wind, he addressed the bird:

"Magpie, Many Quill Woman promises meat to you each day."

The bird leaped into the sullen air and vanished.

Skye wondered, as he always did and always would, if there was anything at all to the Indian mysteries.

six

The wind ebbed, and no sound rose from the blackness outside. But then the snow came, dollar-sized flakes at first, then smaller ones, a white wall of them. Skye could see nothing when he pulled aside his door flap. If he went out, he would have to be very careful or he would lose his way and perish. He did make one last trip while he could, dragging a dozen of the abandoned lodgepoles to his very doorway. Just in case.

Victoria lay inert, in the land somewhere between the quick and the dead. The tiny flame, which he nursed carefully now, kept the cold at bay, but he would have to feed it day and night. Smoke curled lazily upward but an occasional downdraft drove it into the lodge, tickling Skye's throat and nostrils. Tricks of the air sometimes shot snow through the hole, past the wind flaps, and these showered on him, and on Victoria's robe.

With his knife he fashioned some thong by peeling it away from the edge of a robe, and then began tying robes around the perimeter of the lodge, hanging them from the lodgepoles, until he had an inner liner and the small lodge was more comfortable. The Crows often used liners in bitter weather, but this was still October, and he doubted it would grow so cold that trees would pop and crack.

That occupied him through the evening. When he noticed she was watching him, he slipped to her side, examined that cauterized wound and the angry flesh around it, found no bleeding, and felt her forehead. In the chill of the lodge it was hard to say how fevered she was.

"I brought in some bark while I could. I have chokecherry, willow, and hackberry. I can make some tea."

She didn't respond.

"Tea, Victoria? What kind?"

He could not catch her attention.

"I'll try the willow," he muttered.

He shredded the soft inner bark of a willow and set it to steeping in hot water. Time ticked slowly. He impulsively added some hackberry bark. He would try anything, everything, carefully and in small amounts, and he would leave nothing undone that might be done.

He waited impatiently. He had never mastered the Indian way of surrendering to circumstance, and now he felt caged and restless in that small space. A gust of snow billowed down onto the robes, and slowly turned into shining droplets.

At last, the steeping herbal tea in his cook pot acquired a greenish or tan cast, and he judged that the decoction might have some value to her. But it was only a guess. He poured some into a tin cup, let it cool, and then awakened her with a gentle shake.

"I want you to drink this."

She stirred, managed to rise to her elbows, and then sat. He handed her the cup.

"Willow and hackberry," he said.

She sipped, and again, slowly, and finally drained half the contents and slipped down again.

He ached. She had no strength at all, no life force, no vitality.

But there was another tack to try, so he began some buffalo broth, steeping small pieces of the forequarter in the water until he had a thin but nourishing soup. He awakened her, lifted her head, and gradually doled the broth, sliding it into her mouth with a horn spoon. It took a long while, and his arm ached from holding her head up. Then she slid back into the stupor that enveloped her.

Maybe she would die, slide away from him despite his every effort. He thought of burning the Blackfoot arrow that might still take her life. Burn it to ash, destroy it, but something stayed him.

Time stopped. He tried to doze one-eyed, keeping up the flame while getting rest, but soon gave it up. He thought of those occasional people he met, people who had ventured into the wilderness, stuffed with romantic notions about the sweetness of the life far from civilization. In fact life in the wilds was little more than want and hardship, food uncertain, cold, heat, insects, rain, constant discomfort.

Maybe this night, when he could for a change lie on several thick robes, he might sleep a true sleep. But he would not do that, not while she was in peril.

Let them sit in their armchairs with their coal stoves snapping and cracking, a lap robe or sweater adding to their comfort, and a good two-burner oil lamp lighting the pages; let them think this life where there were no houses or stores or stoves was an easy life, full of adventure, without law. Let them think it. They all turned tail, even the Yank trappers, who stayed a few seasons if they didn't die, and headed back to the East, and the comforts of a farm.

He eyed the inert woman he loved, and knew somehow that a crisis was looming. If she saw dawn, it would be after the crisis had come and gone.

He checked the snow; it fell steadily, eight inches, ten inches on the level, and no sign of letting up. The snow was imprisoning him, and could make it impossible to move anywhere for days, maybe weeks.

Her people had a way of making time pass, of dealing with the slow dark minutes. They told stories. The Crows were great storytellers, and many of their stories were bawdy and funny. Often he had sat in a large lodge jammed with Absaroka people, and listened to them exchange stories. The old women told the best ones of all, and made everyone laugh, and soon enough a night had passed, and no one had even noticed the passage of the hours.

"I don't know how to tell stories," he said, "but I guess I will. Maybe you can hear me. Maybe I'll only be talking to myself."

She did not respond and for a moment he wondered whether she lived. But then he saw the faint lift of the robe as breath filled her lungs, and he knew she was still with him.

"I've been thinking about that magpie hanging about here," he said, "the one who's your friend and helper. I wonder where she came from and why she's here. Let's say she's here looking after you. She's the one you saw in your vision, maybe not this very bird. But a sort of idealized bird. I suppose she's up in a branch somewhere, her head tucked under a limb, the snow sliding off of her. I wonder when she was born, and when she learned she was your friend. I wonder how your people know that they can find helpers in the animal kingdom."

It wasn't much of a story. Skye was just speculating, wishing he could know more about the mysterious world known to the tribes, but not grasped by white trappers.

"I think this magpie, the one who's sitting on a twig out there in the dark, must have been told by her mama that she was to take care of you; that a certain Many Quill Woman of the Otter Clan of the Absaroka people was going to need the wisdom of the magpies, and if Many Quill Woman's plea for a spirit guide was just and good, then that little magpie out there would decide to look after you and share the magpie wisdom with you.

"And that's why she's there. She's not with her flock of magpies, holed up somewhere out of the wind and cold. The magpies don't go south, so she has to make her living here, even on a bitter night like this one when snow covers the earth and there's little to eat and it's too cold even to find a bug or a scrap of food."

It wasn't much of a story; for the life of him, he couldn't spin a story or make a plot or put the magpie in real danger, maybe because he knew magpies did well even in brutal cold, and somehow made a living and enjoyed life and made rowdy ruckuses whenever they felt like having fun, which was often. And if they detected danger, the magpies made more noise than a steam calliope. That's one thing about a noisy flock of magpies: no creature on earth can ignore them.

"Well, this magpie should be off with her bunch, strutting and preening and looking for trouble and uproar, but she's not. She's sitting out there watching over my Victoria. Her mother taught her well, because most magpies wouldn't bother. They would be off hunting grubs or bark beetles or pestering blue jays or annoying elk. But not this magpie. That's because her mother taught her manners and duty. If she had a task, she would do it to the best of her ability. So, Victoria, this magpie out there is no ordinary bird."

He paused to slide two or three small sticks into the dwindling fire, and waited for them to catch and flare.

A puff of snow filtered down from above, and it was followed by a soft whir of wings flashing black and white in the firelight. There was the magpie, walking cockily over the buffalo robes. It headed straight toward the bits of meat Skye had cut up for broth and with a few savage jerks of its head it downed the meat.

It peered up at Skye, who sat motionless, and Skye thought he was being scolded though he couldn't quite say why. The whole episode was too startling for him to think sensibly or sort out this great oddity.

Magpie walked about the lodge, as if checking it all out. These birds had an odd, jerky walk, almost a swagger. So Skye sat very still.

Then he discovered Victoria was wide awake, not flushed or dazed but alert and aware. Magpie had waited for this moment, and hopped up on Victoria's robes, and sat quietly in the dark, its head cocked, staring at her. Then magpie lifted its wings and flapped them, as if to fan Victoria's face, and a moment later it popped up to a roost in the smoke hole, and vanished into the night.

Skye sat quietly for a while, uncertain of anything, not trusting his senses, and then he slipped over to Victoria and put his hand on her forehead.

It was cool.

n occasional snowflake fell through the hole and hissed on the wavering fire. Skye saw no light at all up there, and knew a heavy overcast blanked out the stars. It was dark and quiet, but something had changed.

Victoria stared at him. She had barely spoken ever since the arrow had pierced her abdomen and lodged under her lungs. She looked awful: great black circles under her eyes, her flesh saturnine and unhealthy, her jet hair matted.

He discovered the broth in the pot, heated it a while, and then crawled beside her. She struggled up upon her elbows and he spooned some into her mouth. She was swallowing better. She took the rest of it and lay back.

He rose, his limbs aching from long confinement, and pulled his blanket capote around him and plucked up his camp hatchet. He opened the lodge flap and peered into a wall of white. The snow was already high. He stepped into the night, which was not cold, and waited for his eyes to adjust. But there was nothing to see. With the flap closed behind him, he stood in pitch-dark, sensing that if he moved a few steps he would be lost. He felt the snow lick his face and slide under his collar. He probed with the toe of his moccasin for some lodge-poles and found them. He pulled one free of the snow burying it, and chopped it into three- or four-foot lengths. When he was done he could not find the lodge. Nothing revealed itself to him, not even a wall of white. He lifted the longest of the segments and slowly rotated it until it struck something soft. Then, certain he had found the lodge, he kept the pole in contact and felt his way around it until he came to the door flap.

It had been a close call. He dragged the lengths of lodge-pole into the lodge. He had ten or twelve lengths and judged he had enough wood for the night.

"Dammit," said Victoria.

Skye smiled. She was going to get well.

He shed his snow-crusted capote and settled down, refreshed by the exercise. He arranged four pieces of wood so that their ends were burning, and lay back in his robes. They felt good. In all his years of life in the wilds, he had never slept in a truly comfortable bed, but this night he might.

He lay back in them, and pulled two more over him, and felt himself in a cocoon, safe enough even in this perilous place. The mystery of the magpie absorbed him. There were so many things he knew nothing of, and most of all Indian religion, if any of this could be called a religion.

He ached to know if the magpie really was Victoria's spirit counselor and protector, and whether it had powers beyond Skye's knowing. He thought back to the only religion he knew, the precepts of the Church of England that had shaped him, given him his moral and spiritual nature. Even after he was pressed into the Royal Navy, that belief was ever-present for the Sabbath was carefully observed on every ship of the fleet.

Who was God? And what was this lone magpie doing, invading the lodge of a Crow Indian woman and himself, only to fly off into a thick snowfall? He could not answer. Yet something had happened. Victoria's fever had left her. A step toward healing had occurred. She took broth, spoke a little, and lay comfortably beside him.

Was there anything in this unreconcilable with his own beliefs? He didn't know, and felt almost as powerless confronting these great issues as he had been confronting the wound that almost stole her life. He felt the comfort of a bed that gave gently under his shifting weight, the robes forming themselves to his hip and rib and shoulder, and then he fell into a deep sleep, the first since Victoria's wounding. If the lodge grew cold, he did not know it.

When he awoke a gray overcast shone through the smoke hole. He had slept sometime into the morning. He sat up abruptly, worried that he had let down his guard, that danger loomed. He hastily pulled on the fine fringed calf-high moccasins Victoria had crafted for him out of buffalo bull hide, and pushed open the flap, his gaze sharp. A foot and a half of snow, maybe more, lay on the level, and he saw nothing but aching emptiness, a white world under a gray heaven. Not a track marred the smooth surface. It did not seem like a threatening place where Blackfeet lurked, where wolves lingered. Yet it was.

"A lot of snow," he said to her.

"It will keep us safe," she replied.

"Unless it starts blowing," he said.

This could be a country of mountainous drifts, ten or twenty feet high, whipped into walls and barriers by prairie winds. There could be no passage through such a land.

The lodge was cold and clammy with their breath. Not an

ember remained. He stirred the cold fire bed, and found nothing glowing, and the charred wood cold to his touch. She lay under three robes, looking no better except in her eyes, which were brighter this silent morning. He would build a fire if he could. It would not be easy.

He hunted through his possibles for his fire-making kit, and the tiny bit of bone-dry tinder he needed. He found it, and pinched some of the delicate shavings he preserved there. He dropped them into the fire pit, and then carefully shaved slivers of dry wood from the lodgepoles, until he had a small nest of tinder ready. He pulled his flint and striker from his kit, and slid his hand through the bow-shaped striker. Now he was ready. He held his flint stone over the nest of tinder and scraped hard, a practiced scrape of steel over stone, sending a shower of sparks into the cold tinder. None took. He struck again and again, and then, finally, a spark caught, and another, glowing in the delicate shavings. He blew gently, watched the spark glow as air struck it. In a few moments more, he had many tiny glows worming through the tinder, and then at last one bloomed into a yellow flame. The rest caught.

Skye added thin twigs to the tiny flame until at last he had a flame he trusted to live. It brought no heat; that would come much later. For another half hour he nursed the flame until at last it was strong enough to consume the poles he pushed into the blaze. Only then did a faint heat begin to soften the harsh cold of the lodge and drive off the trapped moisture within it.

In the cities, people were using phosphorus lucifers, matches that ignited fires easily. But he could not afford them, and mostly they were not available even at the trading posts. So he lived by the means he had always used, first as a trapper and brigade leader, then as a hide hunter and occasional guide.

He cherished the warmth that gradually permeated the

lodge and the robes that lay thickly about. He hurried the fire along with his breath, wanting it hot because the heavy gray smoke from cold fires was a telltale sign to enemies.

He stepped outside, knee deep in snow, and examined the smoke from his lodge. It drifted gray and heavy into the air but was almost invisible under the cast-iron sky. He studied the distant ridges, the naked limbs of trees, and every dimple in the snow, but saw nothing to alarm him.

There would be work; always work, for constant toil was the lot of anyone living far from the civilized world. He dug up poles from his stack of them and began cutting them into usable lengths, not an easy task with a hatchet. The pop and crack of his all-too-dull hatchet disturbed the deep silence, but that could not be helped. The snow itself damped sound, and in any case his refuge lay in a steep trench. In a while he had what he judged to be a day's wood, and then he cut some more while he was about it. That wondrous sleep infused him with a rare energy, and he took advantage of it to get ahead, to put in wood against a bad time, such as another storm.

He scraped the snow off the lodge, traipsed a path to a latrine area, dug his forequarter of meat out of a drift and dragged it closer, stamped down the snow in front of the lodge, and piled fuel next to the door. By the time he had finished the short November day was dying.

He found her awake.

"It is going to snow again," she said. "I feel it. Skye, go to the People while you can. Leave food and wood with me. I will make do. I have a flint and striker."

He wouldn't hear of it. "Among the British, the captain is the last man off of a sinking ship. He makes sure everyone else is safe first," he said.

"What is this thing, the captain?"

"The chief. The one who commands others."

She laughed, suddenly. "All right then, I am captain of this lodge and I'm ordering you to go."

That was why he loved her so much. He reached across and clasped her hands in his.

"We will do this together, like two chiefs of the mighty Absaroka people."

"Dammit, Skye . . ." she whispered.

"We'll wait this out. You'll be strong someday soon. If need be, I'll make a sled and pull you out."

"A sled?"

"You'll see. I will haul you out of here on a bed if that's what it takes."

He fed the flames again as the light dimmed and the fierce November darkness settled over that small scrap of leather and wood that sheltered them.

A few flakes drifted through the vent and melted on the robes. He rose, opened the flap, and discovered a wall of white falling out of the sky, just visible in the twilight.

"See?" she said. "It's too late for you now. You're stuck with me, Skye."

"That is how I always wanted it," he said. "And it's Mister Skye."

eight

The snow came down through the blackness, smothering the land. It came on the tide of deepening cold. It burdened the buffalo-hide walls of the lodge, bulging them inward. It drifted through the smoke hole, hissing on the fire, glittering white on the robes.

The fire behaved badly, wavering and smoking up the lodge, until Skye finally realized it was feeding on air from above; snow had blocked the passage of air from the base of the lodge.

He pushed aside the flap and furiously pushed the snow out into the darkness. He flailed it away from the lodge. He shook the hide until the snow skidded into heaps. After that the fire burned better, at least for a while. But he knew he must stay awake all night to keep the fire from dying.

Victoria watched helplessly, barely able to sit up long enough to take some broth. There was something eerie about this storm that fell upon them in utter silence. Skye knew that if the lodgepoles he had salvaged for firewood gave out there would be little to burn. The hunting camp had consumed every scrap of deadwood on every tree even before the Blackfoot raid.

Life was running thin, and the silent strangling whiteness was carrying death in its soft wings. He knew what he had to do: stay awake. Periodically sweep snow away from the lodge. Cut meat from the haunches and cook it. Find lodgepoles in the snow-buried stack, bring them in and break them up and feed them to the relentless fire.

And all the while he had to nurse a desperately sick woman who needed broth and warmth and shelter. He stayed awake all that night, feeling he was waging a losing war and this unending storm would engulf him. She lay quietly, awake also, caught in her private thoughts. They spoke to each other without words, and often he knew exactly what she was thinking. It was in her to be testy now; the pain at her side and deep in her abdomen was maddening. She felt helpless, even more helpless than he felt in the face of this silent suffocation falling on them.

But finally a grudging dawn came. Through the smoke hole he saw the gray of low clouds and felt their uncaring. The world had ceased to remember the man and woman in a sea of emptiness.

The lodge had a rim of snow within it. Somehow snow had collected around the periphery, blown down the smoke hole. Only in the middle, close to the feeble flame, was there no whiteness.

He drew his capote close and pushed into the white world outside. Bitter cold air stung his face and sandpapered his throat and lungs. The sky was light gray and he could see no horizons because snow and gray blended imperceptibly together. It was plenty cold for November and would get colder. He had much to do, and hoped his hands wouldn't numb entirely, or his ears freeze, before he accomplished it.

Now, with air so brutal, he needed more wood; he didn't know how long the lodgepoles would last, but not long enough. He had only a hunting-camp hatchet and no easy way to fell limbs. He struck toward the creek-side trees, wallowing every foot of the way in snow that rose to his thighs, found Louse Creek still flowing, giving off steam in the icy air, and began the hunt for deadwood. Enough deadwood to keep Victoria safe.

But every step was an ordeal. He toiled at it, chopping off limbs he wasn't sure were dead or dry. In a short time he was too numb to function, and headed back to the lodge. He would be the worst sort of fool to frostbite his feet or hands. All that effort had netted him only a few good sticks.

He slipped into the lodge, pulled his gauntlets free, and held his hands over the pitiful fire, but they didn't warm. He found some wood, built the fire up, and slowly blood returned to his hands and the stinging in them subsided.

"Cold," he said to her.

"Skye . . . if anything happens, I can't help you."

"I am being careful."

"You should have left me."

"If your magpie didn't leave you, then I won't either."

That sally quieted her.

The next time out, he found a good thick limb, dead and dry, and hacked away until he felled it. He dragged it to his lodge and worked furiously to chop it into four or five long lengths. He could do the rest inside.

He staked the meat, which rested safely under snow, so he could find it. For now, he need not worry about food, but in time scurvy would destroy them both unless he found some roots and vegetables.

Somehow his labor warmed him, and he was able to improve their lot by the time the short day turned into an icy blackness. When he stumbled in, he found her sitting up, and more. She had shifted her bed, moved herself closer to the fire-wood, and was tending the fire on her own.

"You shouldn't be up," he said.

"Go to hell, Skye."

"It's Mister Skye."

"Go to hell, Mister Skye."

He struggled out of his capote, pulled off his gauntlets, thrust his numb hands into her fire, and felt prickles, and then warmth.

"Tonight you sleep. I'll keep the fire," she said. "It's no good if you're too tired to keep us going."

"But, Victoria . . ."

"English, they don't know anything."

He tumbled into his robes, thinking only to rest before he brewed her some broth or cooked a little meat, but next he knew there was light in the smoke hole and she was slumped in her bed. The fire burned steadily but the supply of wood inside the lodge was low.

He could not imagine losing so much time. Nor could he imagine sleeping so long, buried under several heavy robes. In fact, he didn't remember any robes over him when he lay down to rest a moment at the end of the day.

He got up, rested. He ventured out, and found this day cloudless and cold and the snow thick. When the wind came up, as it would on a clear day like this one, it would heap the snow into giant drifts, imprisoning them.

Even as he stood there in the early light, absorbing the white world, he felt the first stirrings of air, slicing heat out of him. In some ways this bright and glaring and windy day would be the worst of all. The firewood was almost gone, but this bitter day he would have to work through heavy snow to find some, and it would be far away.

He was rested at least, and worked north, straight into the rising wind, heading for a thicket ahead. Then he stumbled over something, and found it was a dead cottonwood, limbs shattered and scattered, but under the snow. Good. He would mine that heap of snow for all he could.

She watched him as he dragged piece after piece back to the lodge and then warmed himself. She was keeping the fire now, sparing him one worry. In deep cold it was hard to start any fire, even with dry tinder and flint and steel.

After three trips into that miserable wind, he returned to find that she had heated thick and meaty broth for him. She was well enough to stir about. He drank it gratefully and was renewed. But conditions outside were worsening by the minute. Now the wind whipped the snow into tiny bullets of ice, scouring one piece of land only to pile huge drifts elsewhere. He could no longer walk into it, and was forced to back slowly toward that dead cottonwood while the wind whipped snow like buckshot and plastered his capote with it.

When he returned it was only midmorning, but he was as worn as if he had toiled hard a whole day. He had a little wood, enough for the night, but not much more except a few lodgepoles he was holding in reserve.

She handed him tea this time, something she had decocted, he didn't know from what.

She had been sitting up most of the morning.

"Skye, if you and me get out of here, you're going to get another wife. I'm tired of doing it alone. You get two, three more wives, make me the sits-beside-him wife, so I get to boss the rest."

He stared at her, amazed.

"Dammit, Skye, you get more wives. You're doing women's work, and it ain't right. One wife gets sick, you got three more to help out."

He stared at her over his tin camp cup, feeling the steam brush his face. She was serious even if he spotted humor in those eyes that had been so dull and pain-soaked for days.

"You're all I want, Victoria," he said.

"Then you're no chief. You want to do me a favor? You want to make my life happy? You get more wives. I want some wives myself."

A sharp blast of wind shuddered the lodge, and he wondered if the wind rose so high it might tip the shelter over. There were no rocks pinning it down. This was merely to be a hunting-camp shelter, easily dismantled. There wasn't a rock in sight, and if the wind blew the lodge away, they would perish. As simple as that.

"Some wives, Skye, we could make you comfortable."

"I'll bet."

"Who ever heard of a chief having only one woman? I hold my head in shame in the village because I am the only woman of Mister Skye. It tells them you are no chief, in war or in the robes."

She laughed, wickedly. He had rarely seen her laugh like that, but it was a laugh known and practiced by the Crows, and especially old women of the People. He had heard it many times around many campfires, especially when it came time to tell stories and spin away a winter's day. Her laugh was a bawdy one, and she was thinking of what it would be like in a lodge with several comely women in residence.

Skye sat there, flustered. Where had this come from? How could she be thinking of more wives when their very lives hung in the balance?

nine

Days passed, the early winter weather moderated, but the peril did not diminish. Skye scoured the valley for firewood, stamping trails that took him farther out each day. Victoria took charge of the domestic labor, keeping fires going, sawing meat from the frozen forequarters, and resting in between.

The early November sun crusted the snow so that the giant drifts no longer shifted in the wind. Some were taller than Skye. Each of them formed a wall imprisoning them, keeping them from the Crows' winter camp. Skye feared passage through a gap between the Snowy Mountains and the Belt Mountains where snow always collected and reached formidable heights, all but sealing this country into northern and southern parts all winter long. Somehow, he would have to take his fragile woman through or over that barrier. There was no good way around.

Victoria gained strength but pushed too hard to take pressure off of Skye, and then lost ground. She was right, he thought wryly: he could use a few wives, for it was the Indian women who did the hard work of sustaining life, the women who toiled from dawn to dusk.

There were other things looming on the horizon, and the worst was scurvy. How long could they subsist on meat alone, without greens or fruits? How long before they weakened, their gums bled, they lost strength and even the will to live?

One morning he remembered the cache left behind by the fleeing hunters. It was guarded by formidable drifts that stretched higher than his head but he was determined to find out what was in it and salvage anything useful. He hacked his way toward the creek, sometimes stepping into snow that engulfed him, but he finally reached the creek in the vicinity of the cutbank, and stumbled down a slope. He probed and finally located what he thought was the cache tucked under a river-washed hollow.

He chopped and hacked, using the only tools he had, a camp hatchet and a stick, and finally broke into a hollow area. A great sour odor rose out of it, and he discovered dozens of small eyes peering out at him. He had found a pack-rat city, and the insolent little creatures had made a bonanza out of the cache. He cleared away more snow and peered in. The rats had ruined the robes, eaten leather, soiled everything. There was one treasure: an axe. That simple tool would make all the difference in the world when it came to gathering and reducing firewood. He collected it gladly.

One parfleche caught his eye. It remained tightly bound, and apparently the pack rats had not burrowed into it. He dragged it out, opened it, and found it full of new pemmican. He was overjoyed. It was the great trail food of all the tribes, consisting of pounded dry meat—usually buffalo—fat, and berries. This pemmican had both chokecherry and service berries embedded in the fat and shredded meat. There could be no better food.

Joyously, he collected his axe and the heavy parfleche and wrestled them back to his lodge.

There, Victoria immediately dug into the parfleche and wolfed the pemmican, her body starved for any fruit or vegetable matter. He ate some too.

"Nothing else in the cache," he said. "The rats got it."

"Soon we will go home," she said.

He did not respond; the forbidding drifts that imprisoned them were on his mind.

"I will be ready," she said.

But he saw her weakness. She worked fitfully but always sank back into the robes and lay inert for hours. She was not ready for travel and would not be anytime soon.

He rested; fighting through crusted soggy drifts was the most exhausting labor any man could face, and he was constantly worn out, fighting for breath, needing time to recover.

Then he heard a soft clop of hooves. He couldn't believe it. Not now. He grabbed his Hawken, checked the load and the cap over the nipple, and with the rifle ready, tugged aside his door flap for a look. There, before the lodge, standing in the small area that had been trampled down, stood a gray mare and a colt. The mare had been gaunted by starvation. Her ribs showed. Her backbone formed a ridge. The flesh around her rump had wasted down to bone.

Skye thought he saw a magpie fly away, a flash of black in the glaring winter sun, but put the odd thought aside. The magpie had nothing to do with this. He peered about sharply for Blackfeet, for any living person, and saw nothing. The snowbound ridges hemming this sheltered river bottom were as bright and silent and anonymous as they had been since the storm.

A mare. And near death from starvation. Her head hung low. Brambles had lodged in her mane until it was an unkempt mess that no longer protected her long neck. Her hooves had worn down. She had an ugly roman nose and a look of sorrow in her eyes. She had once been around human beings; she was either unafraid or too starved and close to perishing to care.

"I'll be damned," muttered Victoria.

If the mare was worn, the colt was not. It was six or seven months old and still nursing, and it had robbed its mother of the last of her strength. It was truly the ugliest little beast Skye had ever seen, gray and wild, an oversized jawbone disfiguring its face. Its floppy ears sat in the wrong spot on its skull. It hung about its worn mother, butting her, dancing away.

A mare. Passage to safety for Victoria if somehow Skye could nurse the animal to usefulness, and if she wasn't a complete outlaw.

"Whoa, lady," he said, stepping toward her. He handed the Hawken to Victoria and approached gently, a tentative step at a time.

Then the miserable colt kicked. The little thing whirled, unloosed his hind feet, and caught Skye in the right thigh, rocking him back. And before Skye could recover, the colt caught him again at the groin, staggering Skye backward until he teetered into a snowbank.

Skye boiled up like a sore-toothed grizzly.

"Avast!" he bawled, determined to wrestle the offending colt right down to the ground, tie him up, and show him who was the boss. But before he even recovered his balance, the colt lowered his head, turned himself into a battering ram, and charged straight into Skye, that bonehead ramming into Skye's belly and knocking the breath clear out of him.

Skye reeled backward, gasping for air, and the colt followed his retreat, butting again and again until Skye tumbled into the snow again. Then the colt minced backward, did a little jig of victory, and stood there, watching Skye unfold himself and stand up and catch his wind.

"That's the rottenest animal I've ever seen," Skye roared. "I'll fix him."

But Victoria was laughing, and it was an unkind laugh, a cackle Skye had heard only among Crow old ladies, a cackle that said they were enjoying someone's misery. There was his wife cackling and wheezing, and there was that stupid-eyed colt with the underslung jawbone, ready to nail him again.

There was nothing to do but laugh.

Skye felt a volcano of laughter erupt from his belly; a vast earthquake of joy, which hurt his stomach where the rotten little colt had butted him. But laugh he did, laughed at the whole mad world this bright morning.

But the time came when he and Victoria were looking again at the desperate mare, her head hung low, fighting to stay alive. There was not a blade of grass to be found and the snow was too deep to paw through to feed herself.

"Have to feed her fast," he said.

"Damn lucky you got the axe," she said.

It was lucky. It was almost magical. With that axe he could offer that mare some emergency grub. Maybe the colt would nibble on it too. He circled warily around the horses and headed for the cottonwoods along the creek, where there was a stand of saplings, their bark smooth and green rather than scaled and thick and dry. The smooth bark of young cottonwoods was an emergency horse food, well known to mountain men and Indians. He struggled through deep snow, singled out a sapling, and hewed it down in swift strokes. He limbed it and dragged the green log back to the lodge, then cut a slit down the limb so he could roll the bark away.

The mare tore into it even before he had finished, her big buck teeth scraping the green bark loose and her old lips capturing every green shred. She knew instinctively that she had food before her.

Victoria stood before the lodge, a robe wrapped around her, and watched.

Skye retreated to the cottonwood stand, felled two more saplings poking from deep snow, and dragged them to the lodge. The effort exhausted him. But she was eating. She expertly worked the green bark off that thin log, turning the log somehow, chewing the pliable bark into feed.

Skye watched, gratified. This mare might be their salvation; a fair enough trade. He could feed her; she could carry Victoria away. As for that mean colt, maybe he would shoot it. No man in his right mind wanted a colt like that, full of some insane instinct to attack everything in sight.

The colt wouldn't even let its mother eat, but butted her, poked that thick underslung jaw and snout into her bag, and robbed her of what little milk and life she had left.

Skye watched, disgusted at the little creature's greed. At the rate he was bullying his mother, she would never gain strength or put on weight or be strong enough to carry Victoria out.

He could slit its throat, or he could get the poor mare more feed. He watched dourly, and then headed into the snow once again, and spent the rest of that bright day cutting saplings, until he had managed to drag a pile of green-barked logs to her. The mare never stopped eating, stripping soft green bark off of those wands of wood, and by the end of that day he didn't know whether the tears in his eyes were from snow blindness or something else.

ten

Time was running out. For days, Skye fed the old mare cottonwood bark, which he roamed wide and far to find. She prospered a <u>little</u>, or at least he thought she did, but it was poor food and all it did was keep her alive and allow her to make a little more milk for the ugly colt.

But with each passing day, danger increased. The mare had left a trail in the snow, and what warrior or hunter could resist the trail of a lone mare and foal? There was the prospect of another fall storm, and a hundred times each day Skye's gaze focused on the horizons, looking for an ominous bank of clouds. The forequarter of buffalo meat was dwindling; the pemmican he reserved as a travel food. He had long since consumed the available firewood. This campsite was exhausted and yet he lingered to give Victoria the best chance.

But finally he dared wait no more.

"We'll leave in the morning," he said.

"I am strong."

"We'll see when we hit the drifts. I've made a travois from the last of the lodgepoles. The mare's gentle enough; she belonged to someone once. I'll put the robes on her back, you in the travois, and I'll carry the Hawken, the tools, and the pemmican on my back."

They would abandon the lodge with its comforts. Each night they would have to stay out in the open. He would try to find cottonwood groves, so he could feed the mare more green bark. The odds were bad; he thought they had one chance in ten. Most likely they would suffer snow blindness. The whole world was still white, and only a heavy overcast could save them from ruining their eyes.

They left before dawn to gain time. The mare submitted docilely to the saddle, and then to the travois poles anchored to the stirrups. The colt butted him whenever he approached the mare, and now and then Skye roared at the miserable heavy-jawed thing that kept getting in his way. Then the colt butted him again, just to show who owned that mare.

But the colt might come in handy, especially if it would break a trail. They sadly abandoned the lodge that had kept them alive just as a faint light lined the horizon to the southeast. The snow had crusted, making walking all the more difficult as they punched through, step after step. Skye wrapped the pasterns of the mare in patches torn from old robes to keep them from being sliced to pieces.

Just as he suspected, Victoria lasted a few hundred yards walking and then settled gratefully into the travois and pulled a robe over herself. The travois was easy on the mare, mostly skidding over surface crust, but it didn't take long for the mare to weary. He let her rest. He needed her. Victoria depended on her. They had a long, long way to go.

When the sun rose his eyes watered at once. A squint didn't stop the glare, and only when he pulled the hood of his blanket capote over his face did he find any relief. The mare's eyes watered and so did the colt's. Victoria sat with her eyes closed.

At least he wasn't cold. The temperature hovered above freezing. And Skye was working too hard to get chilled. Behind them a telltale trail unfolded, hooves, moccasin prints, travois tracks. Any passing war party or loner could track them down. And yet it could not be helped. One did what one had to do, and he had to move.

They struck the Judith River, which flowed southwest, and once they reached its valley the going was easier. They were traversing game and buffalo trails, already packed. He kept a sharp eye for pony hoofprints, but saw none. The early snow was a blessing in one sense: the hunters and warriors had taken to their lodges and were probably gathered about lodge fires playing the hand games or bone games or telling stories of their people.

For a while that afternoon they traversed well-stamped ground. The mare perked up, not having drifts to fight, and the travois skidded easily over the glazed surface. The well-worn trail gave Skye the gift of extra miles, but he didn't want to exhaust the mare or Victoria, and called a halt in a fine stand of cottonwoods and willows near the fork of the Judith and Ross Creek.

There, he felled green cottonwood limbs while Victoria chopped willow saplings, wove them into a small dome, and threw spare robes over it. It was little more than a hut, but it would be far more comfortable than open ground, and a fire at its front would throw heat into it.

The ugly colt nuzzled up to his mother's bag and drained it, and then butted it for more supper, but she had given him all she had. Then it began mouthing bits of cottonwood bark, and

Skye was glad to see it beginning to forage for itself. It was old enough to eat any horse feed.

"With that jaw of yours, you could eat whole trees," he said to it. For an answer, the colt whirled and kicked, barely missing Skye's shin.

"You little devil!" Skye roared.

"His name is Jawbone," Victoria said.

"That's a good name! He's all jaw! He has no brains and no back and nothing else of value. Jawbone it is, you little punk!"

They were camped in a trench cut into the plain, and Skye did not worry about a fire. They had come much closer to the Snowy Mountains and the Belts, which brooded whitely above them. In a day or two they would enter the gap between the ranges, and then there could be big trouble. But there was no sense in worrying it to death. For this night they had shelter and pemmican and plenty of green bark for the weary mare.

At dusk, which came all too early, they settled into their hut. Victoria had gathered armloads of reeds from the creek bank and these formed an insulating bed between them and the snow. But this was not the same as the lodge, and they shivered as they slipped into their doubled robes.

"I did not see the magpie," she said. "It is a bad omen."

He lay quietly, gathering what little warmth he could from within the robes. It was important to her to know that her spirit helper was beside her. In her weakened condition it could even mean life or death, despair or the will to live. And he knew he could not cheer her up with bland assurances.

"Victoria, we have given no offense to any living thing that I know of," he said. "We have given food to the magpies, fed the mare, and honored all things."

That was important: she lived in a world in which one must respect all creatures great and small.

"I am just damned tired," she said, but he knew her spirits had slipped into darkness. He rose, fed more sticks into the small fire that threw a little light and warmth into their shelter, and peered into the blackness. No stars lit the heavens, and he dreaded what might come, especially in so rude a hut as this.

He drifted into a light sleep. It was hard to sleep when you had to suck icy air, breath after breath, when your nose and cheeks ached with cold, when your feet remained blocks of ice.

A nervous shuffle outside of the hut awakened him instantly, and he felt around for the Hawken. The barrel was icy to the touch, and the stock had frost on it. He chose his belaying pin instead, and hastened out into the bitter night. Something scurried away. Intuitively he knew the visitors were wolves, and his stirring had probably scared them off. He could not see the mare or colt but knew that if they had been attacked he would have heard about it. The loss of the mare would devastate their chances of ever reaching Victoria's village. But he did not tie her up. She didn't like it, and he finally had learned just to let her be his ally and not his slave. As long as he didn't tie her, he had a partner.

By the time he shook the cobwebs from his mind the next dawn, he was surprised to see a fire burning. Victoria had lit it. She was better and more patient than he with the flint and steel, and sometimes had gotten a blaze going when he had given up and was suppressing a rage at his own ineptitude. She handed him a broth made of boiled pemmican and water, and he drank the hot greasy liquid gratefully.

He pulled on his buffalo-hide moccasins and went after the mare, wondering where she was. He was on the brink of alarm when he found her deep in brush, stripping bark off of saplings. In a place like this she could make her own living. He let her eat a while. Jawbone was butting her bag, getting his own breakfast.

Victoria had dourly dismantled the willow-branch hut and collected the heavy robes.

"Dammit, Skye, there are no magpies here."

He did not try to calm her. If there were no magpies, it could only mean trouble for Victoria. Still, he collected her cold hands in his big ones and held them. "We will do the best we can, and if we always have heart, we will go where we were meant to go."

At first light they loaded the robes onto the mare, slid the travois poles into the stirrups, and set out, following a southerly course. Skye's burdens seemed heavier this day: pemmican in a parfleche, rifle, axe, hatchet, knife, powder horn, capote, and something intangible: an added worry because Victoria was less well than the day before.

Still, they proceeded up the Ross Fork for a while before they abandoned it to head toward the visible gap between the two ranges. But now the drifts were building, and sometimes the crusts didn't hold them and they floundered waist-deep in snow. Ahead was open country, not a patch of trees, not a creek, not a sheltered hollow, not a stand of cottonwoods to feed the mare, no limbs to weave a hut, only a windy snow-covered land in which the wind had rippled the snow into ribs and ridges.

At one final patch of cottonwoods, Skye laboriously felled a few saplings, split and debarked them, feeling as worn out as the mare. He tucked the pliable green bark into the robes. It wasn't but a fraction of a meal. The mare would get no other food, maybe for days. And all that day, no magpie followed them.

eleven

All that bitter day they struggled south, blinded by sun-dazzle but helped by the north wind at their backs. Their course rose imperceptibly toward the gap, and the higher they climbed the heavier the snow. Sometimes Skye whacked a hole in a drift with his axe, and the rest followed single file.

The wind picked up, funneled into a ten-mile-wide flat between mountain ranges. But as long as it pushed them ever south, it was bearable. He rested the gaunt mare often, knowing that Victoria's life depended on that worn old creature. The colt seemed almost oblivious of the hardship, having milked his mother of whatever resources she still possessed.

Often the little fellow dashed ahead, as if to lead this slow procession toward a safe harbor, only to swing around and return again when no one matched his pace.

There wasn't a tree close by, though the distant mountains were black with them. Skye knew a little about this gap. It was bloody ground because it was the only passage for travelers going north or south in the whole area. That meant ambush, war, death right there, most often between Crows and Blackfeet, but other tribes had spilled blood there. It was a stark, treeless place without beauty; there was little to solace the spirit, and the spirits of the dead haunted it.

Victoria mostly traveled in the travois, enduring its lurches and bounces, but occasionally she rose and walked a little, giving the old mare some respite. No one spoke; every word was energy wasted.

They came, late in that day, to a ridge of snow as high as a house, a white wall that forbade a crossing. And yet they had to cross it, fast, before they lost the light for there was no refuge behind them. Jawbone pranced ahead, tentatively sampling the crust. And finding a crust, he began climbing that monstrous drift, ever higher. Then with a pitiful squeal the colt vanished. He had broken through the crust and was trapped in the soft snow below, thrashing about in its prison.

For a moment Skye rejoiced. Little devil! But the piteous wail of the mare filled Skye with shame and regret. He halted the procession at the foot of that drift and studied that slope. The colt was about fifty feet ahead, braying and flailing in his trap. He would soon exhaust himself, freeze, and die.

"Skye, dammit, do something," Victoria said.

"And what?" he snapped.

Skye didn't have the faintest idea what to do, so he did the first thing that came to mind. He shed his gear and prepared to go after the colt. He pulled his axe from his pack and began chopping through the crust, cutting a way to the trapped colt. It was slow, hard work, and after ten feet he was worn. He found that he had some footing well down from the crust, and if he kept knocking the crust with the back of his axe he could work along a narrow trench toward the little fellow, who was sporadically screeching his alarm, but the time between each of its struggles grew and grew.

Behind him, Victoria and the mare stood watching. Skye made slow progress and kept chopping even while his body protested, finding a slow rhythm of axe-swinging and forward movement that sustained him through another ten, then twenty, then thirty feet. But the foal was silent now, resigned to its doom the way animals are when they sense hopelessness.

Skye, too, was in a precarious place, climbing through the soft underbelly of the snow ridge until the crust came up to his chest. But at last he reached the colt, which had worked his way deeper into the snowbank.

He cleared away as much of this soft snow as he could. Jawbone could not even look back at his rescuer.

"Whoa, boy," Skye said, not knowing how on earth to free the colt.

Jawbone did not respond except to rotate his ears.

Skye tried sliding his hands around the colt, intending to lift him, drag him backward, but he couldn't get a grip, and the snow swiftly numbed his fingers.

He burrowed down and cleared soft snow from its hind feet, fearing a sharp kick, but Jawbone didn't move. Slowly he cleared the feet and lifted them, getting a good purchase on the pasterns, and tugged.

Jawbone didn't like that a bit, but it didn't matter: Skye eased him a foot out of his trap. He was so worn he could pull no more, and paused for breath. The sun was just above the southwestern horizon, and they would soon be caught in a black night with no shelter.

He took a firm grip on Jawbone's hocks and pulled steadily. The colt slid along, almost as if he were slipping out of a womb, and in a few minutes Skye, his heart hammering, had pulled the colt out of his trap, down the snow slope, to hard snowpack.

The colt righted himself, shook off the snow, overcame the indignity of it, and butted his rescuer.

"Avast!" yelled Skye, who didn't quite topple.

But the colt had already headed for his worn mother, jammed his bonehead into her bag, and was refueling.

The sun dropped behind a distant ridge.

"I think there is a crossing over there," Victoria said, pointing to a place two hundred yards distant where some juniper seemed to grow right out of the top of the ridge. They headed that way at once, found firm footing that took them around the drift, and out upon a cold flat land.

Ahead was a dark streak, and Skye headed for it in the tumbling twilight. Soon enough he led his weary band into a sharply eroded coulee out of the wind. They could perhaps shelter under a cutbank, and there was enough juniper and other brush to sustain a fire if they could light one in the restless air.

He pushed down the dry watercourse, looking for a good place, and found one in a bend, where occasional spring floods had undercut a bank and piled up some driftwood.

"Here," he said.

They stopped. He had taken them too far this day. The old mare hung her head, her ribby sides heaving. Victoria crawled off the travois, began undoing the bundle of robes on the mare's back, and started to make a nest, gather kindling while the last light held.

The foal, wobbly from its ordeal, stood stiff-legged watching Skye unsaddle the mare and turn her free to make whatever living she could in that little ditch in the prairie. Then the little animal wobbled toward Skye and pressed his bony, misshapen head into Skye's side, and stood there, his head low and tight against Skye's hip.

"You're welcome," Skye said, and found a moment to run a numb hand under that heavy jaw, scratch it, and run his hand under the colt's ratty mane. There was something about that colt, something that set him apart.

He surveyed the cutbank. It wasn't much, but Victoria had summoned the last of her strength to spread robes, gather the heaps of dead juniper brush, and scrape a bed ground clean of stones and debris. Skye found the mare tearing savagely at bits of dried grass poking out of the snow around the juniper. He added his meager supply of green bark to her fodder.

The last glimmer of twilight faded into deep cold night by the time they had the camp readied. But they had no fire. Skye sat down and pulled his flint and steel from a small pouch he carried at his belt. Air eddying up the coulee would make a fire difficult. He settled with his back to the wind, built a little hollow out of Victoria's brush, and began driving sparks into it, with no luck. Once one caught and held, an orange glow, but a moment later it died.

He pulled the robe right over his head, making a shelter. Then he scraped steel over flint, generating a fine shower of sparks, again and again until he saw a dozen of them glowing and curling in the thumb-sized bit of shredded bark tinder he always carried. He blew softly. The little glow worms glowed the more. He blew again, and again, and then the tiniest flame embraced a straw-sized twig. He had fire if only he could keep it. Half the battle was to feed it, keep it going, helping it gain heat. A trickle of smoke stung his eyes but he did not lift the robe. Instead, he edged tiny sticks, smaller than pencils, into the guttering little flame, patiently.

It took a long time, and he coughed a lot of smoke, but at last he pulled the robe away and began feeding larger sticks into the fire, while Victoria lay on her robes, exhausted. The fire would give them hot broth made from the pemmican, a priceless bounty for numb, worn, and cold people. The cutbank at the bend of the coulee was a good place, out of the wind, blocking it from most directions. With enough robes, and enough hope, and enough courage, they would live to the morning.

He tried to heat water but it wouldn't boil. There just wasn't enough heat in that juniper debris. Still, it warmed enough so he could steep some pemmican in it, and then let Victoria drink. It would warm her. He ate his pemmican cold. Then the kindling ran out, and there would be no more light or heat that night. He listened to the night sounds, heard the mare working industriously along the coulee, wherever a sheltered corner offered some dry grass. She would do well this evening, which was not at all what he expected. The colt followed his mother, but now and then trotted through the inky black to check on Skye.

Victoria huddled in her robes. He set his beaver top hat beside him, checked his Hawken and laid it beside him, made sure his belaying pin was close at hand, and then pulled the robes up, not finding any warmth at all in them. It would be a long time, if ever, before they felt comfortable this night.

"It is bad," she said. "My helper has gone away."

"Your helper will return."

"Dammit, Skye, when we get to the village, you go to Fort Sarpy and trade these robes for a jug. I am very thirsty. Firewater! That's what's keeping me going."

"I'll get some from Chambers," said Skye. "You and I are going to celebrate."

twelve

They stumbled south, blown by the north wind, until at last they walked down a long draw and into the valley of the Musselshell.

Skye rejoiced. This night there would be shelter from the wind, abundant firewood, feed for the mare, and maybe even game, a welcome prospect because the pemmican was nearly gone.

The starved mare was failing again; Victoria had walked this day, but she herself was weakening. Never had a river bottom seemed so welcome to Skye. They could regroup and then head down the Musselshell. The Crow winter camp nestled another day's walk downriver, under some protective sandstone bluffs that caught the winter sun and radiated it into the village.

As the short day faded, they hurried over a snowy waste with the wind whipping them until he thought the wind would drive him mad. But when they entered the bottoms they found a great quietness there. Animal tracks laced the old and hardened snow. A lacework of bare branches stabbed the purple twilight. There were jack pines and juniper greening every hollow.

The mare paused to snatch at every dried stem and stalk that poked through the snow. Skye pitied her. She had somehow dragged that travois all those miles and all the while making milk for that boneheaded little colt who ought to be shot.

He found a fine thicket close to the narrow river, deep in a bend curtained by forest and sheltered from the cruel north wind. He unhooked the travois, unsaddled the old mare, and turned her loose. She would make her own living this night. She headed for the river, stuck her nose in the purling water, and drank. The colt followed her, poking his nose into the river and butting her bag. Skye had forgotten how dehydrated animals got in the winter and reminded himself to give Victoria plenty of broth this evening.

She was already picking up loose sticks, breaking them off of trees, for they wanted a fire at once. They hadn't been warm in days, and he was dreaming of a hot blaze that would soak heat through his buckskins. Victoria looked about ready to collapse, but sheer will kept her going. She chopped willow limbs and stripped them and soon had the framework of an emergency shelter, a small domelike affair that would support a couple of robes and give them a sanctuary.

Skye took over the firewood collecting; this grand night he would heap up a mountain of it, and they would enjoy every stick of it. There was dead stuff at every hand, and he needed only to collect it, rap the snow off of it, and drag it to the shelter.

In deep blue dusk they finished their task, scraped snow out of the bed ground, lined it with rushes from the riverbanks, and began to nurse a tiny flame that soon grew into a hot, bright, happy campfire. But no amount of heat was enough. It burned and snapped, but it did not take the cold out of his body. It scarcely even warmed his numb hands. He wished for a rocky overhang, a place that would absorb and reflect the heat through the night, but there was no rocky cliff here. The river cut through prairie and they were camping on a floodplain.

He wasn't getting warm, but at least he could heat some pemmican and make a broth. He set up his cook pot and began a meal while Victoria lay under two robes, utterly drained.

Then he noticed that the mare had stopped gnawing and was staring upriver, her ears cupped forward. He had been around the wilds long enough to respond. He found his Hawken, checked to see if there was a cap under the hammer, and slipped into shadow away from the open-sided hut and the bright fire before it. His old mountain rifle with its percussion lock had never betrayed him. It shot true and faithfully, and now he held it at the ready.

He listened closely and heard the faint clop of hooves and something else, a hiss that sounded like iron tires rolling over icy ground.

"Hello the camp," came a voice out of the darkness.

Usually a good sign. No surprises.

"Come ahead," Skye replied.

Nothing happened for some while. Victoria had slipped out of her buffalo robes, grabbed the belaying pin, and joined him in the spidery darkness of the woods.

Not one but two wagons emerged out of the blackness, following along a river road Skye hadn't discerned in the twilight.

"Thought you might be a white man. Injuns don't make big fires like that."

"Who are you?"

"Sam Fitzgerald, trading man, and my son, George."

Somehow Skye didn't like the tone of all that. He rose, rifle in hand, and walked toward the horses and wagons, which stood dimly at the edge of the orange light. Bearded men stood beside the dray horses, each carrying a shotgun.

"I'm Mister Skye."

"Saw that top hat and figured it was so," said Fitzgerald. "Only man west of the Missouri that wears one of them things."

Skye thought it would be all right. "Fixing some broth; all we've got."

"Well, we've some meat. You have a fire. Sure is cold."

"Why are you out here with those wagons?"

"Hides. We head out to the villages and trade. Operating out of Fort Laramie. We been over to the Flatheads."

Skye nodded. This was the new thing. Traders headed out to the villages during winters, armed with goods and hoping to make a good trade for buffalo hides. It was a more aggressive and successful form of the buffalo-hide trade than waiting passively in forts for Indians to show up with a load of skins to dicker for knives, powder, baubles, and blankets.

Still, Skye was wary and intended to stay armed.

"All right; here's a fire. Warm up. We could use some meat."

"Make a camp here?"

"Maybe down a piece," Skye said. "Not much feed for horses."

"Saw that old plug. That's all you got?"

"Blackfeet," Skye said.

"Thieving bunch! We watch our topknots around them devils."

Victoria quietly emerged from the shadows.

"Ah, so you ain't alone," Fitzgerald said, surveying her too closely.

"This is my wife, Victoria. She took an arrow from the Blackfeet and is poorly. We're going to be glad to get to her village."

Victoria barely acknowledged these two, a sure sign that she didn't like their looks. She headed for the hut where she could oversee the cooking.

The traders steered their wagons ahead a bit and unhooked the dray horses. Both wagons were loaded with stiff buffalo hides, stacked like playing cards and held in place with stakes anchored to the sides.

What looked to be a deer hock hung from one, and this the son untied and brought to Victoria.

"Hey, cookum some grub, eh?"

Victoria rose and walked into the darkness.

"Feisty little squaw, ain't she?" Fitzgerald said.

Skye was having second thoughts but didn't know how to get rid of this pair. He didn't like the way the younger one was eyeing his wife. If he tried to mess with her, he'd find a lead ball passing between his eyes.

On the other hand, this pair was well armed and quick to act and dangerous. Skye settled down to a waiting game, and began sawing at the meat with his knife, gradually peeling away some steaks that could be cooked on a green stick.

"There you are," he said quietly. "Plenty of willow around; cut a stick and cook your meat."

Victoria had drifted toward the laden wagons and was floating around them, studying the contents. She was done with cooking, something he knew but the traders didn't.

"You done trading for this trip?" he asked.

"Yep, we've got over eighty prime hides, heavy devils, stacked up in them wagons. Out of trade goods, so we're heading for Sarpy to unload . . . You got something to trade?"

Skye shook his head. "Blackfeet cleaned us out. You got anything left to trade?"

"Nothing but our own kit."

"What did you start out with?"

"The usual. Knives, some trade rifles, powder and ball, blankets, trade cloth, hide scrapers, flints and steels . . ."

He left things unfinished.

"And whiskey," Skye said. "Where'd you trade?"

"West of hyar, mostly. Some Mountain Crow winter villages, some Bannocks, one Flathead bunch come over for some buffalo hunting."

Talk did not go well around that fire. The Fitzgeralds cooked their meat until it was burnt and then let it cool, while Skye and Victoria sliced theirs into smaller pieces.

"We've got a little sipping whiskey if you can give us something for it," old man Fitzgerald said.

"No."

"Cleaned out. We was going to have us a sip and maybe trade you for a few sips."

Skye sorrowed. If there was anything that would chase away the winter chill and ache, it would be a little sipping whiskey.

"We might work a little deal, Skye," said Fitzgerald, eyeing Victoria.

"Nothing here, friend. We have nothing of value. Now make your camp, yonder, and we'll settle ours. We're pretty well worn out."

But Sam Fitzgerald ignored Skye, headed for the lead wagon, unearthed a pottery jug and a tin cup, and settled at the fire.

"Ah, man, this here's the medicine for a cold night," he said, and poured an inch and added some creek water. He sipped, gave the cup to his son who sipped, and then the bearded young man handed it to Victoria.

"Sonofabitch!" she said, and swallowed a couple of good jolts. "Ah!" She managed another jolt and handed the cup to Skye, who drained off the rest. He felt a good hot fire build in his belly. His old friends the Fitzgeralds smiled and refilled from the earthenware jug and added a splash. The cup made its rounds once again, warming up an icy night; warming up Skye's cold belly. It would be a great evening.

thirteen

*N*ever so cold. Skye stared into a gray dawn. He was numb. Coldness had gathered around his heart. Coldness in his belly. Limbs half frozen and not working. He didn't want to get up but lay stiff and staring at the sky through the skeleton of Victoria's domed hut.

No robes covered it. No robes covered him. No robes covered Victoria. Nothing but deep cold and gray sky. One robe under them. The other robes were gone. He struggled to awaken himself. Now it was urgent. He didn't want to get up. He rolled a little, forcing his body to move. He peered fearfully at Victoria, who lay in her buckskin dress and leggings, looking ashen, a blue pallor upon her.

Get up! He made himself sit up. They were sleeping in open woods. No flame warmed them. The fire was only ash. He did not see his Hawken. So that was it. They saw a weapon they wanted and took it. Along with everything else.

He had to move or perish. He stirred, tried to rise, fell back, and then made himself stand on aching legs. There was no heat in him. He made himself walk, one step, another, then

few. He pushed himself into a lumbering walk, faster and
er, knowing he needed to move before he could help her, if
ne was not beyond help. When he returned she was still inert.
He rolled his half of the icy robe over her, tucked it down
around her. She didn't stir. He didn't know if she was breathing. He shook her gently and was rewarded with a sigh. Alive,
then. He pulled off his capote and spread that over her too.
Anything to catch her in a cocoon.

The Fitzgeralds had taken what they could. Robes, axe,
Hawken. But they didn't bother with his belaying pin, and he
had his hatchet, which was lying beside him. They had missed
it in the dark. His knife was still at his side.

Fire. Flint and steel, still in their pouch at his waist.

He stirred the ashes and found an ember buried under a
heap of half-burned deadwood. One small ember. He blew
softly, and it bloomed bright orange. He could not make his
fingers dig out any tinder. His hands were useless. But he had
breath so he blew and blew, worked his fingers, added a few
dry sticks, and blew some more, because his flint and steel
were worthless with hands that couldn't hold a feather. Some
smoke rose but the ember didn't bloom into flame.

He found a pocket of dry leaves caught in a knothole and
placed them over the ember. They smoked but didn't catch. He
found some reeds and grasses but they didn't ignite. Nothing
but icy ground and a tiny column of smoke.

He sat wearily, worn out by the struggle, and buried his
head in his arms, hardly knowing what to do. Still, he was alive,
and the living have a chance. He made his fingers work, opened
and closed his hands, and found he could hold things. He fumbled his flint and steel out of their purse at his waist and began
striking steadily, showering sparks upon the live coal and the
bits of tinder above it. The sparks caught and glowed orange.

He blew gently, and a tiny flame rose, barely an inch high, wavering but then holding as it bit into the tinder. There was no heat in it and wouldn't be for a long time. Now he hunted for dry stuff, mostly mossy deadwood he snapped off of trees, and laid gently over the worthless little flame, careful not to demolish it. The new stuff caught. Now he had a three-inch flame that wavered wickedly with every freshet that drifted through.

"Burn!" he cried.

There was no way to speed it up. He collected a heap of deadwood and added it, but it was icy and didn't catch. What good was fire when it didn't ignite anything?

Then he remembered his powder horn, hanging from his chest all the while. He twisted off the cap and poured a few grains into his palm and tossed it. There was a satisfying flash. He did it again, and got another flash, and some deadwood caught. He did it over and over, a few grains at a time, not enough to blow the fire out, and saw his miserable little fire expand, eat wood, send up some smoke. But it didn't heat. He held his hands to it, and scarcely felt any warmth.

He turned to Victoria.

She was staring.

"Cold," she said.

Alive. He was gladdened. He stumbled to her, knelt beside her.

"Got a fire started. They stole the outfit."

It was odd how she rolled out of the robe and stood, as if her body could laugh off the iciness. She absorbed the loss: no robes except the one they slept on. Rifle gone. Parfleche with pemmican gone. Cook pot and cup gone.

"They didn't even leave the jug," she said.

"Expensive night."

"I needed that," she said. Strangely, she laughed. "That was pure spirits with a little river water. One sip kicked like a mule. Two sips, dammit, Skye, that was good stuff."

She plucked up the robe, wrapped herself in it, handed Skye's blanket capote to him, and knelt beside the cold fire. He could still feel no heat from it but she was warming her hands over the flames. He wasn't getting any benefit from the fire, so he rose, wrapped his capote about him, and walked.

The old mare was not far, greedily gnawing bark from some saplings, and the colt was butting her bag, as usual. The colt saw him and barreled straight at Skye.

"Avast!" he roared.

The colt veered away and raced off again, enjoying a fine November morning.

Skye settled beside the crackling fire, letting the heat work through his buckskins. He thought he would never be warm again, warm down inside, in his belly and chest, in his limbs, in his toes and fingers.

He had a task. Go after them. He had a belaying pin and an old mare. They had rifles, good horses and wagons, and probably some revolvers and knives too. But he would do what he had to do.

If they were heading for the Crow camp down the Musselshell, he would catch up with them. They would cough up what they stole or learn what a limey with a belaying pin could do to them.

But not now. He was with Victoria, and she was weak and his one duty was to get her to the safety of her village as fast as he could. They were still more than a day from the Crows and didn't have a thing to eat and only one robe to warm them. Vengeance would have to wait.

No food, no rifle, and that meant speed. They had a long

walk to reach the Crow winter camp and he would not stop until he got there. He would somehow do it in a day and a half.

He sliced away some fringes from his buckskin shirt and tied them into a line, and made a string hackamore of it. Then he caught the mare, slipped the hackamore over her nose, and helped Victoria up. He wrapped the buffalo robe over her shoulders and she pulled it tight about her.

Skye looked longingly at the fire: it finally was throwing some heat. The Crows often transported a live coal bedded in moss and kept from the air, and used it to light the next fire. But he had no container; he would have to take his chances.

"Are you ready?" he asked her.

"We will go. I will walk when I get cold. Or the mare gets tired."

"We'll make it," he said.

She smiled. It was a beautiful smile that seemed like a blessing.

He took one last look at this bitter camp and then started resolutely eastward in the valley of the Musselshell, leading Victoria's mare while she clung to the mane.

He had starve-walked before. It required a steely will. An overcast kept him from knowing the hour. He walked slowly at first, letting the last of the spirits burn out of his body, making his cold muscles function. He set a steady pace, with the northwesterly breeze mostly behind him, his battered top hat anchored tightly in his long locks. For a while he followed the tracks of the iron-tired Fitzgerald wagons, the hoofprints fresh in the glazed snow. If he came upon the traders he would give them a fight no matter the odds. And he would have the advantage of surprise.

Maybe he and Victoria shouldn't have touched a drop of the whiskey. Maybe they would still have pemmican, robes, a rifle, and a saddle. But all the maybes in the world did him no good. He and Victoria were bone-weary. The spirits had offered a moment's refuge from cold and pain and trouble and they had imbibed the whiskey with delight. And it wasn't the spirits that had betrayed him, but the Fitzgeralds.

Just when he felt his first ebbing of energy, he redoubled his speed, leading the old mare eastward around river brush, along a natural road or animal trail on the north bank of the stream. He would not give in to tiredness. But he would rest the mare now and then, for Victoria's life still depended on that old cayuse.

The colt, Jawbone, trotted along beside, but sometimes ran ahead or fell behind. Maybe, Skye thought, he could make something of that boneheaded beast but he doubted it.

He came to a place where the wagons turned right, crossed the stream at a gravelly ford, and headed due south for the Yellowstone country. So they weren't going to Victoria's Crow camp after all. That was smart. If they showed up with Skye's Hawken in their arm, or with that parfleche, which had classical Crow geometric designs dyed upon it, they would not have walked out of the village alive.

Skye knew what he would do: he would walk the remaining miles nonstop, through the night, until he reached safety. Only when Victoria was safe in her brother's warm lodge would he himself rest.

fourteen

Skye walked. The mare carrying Victoria followed. He set a steady pace, letting his legs swing easily. If he was tired, what did it matter? He walked along a game trail that followed the Musselshell, thinking about nothing but making his legs work, step after step.

He stayed warm but Victoria, riding the mare, was soon chilled. Then he had to stop and let her walk and stretch, and then hand her up again. She never complained.

Skye had heard legends among the Indians of runners, of amazing young men who could run day and night for great distances carrying news. He had met some famous runners, lithe of body, able to jog along for prolonged periods. But he was not built that way. He was stocky and medium high. A man could walk if he set his mind to it; walk even when his feet began to torment him, his boots or moccasins chafed, his muscles hurt, and blood collected around his toes. Walk and not stop. Walk through twilight into night, walk through midnight and the small hours, walk into a dawn and keep on.

So Skye walked, and kept walking even when hunger

gnawed at him, even when he yearned to quit. There was no shelter at the end of this day, no place to quit, no food. There was water, but no more. He cupped his hands and lifted water to his lips sparingly, knowing it was too cold to sit well in him.

The mare did not disappoint him, but settled into a rhythm that matched his own pace, neither hurried nor slow.

Whenever he tired, he rested briefly. But if he didn't walk too fast, he didn't tire fast, so he moved steadily, sticking close to the river. The wind quartered in from the left, chilling him on that side, but he ignored it. He reached some rocky bluffs and rested in their lee for a while, and then started in again. Here in the bluffs were birds, including a pair of golden eagles, making a riverside living through the winter.

He tried to think of other things, but the weariness of his thigh and calf muscles trapped his mind and focused it on his body. His hunger died away and in its place was a keen edginess, as if he were facing danger. But there was no danger in sight, only the November-quiet valley of the Musselshell with its latticework of tree branches and a gloomy sky.

At twilight he rested in an undercut cliff, not a bad place to camp if he needed to. He lifted Victoria off the old mare and set the horses to scrounging in the brush. Jawbone was learning to get his own feed, and he gnawed beside his mother, finding sustenance in twigs.

"Are you cold?" he asked Victoria.

"Keep going, Skye."

That was answer enough.

He collected the old mare and hoisted Victoria aboard once again, and then set off into the deepening shadows as the November night fell. The next lap was going to be hardest of all. There was going to be no moon for the first half of the night, and when it did rise, it would be nothing more than a fat sliver. This night he would stumble through utter dark and hope he didn't meet disaster, such as falling into the river, which would probably kill him.

He chose open country this time, north of the dense riverbed brush and trees, believing he could make his way better back from the tangle of foliage. And that proved to be true. Nights with open heavens are not black, and the dome of heaven sheds its own faint light, so he walked on, the mare somehow keeping pace. He was never sure about Jawbone, but the little fellow managed to keep track and checked in now and then.

Night travel was not new to Skye but he had rarely traveled in this sort of cold, nor had he ever attempted to cover so much ground. The wind picked up now and then, filtering through his blanket capote. But he kept on. Step by step, through the night. Then the moon rose and he had a little more light and could see the dark wall of timber guarding the river.

He lost track of time. He could walk or he could try to hole up. The buffalo bull-hide moccasins Victoria had crafted for him were slowly opening along their inner seam and he wondered whether to stop for repairs. Some thong cut from the remaining robe might lace up the growing gaps. His feet ached but he would continue. Something in the rhythm of walking kept him going, even if every step shot pain through each foot.

For brief periods Victoria dismounted and walked with him, but she had no strength for it and retreated to the back of the mare. He sensed the mare was slowing now, and he let it happen and slowed his own pace to hers. The goal was not speed but to keep on going.

The landscape was changing and the river was running in a narrower valley flanked by high sandstone bluffs. That was a good sign. But he questioned whether he could go much farther; his body was finally rebelling. He sensed he might be within five miles of Victoria's village, maybe less. He had no way of knowing.

He heard the distant howl of wolves high up on the ridges to the north but heard no answering howl, and then heard only the silence of deep night. He thought it might not be long to dawn, but he saw no streak of light on the southeastern horizon, only the slow-ticking darkness.

The hunger pangs were returning now, not sharp as before, but cold and sullen. His body was telling him it needed nourishment or it would quit on him.

He ignored the trouble; there wasn't a thing he could do about his hunger except push it aside, pretend that his body wasn't howling at him. He was arguing with his body now, trying to impose his will upon it, as if it somehow would heed his wishes. But his steps were shorter and slower, and he knew he was reaching the end. They would have to quit. For a day and much of a night he had walked.

The mare snorted. Then whickered softly.

Skye stopped cold. That was horse talk. He had heard it a thousand times. The mare snorted again, a soft low rumble down in her throat.

Victoria came awake, slid off the mare, and took the lead line, holding the horse in place. Jawbone stood, questioning his mother. Skye edged forward, seeing little, unsure of what he was looking for. Jawbone danced along beside him, sometimes sniffing the night air, smelling something that Skye didn't smell.

Then the colt cut to the right, down a grade, and squealed. Skye hated to be given away by that miserable renegade but padded softly down the slope toward the river, which ran through grassy bottoms. Then he saw the shifting shapes of horses, lots of horses, some of them edging close to him. The colt stopped and snorted.

Now there was a great stirring of the herd. Skye thought he might be in real danger. In a moment he was surrounded by horses, which stared alertly at him, ready to break away, stampede. But they didn't.

Maybe Crow horses. He tried a few words of the tongue they might know: hello, friend, four-foots, and finally Absaroka, the name Victoria's people gave to themselves.

She came up beside him. "We have come," she said.

"How do you know?"

"I know."

These pronouncements had always mystified him. The Indians knew things in ways he could never grasp.

"We're likely to get shot."

"I will walk among them. They know me."

"How can they possibly know you?"

"We are sisters and brothers."

She handed the mare's lead line to Skye, and wandered slowly into the mass of animals, talking softly to them. They did not bolt but soon collected around her. He heard one tiny squeal, and that proved to be from Jawbone, who was being examined by the boss mares of this herd.

He tried desperately to see whether there were herders on this wintry night and worried that they would shoot first and ask questions later. But he saw no mounted form rise out of the dark.

"Come," Victoria said, a sudden lilt in her voice, the song in it celebrating her safe return to her people. She walked ahead, this time with Jawbone cutting through the animals like a ship's prow, and on across a broad but protected grassland bordering the river.

The pale slice of moon caught the quiet cones ahead, which were arranged in a great arc under the shelter of sandstone cliffs. Skye followed; this was now out of his hands. The herd mysteriously stopped, as if some invisible fence lay between the village and the pasture, though no fence did. And then they were clear of the village herd.

Before them stood the stately Crow lodges. Smoke eddied from a few, caught by the pale moon, but most stood silent and dark, the thin walls of buffalo hide protecting these people from all the evils of the night.

She knew exactly where to go, her step lithe and purposeful, and he followed slowly, aware that the mare's clopping behind him must sound like an invading army to these sleeping people. But no one exploded out of a door flap. And then she stopped before a certain lodge. He could not tell one from another, yet he knew this would be her brother's lodge. She scratched softly on the door and waited, while a small cloud slid over the moon and took away the light.

fifteen

gain, according to the polite Crow custom, Victoria scratched softly on the lodge
door flap of her brother Two Dogs and
waited. Victoria's other kin were with the Kicked-in-the-
Bellies band on the Big Horn this season. To Skye, feeling
his own weariness soak him, the wait seemed interminable.
But at last the flap parted slightly, and Skye recognized Night
Stalker, one of Two Dogs' wives. She stared, absorbing the pitiful sight, and muttered something. The flap closed. Skye heard
stirrings and the flap parted once again.

Two Dogs had awakened and was tossing dry grass onto
the coals of the fire. It smoked and then broke into a small
flame, immediately lighting the lodge. The other wife, Parts
Her Hair, was hastily pulling a robe over her hips. Two Dogs
had chosen her for his mating this night.

Two Dogs summoned his sister and Skye with a wave of
the hand, and Skye crawled into the warm and fragrant lodge,
which also contained this family's three children ranging from
infant to teen.

"Ah! Many Quill Woman! We may say your name at last!" said Two Dogs, a greeting that acknowledged that this family thought she had died.

Victoria sank into the robes, and Skye settled down beside her.

Then Jawbone poked his head and neck through the door.

"Aaee!" said Parts Her Hair, scrambling up, mostly naked, to chase the animal out.

Two Dogs stayed her with a barked word.

"Who is this?" he asked Skye.

"It is Jawbone, the foal of a mare that brought us here. He is a horse with medicine. His mother came to us, brought by the magpies, and saved my wife. She has great spirit."

"So he is. Welcome him," Two Dogs said to his wives.

They pulled the flap open and the colt stepped in.

"He is not a handsome horse but he is a horse that is destined to serve you well. Now, Mister Skye, tell us your news while my women heat some buffalo stew."

Skye did not mention his hunger or that neither he nor Victoria had eaten in two days. Their plight was obvious to this family. The children lay wide-eyed in their robes now, studying the visitors.

"My blessings upon this lodge of Two Dogs," Skye said.

It was this ritual that smoothed over the life of the Crows, and Skye remembered it now.

"And the blessings of Two Dogs goes out to his sister and her man."

This called for tobacco, so Two Dogs motioned to Night Stalker for his beaded pouch. She handed it to him, careful not to touch the pipe within, and he tamped tobacco into the pipe, with its bowl of red pipestone, and then lit it with a coal. He puffed and handed it to Skye, who puffed, though he hardly had energy for it. He wanted only to collapse into a warm robe in this safe place.

But there were rituals to perform, and only if they were performed could the peace and safety of the lodge be kept. And so they kept the ritual. It was also a way of preparing the lodge for the story that would follow. These kin and all of Chief Robber's village knew of the disaster up in the Judith basin, but none of them knew Skye and Victoria's story and believed they had perished.

Skye felt the tobacco quiet him, and struggled to stay awake while Two Dogs studied him calmly. At last Skye was able to narrate the story of their struggle against the north wind that had brought down an early winter upon them. How close Victoria was to death. How slowly Victoria's wound healed. How weak she remained. His Crow was rudimentary, but they sat patiently as he struggled for words. His tale of hardship, of wolves, of cold and heavy snow, of hunting for firewood, and of the miraculous appearance of the bony mare and her ugly colt, all caught their fancy, and they listened soberly. Skye told of being robbed by the traders named Fitzgerald and did not neglect to tell how ardent spirits had been employed to rob them.

Victoria, he saw, was falling asleep. No one awakened her.

When the stew was steaming, Parts Her Hair, who didn't bother with her fallen-down robe, ladled it with a horn spoon into two bowls. She shook Victoria gently and when Victoria emerged from her stupor, handed one bowl to her and the other to Skye. He ate gratefully, relishing the hot meat broth. He spooned it into him, admiring Parts Her Hair, whose honey-eyed flesh glowed in the firelight.

The Crows never bothered with decorum, and Skye had been a long while getting used to it. Unlike other tribes, the

Crows mated anywhere and everywhere, in public or in private. Skye's whole instinct had been to back away, turn his head, retreat, but that had only won hoots from Victoria, who thought Skye was being prissy. She often teased him about it, and Skye didn't mind the teasing because it always led to good times.

Two Dogs spoke to his older son, and the youth, clad in leggins and breechcloth, rose out of his robes, steered Jawbone out the lodge door, and pulled the robe from the mare.

"He will take your horses out to the herd, and we will see that they are watched over," Two Dogs said. "When sun returns to light my way, I will go out to the herd with you, and you will show me this medicine mare and this colt you call Jawbone. For mark my words. There has come into my lodge this night an animal unlike any I have ever seen. We Absaroka know more about horses than any other people. We have more and better horses. They live in the mountains south of the Yellowstone River. We have beautiful horses, sleek and fast. But this ugly one . . . it is upon me to tell you that I felt the presence of a power I have not before experienced."

Skye nodded. In truth, he could no longer keep his eyes open. Food, warmth, safety, comfort, all conspired against wakefulness. Two Dogs watched him sharply. "We welcome our friend and kin Mister Skye, and honor the Great Walk, for it will always be known to us as the Great Walk," Victoria's brother said, and Skye's last recollection was someone drawing a robe over him on the right side of the lodge, the place of honor, and then he was lost to the night and to the great village of Chief Robber.

When he woke the next day he was confused, hardly able to sort out the scents and sights around him. Clearly it was midday, not morning. He did not see Victoria. He was uncertain about the young Absarokas who studied him solemnly.

Two Dogs' lodge. Safety. Warmth.

He sat up, rattled, ashamed of oversleeping and impeding the daily life of these people. He wrapped a robe around him and poked his head out of the door, surprised to find the sun behind him. This east-facing lodge had seen the sun rise and begin to set as he slept.

Outside, sitting on a reed backrest, was Two Dogs, wrapped in a red Hudson's Bay trade blanket and enjoying a mild November day.

"Ah, Mister Skye! You have returned from your long trip," he said. "Come enjoy the afternoon. Your story has won the hearts of the People and they wish to see you. All day they have walked by here, looking for a word with you, a chance to see the Walker."

Parts Her Hair, now dressed primly in buckskins, smiled sweetly and began warming some ribs of buffalo for Skye.

"Where is Many Quill Woman?" Skye asked.

"She has gone to the sweat lodge to purify herself. She has some sweetgrass to put on the fire, and its scented smoke will drive the sickness out of her."

Skye settled down beside his host. He discovered both the mare and Jawbone tethered to the lodge and eating some dry grass that had been harvested for them.

"That colt, Mister Skye. I see wings in the sky above it. I see lances and battle-axes. It is a warhorse. It is the greatest of warhorses."

"Your vision is larger than mine," Skye said. "I see an ugly little gray thing with a jaw that is too large for its head, and a madness in its eyes."

Two Dogs laughed. "We shall see," he said.

"I am indebted to you," Skye said.

"There is no debt among kin. You were dead and now are alive. The women are sewing skins and before the sun sets they will have a new lodge for you. My sons are gathering our horses and you will take your pick. You will need four or five. We are rich in horses and you are not. Chief Robber's wives have brought you two robes, and his sons have brought you a forequarter of buffalo cow, killed only two days ago. There will be other gifts in your lodge, including a hackamore and other horse tack, and parfleches filled with pemmican, and a spare dress and leggins for your woman."

"I have no way to repay you."

"You already have. Your Hawken barked many times, felling buffalo for this village, protecting it from the thieving Blackfeet. Someday, we hope, you will have enough robes to trade for another rifle. I hear tell of a new Buffalo gun called a Sharps, but it is only a whisper. No one has ever seen one."

"Never heard of it," Skye said.

Even as he sat, blotting up the mild sun, a band of ponies wended its way through the village, driven by half a dozen Crow boys. Skye knew they would stop before him, and he would be given his choice.

Two Dogs rose and waited, and then nodded to Skye when the herd reached this warm place in the sun, milling and churning, restless at being in the middle of Chief Robber's village. Skye's brother-in-law nodded. Skye stood slowly, doffed his top hat, and studied the horses. He was a seaman, a mountain man, not half the expert with these animals as his hosts, who knew everything there was to know about horseflesh.

Jawbone trotted into the herd, began butting animals, and in a minute had isolated four quivering ponies, a mare and three stallions, two of them yearlings, one older. They were fine animals.

Skye marveled. Two Dogs laughed softly.

"He is telling you," Two Dogs said.

Skye nodded, and watched that colt butt the older horses until they were out of the herd. Jawbone was no horse; he was something Skye couldn't explain, something that had no words to express it.

sixteen

Walks to the Top was in no hurry to receive his visitor so Skye waited in the winter cold. The old man held the office of Tobacco Planter, and thus was deeply esteemed among the Absaroka. He was also a seer, a visionary. Skye had little to give this eminent man but had brought him an armload of firewood for a gift. It wasn't much of a gift from a male, because the gathering of firewood was woman's work. But he had nothing else to give, being a pauper. A gift of tobacco would have served better. A haunch of buffalo still better for the old man was totally dependent on the village to keep him alive and warm and well.

Jawbone didn't like the cold wait, and butted Skye.

"Avast!" Skye bellowed.

Jawbone only laid back his ears and lowered that thick skull and pushed at Skye's midriff. The little colt didn't want this interview.

At last the arrogant old man deigned to open his flap, eye his visitor and the colt, stare at the modest heap of small sticks, and nod. It was not an invitation to enter.

Skye summoned up his rudimentary Crow tongue. "I have come to seek your wisdom, Grandfather."

"I have no wisdom for you."

"It is about this colt."

"That is the worst excuse for an animal I have seen."

"A magpie, the spirit guide of my wife, brought this colt and his mother to us at a time of great need. The mare saved the life of my wife."

The Tobacco Planter stared, and then Skye saw mockery in the man's face. He didn't believe a word of Skye's story.

Jawbone detached himself from Skye and pushed toward the old man until he stood inches away, his muzzle almost in Walks to the Top's face.

"He has something else. Something rare. A will, a force."

"Cut its throat."

"I am seeking your counsel about him. I have given him a name. He is Jawbone. What will he be? A buffalo runner? A warhorse? A hunting horse?"

"No good will come of him. This I see. This animal should be driven from the village. Give him to the Piegans so they may suffer this colt's evil."

Jawbone lowered his head softly and pressed it into the old man's chest, pushing him back toward the lodge door.

"Jawbone!" Skye yelled, and grabbed the colt by the mane and pulled him back. But the insult had been done. The wizened old man, prominent and powerful among the People, had been offended by a colt.

The old Tobacco Planter straightened himself and drew a blue and black trade blanket about him, eyeing the colt, and Skye, with an obsidian gaze that raked them both. He wore the insignia of his rank, including a bearclaw necklace, a powerful reminder that he was not to be trifled with.

"Tell this to The Robber; tell it to the headmen, for I have said it. This village will know no peace, no comfort, no food, no heat, no buffalo, no safety, no new children, no honor until this monstrous creature is removed and the village is cleansed with sweats and prayers."

Skye stood frozen. It would be up to him to report, faithfully, the exact words of the old Tobacco Planter to the headmen.

"I do not want your wood," the old man said. "Bring something that does you honor. Not this." He pushed his moccasin into the piled wood and scattered it.

"Suppose I don't bring this colt into the village but keep him and his mother in the herd . . . I am indebted to the mother. She carried Many Quill Woman all the way here, though the old mare was perishing from the want of feed, and because she was nursing this colt."

"I have spoken," Walks to the Top said, cutting off all further discussion. The old man's eyes betrayed something that Skye had not fathomed before: a contempt for strangers in the midst of this Absaroka village. For a pauper.

He leisurely turned, showing his blanketed back to Skye for too long, and then slipped into his cold lodge. Skye stood there, ripped asunder. Behind him stood the village, nestled under the snowcapped sandstone cliff lining the north bank. Here in a peaceful bottomland the Musselshell River meandered through lush grasses and cottonwood and willow groves. A low autumnal sun heated the sandstone cliff each day, and far into each night the cliff radiated its stored warmth upon these fortunate and comfortable people.

It was Victoria's home, or at least her brother's home. Her own Kicked-in-the-Bellies band was down on the Big Horn River. He wondered whether she would agree with the old Tobacco Planter that the colt must be destroyed or exiled. That its presence would invite disaster upon her People. That he must do as the old man directed or be driven out of this place.

He was a pauper now. The Hawken rifle that had won meat for the whole village had been stolen and he had no weapon save for a knife and his ancient belaying pin. Those were good enough for close-quarters war, but of little value here in this vast plain. He had no grasp of archery and could not hunt with bow and arrow, the way any Crow boy could. Bows and arrows were not weapons known to a British seaman. Just now he was dependent on these people for everything. For every scrap of food. For the lodge the village women were sewing together for him and Victoria. For clothing, moccasins, safety. He had gone from being an asset to a serious liability, someone who needed to be cared for. His rifle had meant meat and hides and a trump against the more numerous Blackfeet and Sioux. Without it, and without skill with a bow and arrow, he was . . . nothing.

He stood in the warm sunlight, absorbing his new status of beggar. The colt edged in and rubbed against him. Well, he would destroy the colt. Slit its throat. Worthless ugly thing. Kill the mare too, because the old creature would be frantic about the colt. Mercy killing. She was starved anyway and her teeth were no good. She couldn't gain weight even if he fed her buckets of oats. He would collect his courage, his ability to do hard things, and do them. They were just strays who happened upon his desperate little camp up in the Judith country. So do what must be done.

But first there were obligations. He walked slowly toward the great lodge of the chief, The Robber, a famed and revered leader of the Absarokas. The Robber and his wives had already given him four lodge skins, and these were even then being sewn into the new lodge that the village would give him and Victoria.

Skye found the fat graying chief warming in the sun before his lodge, enjoying an idle afternoon along with three headmen, every one of them a noted warrior. He paused, waiting for the invitation that would permit him to approach. It came at once, for Skye was still a respected man among them.

He approached, and found the chief and headmen waiting. They had been playing a stick game to while away the sunlight hours. In the evenings they often told stories. The headmen glanced at Skye, but their attention was focused on the audacious colt, which dogged every step and presented himself to the chiefs just as Skye was presenting himself.

Skye studied them, aware that his broken Absaroka tongue was not adequate to the task. But he knew the sign-talk, and decided to employ it.

"I have visited the Tobacco Planter," he began. "The elder has pronounced what he believes. It is this: he says that this colt beside me is a curse upon the people and must be destroyed. He will bring evil upon the village. He will unloose trouble."

"And?" asked The Robber.

"And so I am first to tell you every word of what Walks to the Top has said."

"And?"

"Then I must decide what to do."

"Is there any decision to be made?"

"Yes, sir, there is."

"And what might that be, Mister Skye?"

"To spare the lives of this colt and its mother, who brought Many Quill Woman to safety."

That met with dead silence. It would be an act of defiance. It would signal trouble and sorrow.

"We each must follow our own path, and we each must bear the consequences," said The Robber. It was not unkindly said.

But Otter, the headman, had other ideas. "If that is what the elder believes, then the colt must die."

"Or leave, or be given to other people," Skye said.

"I personally will destroy the colt for the sake of the People," Otter said.

"It is . . ." Skye caught himself. He was going to tell Otter that it was not his to destroy. It was something Skye alone had to do.

Skye glimpsed the black and white flash of a magpie, and remembered suddenly that it was Victoria's spirit helper, the magpie, who had somehow driven and pecked the mare and the ugly colt to Skye's lodge on Louse Creek, clearly a gift of Victoria's helper.

"The horses were the gift of magpie," he said. Every headman knew whose spirit helper the magpie was.

The colt stood quietly and then walked boldly to the headmen and studied them. Skye had never seen such a fearless colt.

Otter didn't like it and growled at the colt. Jawbone didn't budge, and slowly lowered his head and pushed straight at the headman, who was surprised and then enraged. Otter lashed wildly at the colt, who danced away unharmed and bleated cheerfully.

Chief Robber raised a weathered hand. "It is so," he said. "The elder has shown it. Take him from the People. I do not wish to see this colt again, and if I see it, I will have it killed at once."

seventeen

Skye walked away from The Robber's commodious lodge with the strange colt prancing beside him, butting him, and otherwise making a nuisance of itself. Behind him, the chief and village headmen stared, and their gazes were not friendly. Something sour had happened, and Skye couldn't fathom it.

One moment Skye was a hero, renamed The Walker for delivering Many Quill Woman to safety even though she was weak and had been at death's door. Now the village glowered at him and his colt, the foal of the very mare that had borne his wife all that distance.

Was it the colt? The elder had condemned it out of hand, employing his authority as a shaman, to sentence Jawbone to death. And for what? Because Jawbone was unlike other colts? Because Jawbone was fearless? Fear is what governs horses. They sense danger and they run, for their safety lies in escape. But this little fellow marched right into Two Dogs' lodge, butted people, pushed the shaman backward, and didn't behave like a horse. Was that it?

Skye knew it wasn't. An obnoxious horse might be welcomed in a village, but there was something more, something having to do with medicine powers known only to the grandfathers, that had set this village on edge. Jawbone was a dark force, a looming danger, and The Robber had condemned the colt to die, for not even a chief would overrule the verdict of a Tobacco Planter and elder such as Walks to the Top.

Skye didn't know what to do. He could slice that colt's throat, but he knew he wouldn't. He knew somehow that Jawbone was a magical colt who would bring great good fortune to him. The ugly little thing was a gift to a pauper, and it had come to him in a moment of crisis. He would not kill it, nor would he kill the old mare that had rescued them.

Magpies burst away from him, and he thought to tell Victoria who lay abed in the lodge, weakened by the long and desperate trip from the buffalo hunt. But as he walked through the village he felt the hard stares; men who yesterday had honored him and hunted with him and welcomed him now stood silently, their gaze on him and on the condemned colt.

It was a rare and warm late autumn day, with the village nestled comfortably under the yellow rimrock, soaking up the low sun. It was a good day to be alive. Most of the men were out hunting. The disaster up in the Judith country had depleted the supply of meat and hides and robes, as well as horses. The buffalo were nowhere near here, but deer were abundant, and there were elk too. The women were gathering firewood in the thick woods along the river or tending to their cook fires or lacing new moccasins together, or collecting in knots to dress skins and scrape hides and enjoy the mild air. Some of them were out in the woods, cutting willow saplings that could be employed as lodgepoles. Old men and old women, dark and wrinkled, wrapped themselves in grimy blankets and watched the world go by. Blue smoke drifted up from the lodges, which were blackened on top around the smoke holes.

But it was no idyll for Skye, for people paused and stared at him, the executioner's glare in their faces. And some turned their backs, not on Skye but on the condemned animal, who it was believed carried a bad spirit that menaced the village.

Not far from Two Dogs' lodge a dozen women were lacing hides together, making a lodge for Skye and Victoria. It was a tedious process but with so many hands patiently lacing one hide to another the work was progressing rapidly. By nightfall he and Victoria would have a home of their own.

If he slit Jawbone's throat.

He paused at the lodge door, scratched, for he was a guest, and received a word from within. He entered. Jawbone followed.

"Get him out!" said Victoria, who was sitting up in a reed backrest.

Skye grabbed Jawbone by the mane and evicted him. Jawbone contented himself by poking his head inside and observing. Skye thought it was funny but kept silent.

"I have heard it," she said. "You will do it?"

"No. This is my own spirit horse. I won't do it."

Victoria stared, bleakly registering that. It meant trouble, or worse, it meant Skye might be banished from this place.

"I am going away for a while," he said.

"You will not return."

He saw a sorrow in her face and knew what she was thinking. So many women of the People had married a white man only to have that man abandon them and their children and go back to the place where white men lived. She had seen the East; she knew its comforts.

"I will be back, Victoria. I'm going to the American Fur post on the Yellowstone and see about a job. I've traded pelts for years and I think I can get a wage there."

"You will buy a rifle," she said.

"Yes. I'm not much good without it. Without my rifle I am nothing here. I can't make meat. I can't feed us. I can't get hides and trade them for a rifle and powder and ball. I can't help your people in war."

She nodded sadly. "Dammit, Skye, take me with you!"

"I will come for you."

He saw tears collecting in her obsidian eyes, and reached across to her, slipping her cold hand into his big rough ones.

"Every hour that we are parted, I will be thinking of you and dreaming of the time I will send for you. It will be a while. I must earn enough to buy a new rifle and all the rest. But someday I will have what is needed."

"And you will take the mare and the colt?"

"Yes. We are all exiled."

"Exile, what does that mean?"

"Banished. We must leave."

"I am glad. Magpie brought them to us."

"Today, a magpie was flying and flitting around the colt and me."

She nodded. "But you cannot bring them back to this village."

"First I'll get some work if I can at the trading post on the Yellowstone. Fort Sarpy, out on the plains. Get a rifle and an outfit. Then we'll go to Long Hair's village on the Big Horn River, the Kicked-in-the-Bellies, and we will be with your kin. Then I will come for you. We'll end up with your people."

She sighed. "It is so far away."

"It will take one or two moons for you to gain your strength. It will take me that long to buy a rifle."

"Dammit, Skye, you think I am an old woman?"

He laughed, his big voice booming in that small, enclosed cone of leather.

She grinned. "Maybe I will show up at the trading post. Maybe I will surprise you. Maybe I will catch you between the robes with some girl. Maybe I will crawl between the blankets with you. Then you'll see I am well and strong."

He touched her face with his thick fingers, gently rubbing the tears away.

"Will I ever see you again? I am feeling so bad."

"I will be coming for you soon. I must have a rifle. Tell Two Dogs I will come for my ponies some other time. And thank him for caring for them."

It was a painful moment. He kissed her. She smiled at him. He stood, gazed down at her lithe but gaunt beauty, and knew he would never leave her.

He collected his few things: a robe, hatchet, blanket capote, saddle, halters, belaying pin, and some pemmican, enough to keep him going for two days. There were two dangers: cold and Blackfeet, and he would not be well armed against either.

He shooed the colt away from the door flap and crawled into the beautiful afternoon. People had halted their labors and were staring at him. He nodded curtly, not explaining himself though the things he carried told the tale. The colt trotted along beside him, inseparable, and drew cold glances. He continued beyond the village, walking through open bottomland, past young herders riding slowly around the horse herd. The colt squealed and barreled straight toward his mother, who turned her head and watched. She remained gaunt, but somehow looked better.

Skye saddled her, not to ride her but to carry his few possessions, and when he was ready, he walked her to the river, looking for a ford. When he found it he mounted her and she carried him across a flat gravelly shallows. Then he dismounted; from now on, he would walk.

He didn't know this country well, but knew there was a low divide between this river and the Yellowstone, and once he had topped it he could follow any watercourse south and he would end up at that majestic river, one of his most cherished streams and one where he had spent his happiest times.

In all his years with Victoria he had scarcely been apart from her, and only for brief periods. But now he would be gone awhile. He made his lonely way south, a solitary man, half trapper, half native, wearing buckskins, moccasins, capote, but also wearing his battered beaver top hat.

He hoped to earn his way back. He needed a whole outfit, but especially a rifle. With that, he could be a valued guest among the Crows. Without it . . . he was a parasite. He didn't know whether the fur post, Fort Sarpy, would hire him; and if he could not find employment there, he would head for another, either Fort Union at the confluence of the Yellowstone and Missouri, or Fort Laramie, far south. And every step would carry him farther away from his woman.

eighteen

He raised Fort Sarpy just before dusk, when the cold was setting in along with a knife-edged wind. The fur-trading post stood on the north bank of the Yellowstone, below Rosebud Creek, like a grim and solitary prison. It was nothing but four picketed walls of wood, and its bleakness matched the surrounding country.

Skye led his mare and colt along the brushy river bottom, alert for trouble. The Blackfeet had made winter sport of killing any man who dealt with the Crows, and there were often two or three Blackfeet lurking around Sarpy, looking for a chance to bury an axe in the skull of a trader. The little graveyard behind the post had seven mounds of clay in it.

Skye knew that a belaying pin was no match for one of these assassins so he trod gingerly, keeping out of sight in brush, avoiding open trails as much as he could. The forbidding fort rose starkly ahead, on a hill above the floodplain. There was abundant forest in the bottoms to feed its fireplaces and stoves, and river transportation to Fort Union, down a way, where robes and hides could be shipped to the States. It was the most solitary and desolate post in the Northwest.

He saw no Absaroka lodges at the post, but the old, glazed snow was dimpled with hoofprints and other signs of life and passage. The purple twilight settled gently over this land of long rises, tinting the gray smoke rising from the post's chimneys. He walked in utter silence, the sort of quietness imposed by late November on an empty land, hearing not even a crunch of snow under his moccasins.

He had been here several times, usually in fall or summer, when Crow lodges filled the whole plain below the post, like a fleet at full sail. But now he saw not even a raven perched in a branch. He knew the post's bearded and long-haired factor, John Chambers, who scorned and ridiculed the Crow people but was perfectly at ease driving hard bargains with them, a few pennies worth of trade goods for a good robe or hide.

No one greeted him as he walked across the flat in a lavender dusk.

"Hello the post," he bawled.

He saw no one manning the walls.

"Hello the post!" he yelled.

"Someone is talking a strange tongue. We haven't heard it in a long time," a voice returned. "Would you be talking some fool language called English?"

"I am Mister Skye."

"Oh! The damned limey! Living in sin with a Crow slut."

Skye kept the peace. He had heard it all before. It was a way of testing and provoking him. When he was younger, an insult like that always got a fight from him, and he usually gave more than he received. His broken and pulpy nose was mute testimony to his brawling. But now he lifted his old top hat from his head, let them stare through the deepening murk.

"Guess it's himself, all right."

"It's Mister Skye, you bloody damned yellow-bellied Yank."

He heard only a maniacal laughter, but moments later one of the ten-foot-high double doors creaked open and a pair of traders motioned him in.

"We don't let Brits in here," one said. "Now if you were a good honest upright Crow chief with a dozen daughters, we'd let you in."

The other laughed.

The post was typical, with an open yard surrounded by lean-to sheds around the walls.

"Welcome, Skye. I suppose ye want us to put you up."

"You can feed me, water and hay my horses, and give me some floor to sleep on. I want to talk to Chambers."

"That's me, Skye."

"So it is. The darkness fooled me. It's Mister Skye, mate."

"Lord Admiral Skye if you insist."

Chambers opened the gate, let Skye through, then slammed it shut and dropped the bar to keep the redskins out.

"I keep forgetting, you put on them English airs," he said. "We're a little shorthanded here. Lost two men a few days ago. Pesky Blackfeet. You'll have to put up your beasts yourself. The stew pot's full of meat. Good to see you."

That sounded good to Skye, who had subsisted on pemmican for two days.

"I'll be with you directly," Skye said. The horse pen was on the west side. Any animal left outside the walls would vanish and never be seen again. He put the mare and Jawbone in, watched them stir up the half a dozen other horses, and watched Jawbone horn in on some prairie hay that was lying in a manger. Skye found some more hay and fed the mare, hoping she would get it before the others crowded her out.

He watched them a moment, satisfied that his animals had food and drink, and then hiked across the yard to the one lit room, the light radiating from windows plugged with leather hides scraped so thin they were translucent. They were a thousand miles from glass at this lonely place.

He hoisted his few belongings and headed for the common room, a kitchen and dining and social place, the only one in the post. He walked into a wall of warmth. They weren't lacking wood, anyway, and the brightly burning fire in the hearth was throwing heat into every corner.

He set down his robe and saddle and small travel bag and belaying pin and top hat.

Chambers watched him intently. "That's all you've got? No rifle?"

"Two traders named Fitzgerald stole it. And everything else. And I want to talk about that. You got any outfits out in the villages?"

Chambers squinted at him, spat some tobacco, and shook his head. "That'd be the Opposition. Probably the two working for Carson and McCullough. They're hitting the winter villages."

"Father and son?"

Chambers nodded.

"Well, if I find 'em I intend to get my piece back, one way or another. And maybe bang a few skulls."

Chambers looked impatient. "It ain't us and don't you blame us, limey."

"You got any rifles to trade? Real rifles, not muskets?"

"You got any hides or cash?"

Skye laughed. That was a thing about him: anger washed away as fast as it rose.

He discovered four others, mostly so young they looked

fresh out from the States. One scarcely could raise a beard, by the looks of the boy.

"I'm Barnaby Skye," he said. "Call me Mister."

They didn't introduce themselves but he would put names to faces soon enough. The stew pot was hanging on an iron hook over the hearth fire. He hunted for a ladle and a bowl, finally washed out some dirty crockery and spooned the broth into it, savoring the smell.

A much-hacked haunch of buffalo hung from a beam. Meals around Sarpy were plainly self-accomplished. He lifted the bowl, sipped from it, and finally ate with his fingers for the want of a spoon. But it tasted just fine, good meat and salt and some sort of root vegetable tossed in. The rest watched glumly and he wondered just what had gone wrong with this meeting.

Skye finished a hearty meal and took a second bowl for good measure. He hadn't eaten like that for a long time. He wiped his face and turned to his hosts.

"Blackfeet trouble?"

"Never stops. Those two hunters vanished a week ago. We don't know whether they're alive or dead."

"Two of your engaged men?"

"Yost and Parsons. They went out to make meat and never came back. Now we're down to what you see here. No way I can defend this place anymore."

"Crows been around?"

"All the time, but that doesn't mean there ain't times like this when this post's naked."

"You want another man?"

"You?"

"I'm wanting to work to pay for a new outfit. Rifle above

all else. But also powder, ball, and all the rest. I don't have a shilling to my name. I've done a lot of trading and trapping for American Fur, the Upper Missouri outfit. You'll get an experienced man."

Chambers eyed him. "I was thinking of quitting here. Just four men and me against the whole redskin world."

"Nothing I can't do."

"Skye, that's fine, but you'd never save up enough for a rifle and a kit. Not with them horses you'll have to board with me."

"If I cut enough cottonwood bark every day to keep my horses without using your hay, then what do I make a month?"

"Thirty dollars and board."

"And what does a new rifle cost?"

"More'n you'll ever earn here."

Skye laughed. "Then I'll buy a used one. I'll just have to make myself profitable. By the time I was a brigade leader during the beaver days, I was earning a thousand a year. Put me on, Chambers."

"It's Mister Chambers, Skye."

They laughed uproariously, as if that were the funniest thing all fall.

"Now, Skye, I have a question for you. That's the sorriest mare and colt I ever did see. Mare might make a pack animal, but that colt; there's no help for an ugly little cuss like that. What you should do with them is slit their throats and turn 'em into jerky."

Skye stopped his merriment cold. "Anyone who harms those animals will be dealt with in kind."

"That's mighty peculiar, Skye."

"You heard me," Skye said. "In kind. A life for a life, a wound for a wound."

"Mind telling me why?"

"They came to me out of heaven," Skye said.

The factor and his four men stared at the newcomer, hardly knowing what to make of such a man.

nineteen

Skye woke up that mid-November day to find himself an employed man. The American Fur Company owned him now. He had risen high in the ranks of that company, becoming a brigade leader back in the beaver trapping days.

Now the beaver days were gone. The beaver had been trapped out, but fashion had changed also, and the beaver felt top hat had given way to silk. The company had drifted into the buffalo robe trade and continued to dominate the unsettled American West.

Skye felt at home. He knew his value: he could speak Crow, was married into the tribe, and was a veteran of the fur trade, knowing the whole business. He didn't doubt that he could be of service, especially when the rest of this crew seemed to be green youths fresh out of the border towns of Missouri.

Chambers probably thought more of Skye than he thought of Chambers. Through those November days Skye listened to the factor's unending litany of contempt for the Absaroka people. Thieving rascals he called them; immoral, gross, childish. He had a way of condemning everyone and everything about the people who traded at Fort Sarpy. Skye simply shut up and did his work and waited until he could trade his labor for the new outfit he needed.

The morning after Skye arrived, Chambers took him into the trading room to familiarize Skye with the stock. There were the usual striped trade blankets, kettles, awls, knives, arrow points, powder, pre-cast bullets, lead and bullet molds, calico, flannel, beads, thread, needles, flints and steels, and rifles. It was those rifles that absorbed Skye. His old Hawken was gone, though he·intended to get it back if he ever saw it again. He knew that rifle better than he knew his own face. But here was a battered Hawken and assorted muskets and Indian trade rifles perched on a rack.

One new rifle caught his eye instantly: it had an octagon barrel and was made of blued steel, and was unfamiliar.

"A Model 1852 Sharps," Chambers said. "Fifty-two caliber. Anything hit with a ball that size stays down." He lifted the rifle off its rack and handed it to Skye. Everything was unfamiliar. It had a sliding breech action and used linen or paper cartridges. When the breech closed it tore the paper, exposing the powder to the cap. But even the caps were different; they came ten to a small rotating disk.

"A man can fire this rifle ten shots to a minute," Chambers said.

"Ten shots? One minute?" Skye had never heard of such a thing.

"The capper rotates. You slide in a cartridge, close the breech, aim and fire."

"A shot every six seconds? That's faster than an Indian can nock an arrow and shoot it."

Chambers nodded. "Evens the odds, don't it?"

It certainly did. Skye thought through the long roll call of dead trappers he had known, men who died because it took so long to pour powder down a muzzle-loader, jam the patch and ball home, pour powder in the pan or slip a cap over the nipple, aim and fire.

Skye hefted the rifle, felt the sliding breech snap shut, dry-fired, and suddenly wanted it worse than he had ever wanted anything in a trader's store. "How much?"

Chambers laughed. "More'n you'll ever earn, Skye. Over a hundred dollars for the bare rifle, and the rest, the caps and cartridges, cost a pretty penny."

"We'll see about that. Now, Mr. Chambers, what's a carbine like this doing here? Not an Indian on the plains can afford it."

"Wrong, Skye. The fur company knows better. Some chief walks in here, finds a rifle he can shoot like that, every six seconds, and he wants it so bad he'll bring in a thousand dollars of hides and pelts, kill half a buffalo herd, and throw in all his wives in the bargain. Company figures one of these will fetch a thousand percent profit."

Skye didn't like that. Chambers probably wouldn't sell him the rifle even if Skye came up with the cash.

"If I bring in enough hides, you'd sell it to me?"

Chambers just laughed. "Skye, those shelves need cleaning. Pesky thieves made off with half our sugar and coffee last time."

"I'll hunt, Chambers. You need a hunter?"

"They'd kill you too."

"Not if I use the Sharps."

"I'm not letting the Sharps out of here unless it's paid up. A Sharps in the hands of some Piegan or Blood could just about knock the props from under the fur company. Bad times, Skye. No one's making much."

"I've heard that before," Skye said.

Skye found himself doing whatever needed doing. There were hides to be graded and protected with bug powder. Firewood to be felled and chopped and hauled. Stores to be inventoried. And once in a while a Crow party showed up, wanting sugar or coffee or candy or firewater. The spirits were illegal, but Chambers no doubt had a private supply hidden somewhere. Skye guessed it was kept in a cellar under the factor's own room. Skye wished he could trade a few hides for some of that stuff himself. But he knew if he just waited around that post, there would be a fandango sooner or later. Meanwhile, he went dry.

Chambers soon gave Skye the tasks that required some experience. Skye sometimes did the trading, but Chambers didn't like it: Skye always gave an honest weight of gunpowder or coffee or sugar, and failed to stick his thumb into the measuring cup.

"Skye, you'll never earn anyone a profit," Chambers said.

"It's Mister Skye, mate."

So Chambers pulled Skye from the trading counter and sent him out to make meat while the greenhorns around the post did the menial work such as loading in the firewood and bug-powdering the hides in the storeroom and feeding the horses.

Skye borrowed one of the Leman muskets to hunt with; it was made for the Indian trade, and shot true enough. There weren't any buffalo close to the post this winter, but he found plenty of elk and a herd of antelope.

Whenever he headed out, he took the mare and Jawbone

with him. They always enjoyed themselves, nipping at dry grass and twigs, enjoying the liberty of the open country. Skye kept a sharp eye for trouble but the November days paraded peaceably by, absorbing him in the routine of the trading post. It took an awful long time and a lot of labor to fetch thirty dollars.

The darkest days of the year arrived, and Skye heard nothing of Victoria. Was she healed? Did that wound and scrape with death change her? Did she still hurt? There were some wounds that never ceased to torment. A deep December cold settled over the north country, temperatures far below zero on Fahrenheit's scale, and Skye hoped she was warm in her brother's lodge, or her people were caring for her in her own lodge. This winter the Blackfeet were especially aggressive, and reports filtered in from all over, Piegans, Bloods, killing a Crow here and there, stealing horses, causing trouble.

Evenings, Skye listened quietly in the small kitchen room but said little. Chambers mostly railed against the Crows. For most of a week he complained about Crow mating habits, calling the whole tribe debauched, corrupt, scandalous. Skye listened irritably. The man was applying his white man's morals to a people who lived and believed other things. The Crows were a bawdy tribe, and none more so than the old grandmothers, who could tell yarns that made him blush. But Skye had rarely seen the sort of open and public mating Chambers claimed was commonplace.

"Them Crows, they got nothing else to do all winter, so that's why they get a mess of babies along about October, November, December," Chambers said.

Skye kept his silence. It wasn't so different among European people. The greenhorns, Rufus and Jasper and Billy and

Ezekiel, mostly listened and blotted up the lore of the fur trade. They were all good enough youngsters. But they had little commerce with a squaw-man, and Skye let it stay that way.

Each day, Skye headed into the trading room, hefted the blue-steel Sharps, slid a cartridge into the chamber and slid it out again, lined up the sights, learned how the rotary capper worked, and ached to own the rifle that would make him king of his world once again.

"Forget it, Skye," Chambers said, just as Skye dry-fired at a raven outside.

"I will own this rifle," Skye replied.

Jawbone began filling out as he headed into his yearling stage. The colt put on weight and began to bully the other horses in the pen, especially his mother, who wouldn't take it and nipped Jawbone hard. Also, he began to grow in his adult hair, and began to show the color of a blue roan. If anything, he turned even more ugly. That underslung jaw projected outward from his muzzle. His narrow-set eyes seemed to bore into the surrounding world and intimidate it. He learned to bare his teeth and squeal, and that was all it took to stir up the post's horses.

"Skye, if that colt causes me any trouble, or I end up with injured stock, I'm holding you responsible," Chambers said one day as they watched Jawbone herd the rest of the animals round and round the small corral.

"That's fine. He's my responsibility," Skye replied.

"I should charge you for feed."

"Every day I bring more cottonwood bark into this pen than both of my horses eat. Look at your stock. They're fat, and it's the leanest time of year for horses."

Chambers wasn't done with ragging Skye. "I'll tell you, Skye. That colt is nothing but trouble. You'll wish you took my advice and knocked its head in. The first time you climb onto that outlaw, that's gonna be the last day of your life."

"Good," said Skye. "Then no one else will ride him. And call me Mister or I'll quit."

Chambers backed off. Skye was obviously his most valuable and experienced man. But Skye had his fill of Fort Sarpy and Chambers, and thought maybe it was time to move on, rifle or not.

twenty

kye preferred to hunt alone. It had fallen to him to keep Fort Sarpy in meat, especially on days when no Indians drifted to the trading window. Chambers saw the value of it. More often than not the former mountain man returned with a deer or an antelope, and sometimes even an elk. The others were mostly hooligans recruited from the waterfront dives of St. Louis, and likely to scare game off.

But there was one of those young ones who wanted to hunt, and resented it when Chambers sent Skye out. His name, Skye gathered, was Rufus. He particularly didn't want Rufus along. The young man had killer eyes. Dead eyes. What was there about some males that gave them that look? Skye couldn't imagine. He only knew that some men liked to kill, and he usually could see it in their faces, in their cold dead gaze, in their view of animals, and sometimes in their view of people as well. He did not want this dead-eyed Rufus with him or around his mare or Jawbone.

He did not want Rufus killing more meat than he and Skye could haul back to the post. He did not want Rufus orphaning a fawn. He did not want Rufus standing around and gazing at the birds while Skye butchered and loaded meat.

When it came to killing animals, Skye preferred to be alone. Long ago, he had adopted the Indian ritual of asking forgiveness of the creature whose life he was about to take. He wasn't sentimental; a quick death from a bullet was easier than the torment of wolves. But Skye had come so close to perishing so many times that he respected the living, and honored the living, and took no comfort in destroying any creature's life.

He set out most days with the mare and Jawbone, often under low gray December skies, and usually headed downstream into country less traveled by the Crows or others. It was always a relief to escape Fort Sarpy and the endless scornful comments about Victoria's people. Skye endured it, kept his mouth shut, and saw his back-wage build. He was getting close now, close to abandoning this melancholy place, this lonely life, and rejoining Victoria.

From time to time he did receive word of her. The Absaroka bands did not neglect each other during the long winters. She was well. She was even more crabby than usual. She was living with her older brother and making her sisters-in-law unhappy. Those snippets of news heartened him. He had come to the realization he was more at home with his wife's people than he was with these white men, no matter that they spoke his tongue. His beliefs had changed and he would never be wholly a European again.

On this overcast morning just ahead of the New Year he set off once again. Chambers usually required him to stay close at hand when there was trading to be done. But on this morning what little snow remained on the flat was glazed, dimpled, and devoid of life.

He set out with Jawbone, who carried an empty packsaddle, and the bony old mare, who dragged an empty travois. By these means he brought meat home and sometimes that saved him a return trip.

"I'm tired of antelope, Skye," Rufus said just before Skye let himself out of the gates.

Skye lifted his top hat and settled it. "It's Mister Skye, mate."

"Putting on airs, that's what."

"No, it's my way of saying I'm worth something in this world. In the Royal Navy no man was mister except an officer."

"So you deserted, and now you can call yourself whatever you want, and bring us rabbits for dinner. If you was a Yank, we'd be eating buffler hump every night."

Skye smiled and refrained from a retort. If Rufus was the post's hunter, they would be boiling bones for some thin soup most nights.

Rufus laughed nastily, no doubt feeling he had put the Brit in his place, and slammed shut the massive gate behind Skye.

Skye headed east again into a desolate emptiness. The river bottoms bristled with a latticework of naked branches. Animal trails laced the rotting snow. He studied them, wanting to know what sort of creatures had threaded through.

The lonely white ridges that guarded the broad valley blended into a gray sky. He saw no movement this morning, not even a raven or the flash of a magpie, both of them wintering birds. No wind plucked at him, and he knew he would be warm this time. Some hunting trips had left him so numbed he thought no fire on earth could restore his heat.

His horses followed dutifully behind. He didn't need to lead them. Jawbone had accepted his packsaddle easily and seemed proud to carry meat. Sometimes Skye would hang two quarters of a deer from the pack frame. The little fellow was filling out. He was still fearless, facing danger by plowing toward it rather than fleeing, the way any ordinary horse would. That worried Skye. But something mysterious still clung to Jawbone, as if there was a Destiny about him beyond Skye's fathoming.

He checked his borrowed Leman rifle now and then, making sure a cap was seated and no snow or mud plugged the muzzle. It was a good enough weapon and he could afford to buy it now, after almost six weeks of service. But he wanted that Sharps and the cartridges and caps that it required.

He walked quietly, his gaze alert for the flash or color of game. In their winter pelts, animals blended into the black and white world they inhabited. Hunting always made him lonesome. He enjoyed being out on a good day, matching his wits against a wily deer or a distant herd of antelope. And yet there was a sadness weighing it not because the animals anticipated death, but because he did. Animals lived in the moment. It was he who foresaw the yearling without the mother, the calf without the parent, the pregnant mother carrying a creature that would be born only two or three months into the future.

He topped a rise and was startled to discover a dozen buffalo a thousand yards away pawing through crusted snow and snatching at prairie grasses. They were black dots in a white hollow. It had been weeks since he had seen a bison, and now he had a chance to kill two or three and bring in meat for two weeks. He would carry what he could and send an *engagé* back for the rest. They were all facing away from him, save one. He saw no calves. This probably was a bachelor band, yearlings or two-year-olds, driven off by the old bulls, awaiting their turn to lord over a harem. Good tender hump meat tonight! Buffalo steaks for days to come!

He felt no breeze, and wished he might because he didn't

know what direction the air was eddying. The animals were not on the alert, and were placidly pawing and eating, black behemoths under a leaden sky. He could not get close from this point of view, but to the left an intervening slope would give him cover. He backed off until he reached a coulee with brush in it, and tied his horses there, out of sight.

Then he slipped leftward and worked around the slope until he found a small dip where he might approach without being seen. He wanted three or four good shots and he would have them. He stayed low, out of sight, knowing that buffalo had weak eyes and an excellent nose. As far as he could determine the air was lifeless. No breeze would carry ahead of him.

When at last he spotted them again, two or three hundred yards away, they had stopped grazing and were all staring southward. He feared it was too late. He readied his Leman, choosing a big male on the far side of the herd, when on some sort of signal they all snorted and ran, scattering east and northeast. And moments later half a dozen Indians pursued on horseback, each after one or another of the buffalo. He could not make out who they were; only that he was in some company he may not wish to entertain. Men clad in buckskin; men with black hair, some braided, some loose, some pinned in place with red headbands. Men on good ponies.

The ponies were slower than the buffalo, which were now running swiftly and oddly silently. Skye had always associated the sound of a buffalo running with thunder, but not this time. They were phantoms, easily racing away, with the Indian hunters not far behind. He could see several rifles and one or two bows among them.

There went the buffalo steaks. He would have relished dropping a haunch of buffalo in Rufus's lap this evening.

He backed off and circled around the slope. He might yet

bag a deer if he was lucky. He rounded the bend that led down to the coulee and froze. Two of the Indians had found the mare and Jawbone, grabbed the leads, and were hastening over the top of a grade and out of sight.

Skye started to yell, and curbed the impulse.

Not the mare, not Jawbone.

He ran, his body thumping through brush and up the far hillside, his heart banging, his lungs pumping. He would stop them. He would catch up. He would shoot those thieves off their ponies. He topped the grade and saw them again, maybe a half a mile distant, mounted now, dragging their prizes behind them, looking backward to see if they were followed.

Skye raised the Leman, sighted on the more distant of the pair, and lowered it. He didn't know how many more were nearby, friend or foe. He hadn't the faintest idea who they were.

An anger welled through him. He was a walker. He would walk. There would be a trail. He would follow. He knew Jawbone's hoofprint. There was a little snow to reveal it. He would walk until he dropped. But he would get his medicine horses back. He peered about carefully, looking for trouble, saw none, and began a slow, steady, methodical pace that would mount into miles and leagues. So far, at least, the thieves were sticking to the valley of the Yellowstone, and heading toward the fort. That was a bit of luck even if he was out of luck.

twenty-one

Skye stopped dead. He had neglected a cardinal rule. Now he studied every ridge and valley looking for the rest of them. He didn't know whether he was among friends such as the Crows, or foes. The hunting party could have been Sioux, Blackfoot, or Assiniboine, and not a bit friendly.

So he stood quietly and took the measure of the land and all upon it, noted places he might find cover, places that might conceal danger. But he saw no more movement this overcast day when the snowy ridges evanesced into dreary cloud. The rest had been chasing buffalo and were probably far away. Far enough so that he heard no shots, no rumble of hooves.

He checked his Leman rifle. A cap rested over the nipple. He studied the route taken by the thieves, one that took them through river brush, concealed them from view, and afforded them endless opportunity to ambush pursuers. He would need to be doubly careful because he would not be trailing through open country with good views, but through the dangerous woods of the river bottom.

Satisfied, he began the long walk. The prints were easy to follow, fresh in patchy snow. He walked into the river flats, wary of every thicket, every chokecherry or willow copse, every fallen cottonwood. But then he realized he would do better on the bluffs where he could see the whole country again, so he abandoned the trail, headed away from the great river until the land rose and the forests gave way to grassy slopes. He saw no evidence of the thieves and knew they were well ahead now, mounted and making good time.

But he walked. He liked it better there just above the bottoms, the formations distinct, his gaze able to measure what came ahead. Now and then he could see the river, a great gray slab of water hemmed by timber. What he did not see was his horses or the thieves. But he did not give up hope. A man who had been left with nothing as often as Skye had realized that luck turns, a determined man rebuilds. Even so, this loss was acute. His medicine horse, his mare, his future . . .

Then he did see them a mile or more ahead, fording the river, distant dots so small he had to focus hard, strain to make out what he was seeing, for the tiny figures working across that wide flowage could have been anything, elk, buffalo, even mustangs. But it was the thieves, both mounted, both leading Skye's horses. That deepened his melancholia. Unless the ford was shallow, and there were few of those on the mighty Yellowstone, he could not wade across. It was one thing to cross a river in winter on a horse that never got belly-deep in water. Another thing to wade across naked, carrying one's rifle and clothing high above one's head, hoping to build a fire and dry out on the other side before freezing to death.

He continued along the bluffs until he came to the place where the thieves had forded, and there he cautiously descended into the thick cottonwood forest, and made his shadowed way to the riverbank. It didn't take long to find the place. Prints in rotting snow told him what he needed to know. The Yellowstone was wide and ran fast there, rippled by a few rocks that broke the surface. But on the far side was a deep channel carrying gray water topped with foam. Death to a man on foot.

The thieves had escaped.

He stood at water's edge, aching to cross, watching the turbid water roll by, and then slowly backed away. This was not done. Somehow, some way, he would find Jawbone and the mare and he would care for them the rest of their days. Somewhere someone would know, would show Skye the way.

He took off his top hat, wiped his battered hand through his mop of hair, and stared across the barrier. He was familiar with water. For years, water was what imprisoned him. He could always jump off the ships that carried him; it was the water that robbed him of life and liberty and hope. Now he was thwarted by water again.

He studied the distant ridges, and then began the slow, steady pacing that would take him back to the fort in perhaps three hours. He didn't walk easily, the way some Yank frontiersmen walked, with a swinging gait and a way of galloping over the surface of the earth. But he walked, stocky, solid of limb, determined as a bull moose, and gradually he covered the miles that had separated him from Fort Sarpy. This night he would bring no meat. A pity, too, because he had buffalo in the sights of his rifle. Rufus would scorn him. Lost his horses! Returned empty-handed!

But Skye knew something about young men like Rufus. They didn't last in the wilds. They were killed as the result of their own recklessness, or driven out of stockades and posts by others, or they wandered back East to brag about their times out beyond the borders.

He reached Fort Sarpy an hour before dusk. The gates were still open. There was a scatter of Absarokas outside along with horses and travois. Skye looked sharply among these but did not see his mare or Jawbone. He hailed a warrior he knew, one of Long Hair's band, an Absaroka version of Beau Brummell who was parading his new red and black blanket before his woman.

"It is a good day when I see you, Little Horse."

"Ah! It is the man named after the heavens above."

"Have you word of Many Quill Woman?"

"I hear nothing, man named after the heavens."

"Or her family? Are they here?"

"No, they are in winter camp. We came to trade."

"Did some of your party hunt this day?"

"No, Sky Man. We came to trade. Why do you ask?"

"I saw some hunters and they had found a few buffalo."

"The shaggy ones? Are they near?"

Skye pointed downriver. "Half a day," he said. "Are there any other of the People nearby this day?"

Little Horse pondered it and finally shrugged. "It has not come to my ears," he said. Skye thought his response was oddly secretive. But he knew he was in no mood to judge others fairly.

"We are preparing for a great feast," Little Horse said. "Our son is coming into his manhood. Even now, he is doing the manly things the elders and Tobacco Planters have given to him to do, and when he is called he will go upon a vision quest, and if his pleas are heard, he will receive his protector and learn of his medicine. And then we will hear what name he has taken."

"Congratulations," Skye said. "Is he with you?"

"No, he is preparing his way."

Skye nodded, bid the Absaroka good day, and headed into the post, where the high stockade was throwing cold blue shadow across the court.

"Make meat?" Chambers asked.

"Lost my chance at some buffalo."

"That's not good, Skye. I've been feeding these big-bellies whatever chops we had lying around, so's to get more trade. You know how they are. Give 'em a rib and they'll eat a haunch. If I don't watch 'em, they make off with half my stock. Bunch of thieving redskins."

Skye had heard all this before and turned away. Chambers wanted to gouge some headman a thousand percent profit for the Sharps, but complained when an Indian lifted an awl.

"Where's your plugs?" Chambers asked.

"Stolen."

"Stolen? You let 'em get away with it?"

Rufus, at the hide press in the court, stopped his labor and stared.

"If that's how you want to put it, yes."

"Well, as long as you're not doing anything, go cut some cottonwood bark for the rest of the nags. That's a good little way to keep some meat on 'em in the winter."

Skye nodded. He returned the Leman rifle to the trading room, and dropped his powder horn and other personal gear in his bunk, which was fashioned from some buffalo hide strung between two poles. The employees shared a common, ill-heated lean-to room against the rear stockade. Only Chambers had quarters of his own. Skye was weary after the long hike back to the post.

Skye found an axe among the post's tools and headed out

the gates, his destination a thick grove of cottonwoods near the banks of the Yellowstone. Cutting bark for horse feed was hard work. He didn't shy from it. But Chambers's command was spiteful and had little to do with the welfare of the post. The Absarokas had pulled out, and the river valley was a solitary place now, in the lavender shadows. He found some suitable saplings, smooth green bark all the way, and slowly hacked them down and limbed them. Then he dragged the three poles back to the gates, carefully slitted the bark, and then peeled it off in large chunks. By the time he had finished and fed the fodder to the post's horses, it was dark.

"I want some more bark, Skye," Chambers said.

"In the morning?"

"Now. There's a moon coming up."

There was a post rule against needless night activity when Blackfeet and others were waiting their chance. Chambers was deliberately flouting his own orders and ragging him.

Skye lifted his top hat and settled it again.

"I guess I'll be drawing my pay. There's over six weeks of wage owing," he said.

"Draw your pay? You quitting me?"

Skye nodded.

"Your pay comes outa St. Louis. You walk out, you walk out with nothing. I always knew you couldn't be trusted, Skye."

"Forty-five dollars," Skye said. "And it's Mister Skye."

Chambers laughed and walked away.

twenty-two

Forty-five dollars would buy him an outfit even if it wouldn't buy him the Sharps he coveted. For starters there was the battered Hawken on the gun rack, not in the excellent condition of the one stolen from him, but a Hawken even so, rock solid with the thirty-four-inch barrel, low sights, and a fifty-three caliber bore. Seventeen dollars. The back wages would buy him that, a one-pound can of Dupont, a pound of precast balls, a box of caps, and some patches. And a pair of five-point blankets thrown in. He knew the prices; he worked most days in the trading room. He would take his wage in goods.

He collected his capote, belaying pin, and buffalo robe, the meager possessions he could call his own, and headed for the trading room. There he lit an oil lamp with a lucifer and began laying out what he would take. He hefted the old Hawken. He had looked at it a dozen times before. Its stock was battered and the basket protecting the nipple was damaged. No matter. He set it on the counter along with the rest and began scratching a receipt. Let no man accuse him of theft.

At that moment Chambers roared in, saw what was in progress, and yelled at him to stop right where he was.

"This comes to thirty-nine dollars and forty cents worth of trade goods, and I am taking my pay this way," Skye said.

"You are not. You walk out of here and you get none of it."

Skye thrust the receipt at Chambers, who backed away from the counter and reached for a huge dragoon pistol he kept under it for emergencies.

Skye's belaying pin pushed the factor backward so swiftly and steadily that Chambers found himself staring helplessly at the pin as if it were a snake, lashing slowly back and forth.

"Sign here," Skye said.

Chambers twisted free, bolted from the dimly lit room, and Skye heard shouting. The factor was marshaling his troops, who were in the common room starting in on an evening's meal.

It would be no easy task to get out of Fort Sarpy along with his new outfit. He would have to take what he could on his back. There would be no second trip to pick up anything left behind. He slid into his capote, rolled the blankets into his robe for a bedroll, and hung it around his neck. He stuffed the powder and ball and caps inside his buckskin tunic and didn't forget the unsigned receipt. Then he plucked up the Hawken and the belaying pin, one in each hand, and emerged into the court just as the engaged men burst out of the common room. Skye backed steadily toward the gates. Unbarring them would be a problem. He needed an extra pair of hands. But he would deal with that when the moment came. First, he would show them what a limey seaman with a belaying pin could do in close quarters. This was familiar ground to him, up close, his wooden club against sharp-edged steel.

He dropped his gear before the gates and watched them

boil across the court, the dim light from the hearth of the kitchen turning them into bobbing light and shadow. He didn't wait; he pushed into them, bulldog strong, jabbing and whacking, spinning to crack one over the head. Chambers stood aside, watching, a coward. These were youngsters mostly, tough as warts on a toad, but they had never brawled on the bobbing decks of a man-o'-war. It was Rufus who worried him. Rufus didn't plunge in but circled behind. Skye caught the glint of steel. Dead-eyed Rufus, the killer.

Skye danced away from the rest, took a hit on his right shoulder, and almost dropped the hickory stick. Then he cut it upward into Rufus's groin just as the lout jabbed with the cutter. The knife ripped leather in his sleeve. Skye jammed the belaying pin into the man's crotch and watched him fold up. Rufus tumbled to the icy ground and howled, the big knife lying ten feet away. Skye took a whack along the head from one of the others, lifted his belaying pin into the man's jaw, and heard the crack of teeth and bone. Then suddenly they quit.

And Skye found himself staring into the bore of Chambers's hogleg pistol.

"Very good, Skye. You've disabled more of my men. Now walk out and leave the goods."

Skye laughed suddenly, relaxed his stance, and reached into his pocket. "Sign the receipt," he said. "Trade goods for labor."

"You step back now, step toward that gate, lift that bar, or you're dead."

Skye started to obey, took one step back, and then dodged to one side and plowed into the factor, knocking him over. The piece exploded with a flash. Skye felt the burn of gunpowder sear his face, but Chambers was disarmed and sitting on the cold and filthy ground.

Skye's top hat lay on the clay, a perforation through its crown.

Skye pulled out his paper and a stubby pencil. "Sign here, Chambers," he said.

Chambers glowered. "I will hunt you down. The company will hunt you down."

"For what? Taking my wages in goods after you stole my labor? Let me tell you something, Chambers. I was pressed into the Royal Navy, and for seven years the Admiralty stole my labor. I'm a little tired of people stealing my labor. I'm so tired of it that I'm ready to knock your head in. So sign."

Behind him, one man was sobbing. Two stood apart, not wanting to try Skye again. Rufus clutched his groin and groaned softly. Chambers still exuded contempt, but now it was leavened by a little respect.

He turned the paper so it caught the light from the kitchen hearth. "All right," he said. He scribbled a signature. Skye took the foolscap and studied it. He had seen plenty of Chambers's signatures. There was nothing tricky about this one. Now he had a bill of sale, one expressly saying his wage was paid in goods. The paper vanished into a pocket within his tunic.

He tucked it into the quilled buckskin tunic that Victoria had lovingly fashioned for him. He felt alone here, alone among these English-speaking white men.

He turned to them. "Remember the Golden Rule," he said. "Treat others as you want to be treated."

They stared.

He tested his limbs. Except for a hurt shoulder and a nasty welt on his head, he was whole. He deliberately turned his back to them, a sign of his triumph over them, and unbarred the massive gate. Then he collected his gear, the old Hawken, the bedroll, the rest, and stepped into the cold March night.

A deep chill had settled over the flat. There was little light. Behind him he heard the gates creaking shut and the heavy bar fall, locking him out. He didn't mind. He had a kit, the result of toil and insult. He was alone now, but he had been alone ever since he had been snatched off the streets of London's East End by a press gang. He knew where he would go, straight upriver to the Big Horn, and then start looking for the Kicked-in-the-Bellies band, Victoria's people. Her younger brother, Arrow Giver, was there, and her younger sisters, Makes-the-Lodge and Quill-Dye-Woman were there also, married to warriors he knew. But they were a long way away.

He carried a heavy burden. The bedroll on his shoulder consisted of two new blankets and a robe; the belaying pin hung on a leather thong from his waist. His capote kept him warm. The Hawken felt good in his hands. He had his knife, hatchet, flint and steel, powder and ball, as well as the powder horn that hung on his chest.

He hadn't a lick of food but he wasn't worried. The river bottoms would provide. He knew of an excellent emergency food sometimes used by the Indians. Cattail roots were thick, starchy, and filled the belly. They were awful, redolent of the swamp, but they would serve. Ideally they needed to be mashed and boiled into a white paste that was edible with the fingers, and served to stay starvation and weakness. But for the moment he needed nothing, and was anxious to put miles between himself and the rotten traders at Fort Sarpy.

He did not mind the wintry night in a land without shelter. He had begun his career in the mountains thinking of wilderness as a hostile and alien place, as most white men did. Now, many years later, he viewed the wilderness as his natural home, friendly, embracing, filled with resources. He had begun not only to live in the manner of the Absarokas, but to think in their fashion too. The Crows treasured this very country as the very best place on earth, neither too hot nor too cold, with abundant game, mountain vistas, rolling prairies, and endless comforts.

He was weary. All day he had hunted, lost his horses, walked back only to find the factor resentful because he had not made meat that day, gotten into a brawl, and now was walking west through the thick darkness with only an occasional howl or the bark of a coyote to tell him that others, too, were out upon the night.

He felt the belaying pin thump against his leg. The Yanks thought it was merely a stick. It was a long shaft of polished hickory, slippery and hard to grab. Any good British seaman knew how to use it with great effect. And fists were no match for it, which is how he settled the question of whether he would leave Fort Sarpy with his wages.

When dawn broke he had made another eight or ten miles upriver. He located a cattail swamp and soon was pulling the sere brown cattails out of the half-frozen muck, collecting a heap of their thick roots. He built a small fire, nursing a spark in the bosom of the dry inner bark fibers of a dead cottonwood until it flared into flame. Then he patiently cleaned and mashed the roots with the back of his hatchet, and roasted them on rocks set close to his cheery fire.

His cheer departed when he tried to eat the stuff, but it would do, and keep him alive another day, another week, another month until he could find the treasured old mare and Jawbone. In a day or two a new year would begin, and he would make it his own best year.

twenty-three

Skye worked west along the great river, at one point circling widely around an ice floe dam that had backed water across the entire valley. The weather held. But he had seen no game and subsisted himself on roots. He was so sick of roots that he yearned for meat, any meat.

His wish was granted, or so he thought. Ahead, motionless, white on white, sat a snowshoe hare, almost invisible on a snow patch. Dinner. He lowered his plains Hawken, lined up the low sights until the hare was directly in line, and squeezed. The Hawken bucked. The hare raced away. Skye peered about sharply, looking for observers, but saw only a crow or two riding an air ladder. Missed. He had not test-fired the weapon but knew he needed to, at once, to find out what was wrong. Carefully, he ran a patch through the rifle to clean it and then measured powder and poured it down the barrel. Then he jammed home a patched ball and slipped a cap over the nipple, making sure the nipple was not fouled. He gouged a cross in a cottonwood tree and paced a hundred yards, found a log for a bench rest, settled onto the hard frozen earth, and aimed. He took his time, resting the heavy barrel on the log, until he was satisfied that his sights were squarely aligned with the mark on the tree. He squeezed. The Hawken bucked. He carefully reloaded and then walked to the tree. The ball had struck three inches low and to the right. He felt betrayed. Hawkens shouldn't do that. His own had shot true. Still, it was valuable knowledge and he was glad he had taken the time.

The next hare might not be so lucky.

He soon found himself in deep woods across from the confluence of the Big Horn and the Yellowstone. He continued upstream along the much diminished Yellowstone, looking for a ford, usually a wide place, often braided, with rills showing, and water only a few inches deep this time of year. But he had no such luck. A man with a horse could have crossed at a dozen places; a man on foot would have to face the worst ordeal that winter travel could offer.

He studied the river, selected a spot that was shallow except for the far side, where a channel of clear green water ran swiftly. He could not fathom how deep. One misstep would send him into a hole, up over his head, drenching everything he would carry, including his blankets. That would probably prove to be fatal, though some of the hardiest of trappers had survived similar drenchings.

He studied the far bank, wanting plenty of firewood, and saw an abundance of ancient cottonwoods. He hated what he had to do, but did it. Crossing would require two trips. He stripped, rolling his clothing and capote into the bedroll. He felt the icy air upon his flesh. He left his moccasins and hardware on the riverbank. Then he waded out, feeling the numbing water pour over his feet and ankles, wobbling as he walked over slippery rock, step by step. The water did not come to his knees but even so his lower legs were afire with cold. He reached the channel. It looked mean and swift. He tentatively stepped out, holding the roll high above his head. He felt the bottom descend swiftly and ice water boiled over his thighs, making his heart race. His whole instinct was to retreat, but he felt his way along, dreading a hole. The water slid up his torso, maddening him with its cruel cold. He almost slipped as the swift current tugged him, but then he stepped to higher ground, rough gravel that hurt his feet. He took three bold steps and a lunge and clambered up the south bank. The blankets and clothing were dry.

He was tempted to wrap himself in his robe for a while, but resisted the seduction. Instead, he steeled himself, stuck his numb limbs back into that brutal current, and made his way to the north shore. By then he was so numb his muscles weren't working, but he had no choice. Every stitch of clothing and warmth lay on the south side. With a thong he draped his moccasins around his neck, then his belaying pin and hatchet, flint and steel, and knife and powder horn. He picked up the Hawken last, checked its load, and started for the brutal river. He had never known such dread of cold. He stood on the bank in browned grass, unable to make himself step into that current; not even the shallows that would take him three-quarters across. But he knew he was not far from the sort of cold that kills, and if he delayed he would never see another sunrise. He was quaking now, unable to stop the shudders that were unbalancing him.

There was only will, the steely determination to carry through that is our last resort. He stepped again into the river, forcefully strode through the shallows, stumbled once and again, righted himself, and came at last to the grim channel. He did not stop, for stopping would have paralyzed him. He felt the bottom decline away from him, stepped fiercely forward as ice water rose to loins and belly, and then at the middle, he did step into a hole, felt himself submerge, ice water over his chest and neck. He thrashed, plunged his Hawken into water, and made himself continue. The shore was only yards away. He stumbled up and out, shaking so hard he could not control the spasms.

There was no time. With water rivering off of him, he reached his bedroll, yanked it open, dumped his burdens, pulled the buffalo robe fur-inside around him, and shook violently, feeling no heat at all from it.

He thought he was a deadman. He felt ice clutch his heart. He clung to the robe, but it did little for him. He found his moccasins, which were largely dry, and somehow tugged them over his feet, and swiftly knew that was the right thing to do. It was as if his feet governed the rest of him; warm them a little and the rest would follow. But he could not stop his violent shaking. He rose, kept the robe wrapped tightly around him, and walked, kept on walking, made his body work. Some while later the quaking diminished to tremors. But he was still so cold he knew he would not live long without fire.

There was plenty of deadwood everywhere, but whether he could make something of it was the question. Much was half wet or icebound. He found a knothole in a willow trunk, and gingerly reached in, finding soft dry debris. This he tenderly placed under a heap of thin sticks. He found his powder horn and poured a bit of powder into the tinder. He could not control his shaking hands and arms, and feared he had poured too much, so much it would blow the tinder apart.

He found his flint and steel in their wet pouch, and now began the hard part. He could not make his hand strike the steel against flint in the practiced way, but he had to. There was, again, only will, the fierce determination to make his muscles obey him. Three strikes failed even to yield a spark from the wet flint. But then the fourth strike shot sparks into the tinder, into the powder. It hissed, flared, flashed, but did not blow the tinder apart, and suddenly he had a tiny, tentative blaze.

"Burn!" he cried hoarsely, for there was nothing he could do but wait and see. His hands trembled too violently to be adding twigs. He wrapped his robe tight again, protected the tiny fire from the breeze with his bulk, and waited an eternity, shaking badly, growing more and more weary. Would his body fail him even as the cold little fire burned?

He watched smoke curl upward. A twig flared and another. A tiny piece of deadwood caught. Then the flame seemed to retreat, and he feared it would die. He made himself rise up, dig for more tinder from any likely spot, the fiber under dead bark mostly, and fed it into the struggling little flame. It caught at once, and he knew he had won. The fire flared orange and another half a dozen deadwood sticks caught. He could live now on hope. It would be half an hour before he had heat, but he had hope and hope preserved life.

There was no warmth. He shook inside his robe. For the first time he surveyed his situation. His goods were safe; his rifle wet and probably useless. He had two blankets he didn't touch because he didn't want his wet body to dampen them. He saw no one. It was not yet afternoon. A weak sun, obscured by a veil of cloud, cast cold shadows.

He fed his flame more sticks. He rose, still trembling, and gathered a pile more. He would burn this whole cottonwood grove if that would warm him. He would build a bonfire ten feet around and ten feet high if that would warm him.

He jammed his beaver hat onto his head again, over wet hair. Maybe that would warm him. It did warm him; he felt it almost instantly.

He fed the fire, returned to its side, opened his robe to its radiation, and let the snapping little flame ply his damp icy flesh with the first friendly warmth it had felt. He opened his robe and spread his arms, making bat wings out of his robe, collecting every scrap of warmth coming his way. His flesh dried. He bathed in the heat, heaped more deadwood into the fire, breathed the foul cottonwood smoke, the bitterest of all wood smokes but didn't mind. Smoke was fire, fire was life.

He brought his clothing to the fire and let it warm. He brought his Hawken close, and let it dry, making sure the octagonal barrel was pointing safely away.

He felt prickles in his flesh, but his inner torso remained numb. He needed hot liquid and had no way of heating any. He needed food, something to heat his body from within. He had seen Crows heat water within some curving green bark placed close to flame, and knew he would try it when he was able to make his arms and hands cut a piece of green bark. But for now he had nothing.

He found more firewood and added it. The fire leaped high now, sending telltale smoke high, but he didn't much care. It was fire or death.

For an hour he sat absorbing heat, gaining ground, staving off a weariness that made him ache to lie down and tumble into oblivion. But finally, he dressed in his warmed and smoky buckskins, swiftly feeling warmer for it. Then he wrapped himself in the two new blankets as well as the robe. He had crossed the river. He was alive.

A while later he lifted the warmed Hawken, sighted on a distant tree, and squeezed. The cap popped. A faint smoke leaked from the nipple. The ball remained in the chamber, and behind it a mass of soaked powder. He had no extractor, a corkscrew-shaped device one could use to pull a ball. His Hawken was useless.

twenty-four

The trick was to heat the barrel without scorching the half stock or stock. It needed doing at once. A working piece was more important than his own comfort. He found some flat sandstone that might shield the half stock from the glowing embers, and devised a way to heat the Hawken and draw off the water in the powder. He hated doing it. This was no way to treat the finest rifle ever made. He was so weary that the slightest effort drained him of what little reserve he had, but bit by bit he gathered some sandstone, fed the fire, and finally laid the barrel over hot coals while the flat stone protected the rest of the weapon.

He sat and watched. He knew he should try to make a cup from green bark and heat some water and warm his innards. Instead, he slipped into his capote, rolled up his bedroll, and sat and waited, so devoid of energy that he could do no more. From time to time he fed small sticks to the flames near the barrel. Nothing happened. He hoped for a small, satisfying snap, a puff of smoke belching from the muzzle, a sign that the piece had discharged. But even after what might have been a half hour of careful roasting, nothing happened. Wearily, he found a small copper cap, slid it over the nipple, burning his fingers, and then hunted for his gauntlets. He could not handle that hot steel with bare hands. At last he was ready. He pulled the hammer back to cock, held the weapon, and pulled the trigger. It cracked. He felt the soft recoil. He set it aside, even as the barrel heat threatened to burn through his gloves. He would soon arm it and have a weapon again.

That heartened him. He found his hatchet, headed for a grove of young trees, found an elbow in a limb, and began slicing the bark from it. The task exhausted him but in time he had a hollow green-bark vessel. He dipped it into the icy river and then settled it on some of the burning-hot rock, just apart from the flame. A while later he clumsily drank warm water. After a second try, in which he heated the water longer, he downed a gill or two of good hot water, and rejoiced. He felt that heat work through his middle. He started another gill of water heating on the hot rocks, and carefully reloaded his Hawken after swabbing it. He was armed.

Three more times he heated water and downed it, and felt his strength tentatively return to him. But the river crossing had exhausted him and he could not travel until tomorrow. He judged that he was one full day's walk from the Absaroka village. He hoped so, anyway. He found cattails in a backwater, roasted as many of the knobby roots as he could manage to push down his unwilling throat, and called himself fed, though it wasn't much of a meal.

He knew he shouldn't stay there in plain sight beside the river. Blackfeet prowled. He studied the country. Heavily forested bottoms, steep lightly forested bluffs, maybe some good cover from predators and weather.

He trudged slowly into the bare-limbed forest and then

found himself walking onto a lush meadow. A log structure loomed ahead. It was roofless but had a sandstone hearth at one end and thick cottonwood walls. Some history came to him. This confluence with the Big Horn was where several trading posts had risen and fallen, including the earliest of all. Soon after the Lewis and Clark Expedition Manuel Lisa of St. Louis had come upriver to this point, and did a lively trade.

Skye entered, found the enclosure empty except for a scatter of animal offal. Others had long since burned the fallen roof in the hearth. He examined the hearth and chimney, well aware that such a structure could hold fire and throw heat at him all night. He decided to stay. It took his remaining strength to drag deadwood and driftwood to the hearth, build up a fire there, carry his few possessions, cut some boughs for a bed, and start more hot water heating, for he was still bone cold. But at last, as the afternoon light waned, he was settled there, out of the wind, the entire heat of the fire thrown his way by the hearth.

He was grateful and felt a kinship with those who long ago had felled these logs, raised these walls, built a mud-mortar and sandstone hearth, and did a business here. He realized he did not feel alone at all, though he was a solitary man in an empty place. He felt a kinship with so many people. He remembered his parents and his sister in London. His testy father who was always lecturing him. His ironic mother, love and mock in her face as she dished the porridge. How could memories so simple give him so much delight? Who was alive and who had died he did not know and might never know. But he remembered their hopes for him, their patience with his youthful foolishness, their belief that in him something of themselves would be passed along to the future. And he remembered their furrowed brows and sly humor. They were present here. They were beside him when he crossed the river, as was his beloved Victoria.

He felt his own goodwill being returned to him. Those men at Fort Sarpy, Chambers and the rest, they were the true loners, for they had nothing to share with others and were divided between themselves and apart from all the world by their own sourness. They might have a wage and live in a safe place, but he would not trade his life for theirs. For he had friends. For he loved. And they could not. And finally, as he sat there absorbing warmth in the twilight, he felt that he had never been alone, that some great Being was his friend and companion, beside him even in his most harrowing moments.

"Thank you," he whispered. It was a prayer.

Night settled, the stars emerged, and the sandstone hearth threw heat his way. He liked it there. A good buffalo hump steak might have helped, but he was alive. He had Victoria. He had an outfit. He could make his way, care for her now with that old Hawken lying beside him.

He picked up the weapon, rubbed the soot off the barrel, sighted down it. If he could find a file among the Kicked-in-the-Bellies, he would file down the bead and alter the notch a bit, and then it would shoot true.

He was rich. What more did a man need than friends, a good rifle, two blankets, a robe, and a hearth with a good fire throwing joy at him?

He slept well and undisturbed, though once when he replenished the fire he saw a pair of eyes glowing in the dark, outside of the open door. A wolf maybe; coyotes were too shy, and no deer or antelope or buffalo or elk would come close. By the time the slow dawn of a winter's day quickened the world, he was rested and his worn body had recovered from the crossing. With luck, he might reach the camp up the Big Horn River and find succor among Victoria's kin.

He was ravenous, but thought to make time during the

short cruel winter's day rather than wait upon his belly. He loaded the heavy burdens over his shoulders: bedroll, belaying pin, powder horn, and hung other things from his waist, including his fire-making pouch, hatchet, and Green River knife. He felt like a beast of burden.

He thought of Jawbone and the mare, and knew his life was not complete. Somewhere not far away were his medicine horse and the mare, and he sensed they were eager to return to him if only they could. He did not know why he needed them so much. Horses were horses. And yet, something that reached into his very heart told him he must find the pair, that he and they were destined to face the world together, that Jawbone was more than a horse; he was, in the terminology of his wife's people who had condemned him, a medicine animal.

He hiked slowly south along the Big Horn River, itself a formidable stream oxbowing northward toward its marriage with the Yellowstone. There were easy trails to follow, showing signs of passage by horse and man and wild game. He had to rest every little while. A man who had come so close to perishing the day before was a man whose heart and limbs and lungs had not yet restored themselves. But he soldiered on, resting at midday beside a giant slab of sandstone that had caught the sun's heat and was warm to the touch.

Later that afternoon he began to find signs of traffic, and walked warily, his old Hawken at the ready. Then he passed some women who were gathering firewood in the cottonwood timber. They stared. He raised his hand, palm forward, the Friend sign. Soon some boys swarmed up to him, several armed with bows and arrows that were not toys.

"I greet you," he said in Crow.

They swarmed beside him, sometimes tugging on his bedroll, mocking him with drawn bows. It was not comfortable nor was it intended to be. But then he rounded a river bend and beheld the village, spread comfortably against deep woods and under protecting northern and western slopes. The blackened peaks of the lodges leaked gray smoke. But around the bright tawny bottoms of the lodges life teemed. Women scraped hides or sewed with their awls. Oldsters wrapped in blankets or robes sat idly, taking the sun and smoking. An arrow maker patiently anchored metal points to the shafts with slippery wet sinew.

Young men greeted him. He was known at once, and the youthful warriors greeted Many Quill Woman's man with delight. Ahead, a town crier, already informed, proclaimed the visitor. People swarmed about him now, delighted at this novelty, a white man and friend who had come to the Kicked-in-the-Bellies. One of their own.

Their gaze noted that he carried his burdens, that his step was unsure, and that fatigue lined his face and furrowed the brow under that famed black top hat. They waited silently, for he first must seek Long Hair's permission to stay among them. He saw his brother-in-law Arrow Giver, and then spotted one of Victoria's sisters, Makes-the-Lodge, and they greeted him with a slight nod. Soon he found himself before the great lodge of Chief Long Hair, whose locks had never been cut, so it was said, and extended many feet when unbound.

The chief was waiting; he, too, had been apprised by the crier, and now greeted Skye, observed Skye's desperation, and invited his guest to have a smoke, which was a way of preparing to receive Skye's news. Skye lowered his heavy burdens, nodded, and followed Long Hair into the great lodge. There would be much to talk about.

twenty-five

C hief Long Hair was obviously a vain man. He bestowed glimpses of his legendary hair, folded into hanks and tucked into a quilled pouch he carried around with him, all the while grilling Skye. His vanity extended not only to his odd affectation, but to knowing more than anyone else in the band knew, so that he might be the fount of all knowledge.

Thus did he detain Skye through the rest of the afternoon, oblivious of Skye's hunger and weariness. Nor did it matter to Long Hair that Skye might want to see his in-laws and discover if they had news of Victoria.

"It is said, pale man among us, that you worked for the traders at Fort Sarpy. Tell me what you think of them. Are they just and good, and do they treat us well?"

Skye, whose stomach churned just from the scent of boiling meat wafting through the village, thought over a judicious reply. He had been thinking up judicious replies for what seemed like hours, but wasn't that long a time. The ritual smoke, the slow deliberation of Indian social commerce, seemed lengthy to any white man.

Skye decided on candor and summoned up his limited Crow words, which he supplemented occasionally with finger-talk. "I left them after a fight. It was about my failure to bring back meat. But it was about much more."

"Ah, a fight! And you won this fight?"

"No one ever wins a fight for little is settled by one. But yes, it was necessary for me to tame them in order to receive what was owed me and leave. That very day I lost my horses, a mare and yearling colt. So I walked away."

"And how many of them were there?"

"Some fought. Some didn't. I fought two or three."

"And then you walked for days. And how did you ford the river?"

"I almost didn't."

"It has been said in this village that your mare and colt rescued you and your wife, Many Quill Woman."

"They appeared in our camp when I needed a horse to carry my wife. A Blackfoot arrow almost killed her."

"So it is said."

The conversation droned on. The chief never let Skye go. The chief's appetite for news exceeded even his appetite for food, wives, honor, and notoriety.

By the time evening settled in, the chief had acquired an exact knowledge of the Blackfoot raid, Victoria's wound, surviving alone through the blizzard, the miraculous appearance of two nondescript horses somehow steered there by her spirit helper the Magpie, the trip south, and the encounter with white traders who stole Skye's outfit. There, at least, Skye learned something.

"They passed here, heading for Fort Laramie," Long Hair said. "We did not encourage them to stay. They tried to trade the rifle for robes, but it was recognized as yours."

"I am not finished with them," Skye said wearily.

The chief questioned him about the horses, their color and looks, and turned oddly silent. Then he elicited from Skye the whole story of his hunt for buffalo, the discovery of other hunters, and the theft of his horses, taken by two Indians who crossed the river at a place where Skye could not follow. And then the chief kept returning to the fight, the unhappiness at the post, and what might have caused it.

Some intuition told Skye not to tell Chief Long Hair about Chambers's contempt for the very people he traded with, but the chief relentlessly ferreted it out, mostly by saying it himself.

"This headman Chambers has the bad eye for us," he said. "This man tries to steal robes and pelts from us by cheating on weights. His thumb is always on the balance. My people trade for one cup of sugar and get less. One cup of the bean that makes us crazy, you call coffee, and get less. He is a thief."

Skye couldn't agree more.

This consumed yet another strand of time, while the evening deepened. Skye had received not a drink of water, not a dish of stew, not a slice of meat. Long Hair's wives sat patiently, eyeing their guest with blank faces.

Skye decided it was time to escape, knowing he might well insult the chief. But he could no longer endure the grilling, or sit still, and he was dizzy with hunger and need.

"It is time to see my kinfolk," he said.

The chief stared sharply. "Is the company of Long Hair not enough?"

Skye was afraid of just such a response, and met it head-on. "It is always enough. But I wish to see my kin."

Long Hair nodded curtly, a dismissal that boded ill for Skye in the future. Skye had arrived with no gift for the chief and that didn't help either.

Gratefully, Skye nodded, retreated through the lodge door and into the night. Arrow Giver beckoned. Skye followed, and his brother-in-law steered him into a commodious lodge where two wives and a younger woman and two small boys crowded around the fire. He barked some commands and the younger of the wives ladled some steaming venison stew into a wooden bowl and handed it to Skye. He lifted it, sipped, felt hot nectar slide down his throat, and rejoiced. It didn't take long for him to demolish what lay in that bowl.

He would have liked a few more bowls but no more was offered.

"Long Hair talks," Arrow Giver said. It was a way of saying more than the words implied.

Skye smiled.

"Now you will have to talk all over again," he added.

"Have you word of Many Quill Woman?" Skye asked, relying more on his sign-talk than on his limited Crow tongue.

"She lives alone in the new lodge and puzzles the people," Arrow Giver said.

"Is she well?"

"It is said her mind is changed. The wounding and the visitor from the other side changed it."

"How changed?"

"She is very cross, and uses trapper words, bad words, upon all the people there."

Skye started to laugh and then contained himself. "That is a sign she is getting her strength back."

Arrow Giver tamped tobacco from a pouch into a long-stemmed pipe and lit it with a coal he plucked from the fire, and then handed it to Skye, who drew the tobacco into his lungs and felt its calming.

Once again Skye told his stories, while Arrow Giver listened. When it came to the story of the mare and the colt, Victoria's brother had Skye repeat it again, though Skye was so weary he thought he would tumble to the robe he was sitting on and fall instantly asleep.

"This colt, is it the very colt that the Tobacco Planter, Walks to the Top, said would bring great trouble to the Otter Clan people?"

"It is."

"And this is the very colt he said must be killed for the sake of the People?"

"It is. But I would not permit that. I left instead. It is my medicine colt. He is unlike any other horse. Other horses run from trouble. This horse heads right into it. I knew at once that this horse was destined for me. If a white man can also have medicine, then this horse is my medicine, for it will bless me all of its days."

Arrow Giver stared sharply at Skye. "But now the horse is stolen?"

"I will find that colt and that mare. The mare brought my wife to safety, dragging her by travois and carrying her. It was our salvation. My wife had no strength. The Blackfeet had taken the horses. We were alone and surviving on our last meat and wood during a blizzard. But then just when she was well enough to be carried, and the weather warmed enough so it was possible, there came the mare, and the colt I have called Jawbone in honor of his great jaw, which protrudes from his head and makes him look misshapen. I would not let our medicine horses perish. So there was no choice. I left the Otter Clan people, and brought my horses this way, intending to come here. But my rifle and most everything else was stolen by white traders. I headed for Fort Sarpy, where I hoped to earn enough as a trader to outfit myself again."

He wasn't sure whether his words and signs were fully understood. How could he explain about Jawbone, a horse unlike any other, a horse that was meant for him, and only him.

Arrow Giver stared into the dying flames. The night had thickened. Some of his wives and children and nephews had slipped into their robes.

"The mare and the colt are here, in the herd," he said at last.

"Here?" Skye's spirit soared.

"Here. But it is not possible that the horses will ever be returned to you."

Skye stared, unhappily, wondering what was happening here.

"It was taken from you by the son of Little Horse, Badger Tail, and his friend Wolf, son of The Hawk Watcher. They are both boys entering manhood. They have gone to the hills to seek their spirit guardian, which is also part of becoming an Absaroka man. They will cry for a vision high in the high place that is known only to the People. They have done all else to enter into manhood and into the warrior society. Taking horses from others was the act of war and bravery both needed to enter manhood. It is the most important thing they have ever done, and celebrated by all the People."

"But I am one of your people by marriage. And adoption."

Arrow Giver ignored that. "What is done is done and cannot be changed. If they took your horses, those horses are theirs. There is nothing you can do. The young men will be honored. If you shame them upon their passage to manhood, the People would not forget. You will have bitter enemies. Do not shame them. Let the horses go. They no longer belong to you. If the issue is pressed, Mister Skye, there would be no welcome here or in any Absaroka village for you . . . or for my sister."

twenty-six

Soft light in the smoke hole awakened Skye. He had slept badly in spite of his exhaustion. A lodge filled with people always left him restless. There were usually noises in the night he could only guess at, people moving, slipping in and out.

Now they all lay motionless, the fire down to a few coals, a dawn coldness heavy upon the air. He threw back his robe and blanket, slid on his moccasins and tied them, found his capote and threw it over his shoulders, and slipped into the gray morning light. Smoke lay heavy over the village, drifting lazily from dozens of lodges. He saw no one about, but there were always a few, the warrior clan acting as village police and guardians, watchful even in the dead of winter.

A deep peace reigned here. He stretched and headed south along the purling river, seeking the horse herd. The Crows were rich in horses, which is one reason other tribes were constantly raiding them. He realized he was not alone. An old woman bathed at the river. Several young men stared. He found the herd grazing semitimbered meadows half a mile south, dining on leaves and bark as well as grass and sedges along the river. There were all sorts, lineback duns and grays, paints and spotted horses, a few blacks and some chestnuts. They weren't pretty horses, and yet they seemed vital and capable. Some had potbellies or oversized heads or broom tails. They served their purpose, which was not only to provide war and hunting mounts to the men, but travois and pack transportation to the whole village.

He walked quietly among them, and they didn't stir; it was as if they knew him, though most didn't. Then he spotted Jawbone and his mother just as they spotted him. The yearling raced to him, squealed, lowered his big ungainly head, and pushed it hard into Skye's midriff, forcing Skye back.

"Ho, there, you bloody devil," he muttered, overjoyed at the sight of the medicine colt Skye ached to call his own. He knew he must be patient, cautious, and terribly circumspect if ever he would get his horses back. Anger filled him. These were his own horses! He pushed back a fierce notion to take them and get out. The Crows would catch him in no time. This needed diplomacy, something he hated.

Jawbone kept butting Skye and expressing his joy with odd little bleats until the mare whirled, planted both rear hooves into Jawbone's butt, and drove the little rascal away. Then she bared her teeth at him just to show him who was still boss.

Skye laughed, albeit sadly. There was now an aching void between these horses and him, a gulf he had no way of bridging.

He knew he was being observed. Warriors, herd watchers, studied him. This was no secret. Everyone knew whose horses they had been, who took them, and what Walks to the Top had said about the colt in that faraway village on the Musselshell.

So, if anything, young Crow males watched and waited, and Skye felt himself being weighed. He ran his hand under the mane of the colt, and then turned to leave. The colt followed.

"Avast!" he growled.

The colt, looking wounded, stared. Skye walked away and downriver, feeling miserable. The only good thing was that he had seen his horses and they were healthy. Maybe he should just try to forget, abandon them. But he knew he could not. They were his. There was some strange destiny about them, something larger than the reality of the day or the hour could voice.

He performed some simple ablutions at the river's edge and walked back into the village. It still barely stirred. Especially in winter, people slept late, except for the ever-busy lesser wives, who were constantly burdened with dreary tasks, such as gathering loads of firewood and hauling it on their backs.

He would talk to Long Hair. That would be the first step, but he had no illusions about any of it. It would be late morning before he would be admitted to the chief's presence. The legendary chief followed a well-known ritual. He slept late while his several wives did the drudge work. When he arose, his first business was to primp. His wives unfolded his hair and spread it on the ground, and sometimes measured it to see if it had grown longer. Usually this was done out of doors unless the weather was bad. After the hair was stretched, the wives curried it with a porcupine-quill brush until every strand was unknotted. Woe to the young wife who pulled a strand out of Long Hair's head.

Then the wives folded his hair into hanks and returned it to his carrying case, which he kept at his side, or on occasion slung over his back. After the wives had attended him his next

ritual business was gossip. It wasn't called that, but that's what
it was. News givers brought him every detail of life in the village, every scrap of information. This morning they would tell
him all about Skye's trip to the herd, and how the medicine
colt butted him and was disciplined by the mare. This morning
Chief Long Hair would learn who visited whose lodge in the
night, what the medicine seers had said, who was out of meat,
whose wives were quarreling, what children were teasing
whom, and on and on. By late morning the chief would know
everything worth knowing, and everything not worth knowing, and he would use his vast knowledge, brought him by a
whole network of talkers, to lord over his people in ways that
seemed miraculous to them.

So Skye waited. Back in Arrow Giver's lodge he noted that
Victoria's younger brother was paying close attention to his
youngest woman, with smiles and merry little jokes, and Skye
surmised who was his host's favorite at that moment. But if
anything was true of the Crows it was their fickleness. Tomorrow that wife, Sow Black Bear, might be flirting with someone
else, and Arrow Giver would probably be favoring two or
three others.

Meanwhile, he had a rifle to look at. The Hawken didn't
shoot true. He pulled the charge and studied it. The rifle had
been abused by someone, and its bead, the little ridge of metal
at the muzzle used for aiming, had a left tilt to it. The rifle had
been used to pry something and the bead had been damaged.
Actually, Skye's heart lifted. If he could find a file he would re-
shape that bead. It took some while to convey to Arrow Giver
what he wanted, but in time Victoria's brother produced a
rough wood file. It would have to do. Skye found some sunlight and patiently scraped away the cant in the bead, and
hoped he could center on his target. Then he scraped at the top

of the bead to lower it, hoping that would raise his aim slightly. It was good steel and his work went slowly, and the sun climbed and arced around the southern sky.

Something changed in camp: it was, in fact, the time when Chief Long Hair would hear petitions or counsel of whatever a Crow wanted to say to the headman. But this time there was more: the whole of the Kicked-in-the-Bellies were waiting for Skye to make his petition. This moccasin telegraphing was a thing Skye hardly understood. How could everyone know his business?

He finished his work on the rifle and thought to aim and shoot it later, but now he had a case to make. He wondered how to make it. He set the rifle aside and started toward the chief's oversized lodge. There he discovered the village elders gathered outside in the bright winter sun, and all of them in ceremonial dress. This was no ordinary occasion.

Skye stood and waited for the summons, which came at once.

He knew there would a great deal of talk. They would seek to hear his case, there would be a lengthy debate, and then a verdict. He would need to summon all his Crow words and add some sign language too.

He decided on a simple approach: the young men took his horses, the horses of a friend and adopted son of the Crows. He wanted them back. He would honor their bravery, but he wanted his horses back.

Thus he approached the chief, who sat in a reed backrest, with several robes scattered about him. His hair pouch rested in his lap.

"You who married one of my people, approach," he said. "I have heard your story and will decide now."

"But I haven't told it . . ." Skye suddenly realized he would not be allowed to tell it. This was not a matter for debate nor did he have standing. This was going to be something directed at him, and he would have only the choice of heeding it or leaving the village.

Skye stood awkwardly and removed his hat. He was the center of attention. Headmen at the innermost circle, then warriors, and then women and children, as was the custom in Crow life.

Long Hair was plainly enjoying the moment.

"Our fine young men, Badger Tail and Wolf, have acquired a mare and a colt. This mare and colt were taken in an act of war, and now belong to these young men, who are entering into the manhood of the Crow people. These horses are said to be medicine horses by the visitor among us." He did not refer to Skye by name, which was a bad sign. "But we know that the Tobacco Planter, Walks to the Top, has said this colt is a bad omen and will bring evil to the Otter Clan people who are wintering on the Musselshell. He required of you that you destroy the colt so to spare the people his evil. You brought the colt and its mare here, intending to escape that verdict.

"Some of my headmen think it should be heeded. The colt should die. Others say that Walks to the Top was speaking only about the fortune of his village, not ours. And so we are divided. Some say when Badger Tail and Wolf return from their crying for a vision, they should heed what was said by the Tobacco Planter. Others say that the young men won war honors, and the horses are the sign of it, and it would dishonor their victory and dishonor us if we require them to destroy their prize.

"I have decided. Let my word be heard. The horse colt will belong to Badger Tail, the mare will belong to Wolf. I will wait and see whether the presence of this pair of horses harms my people. You visited the horses this morning. You will not visit them again. They must be left to the young men. If you visit the horses you will not be welcome here. I trust you have listened."

Skye nodded. "I have listened," he said, "but I wish to talk about those horses. They were the gift of Magpie to Many Quill Woman and me."

"Enough," said the chief.

The horses would live for the moment but only until the next trouble. Skye turned slowly and walked away. He had not been allowed a word of explanation, not a word about how Victoria's life had been saved. Not a word. It was most unusual and bespoke some strange chill, or fear, or dread, soaking through these people. How could a feisty little colt like Jawbone evoke all that? Skye didn't know, but he knew he must not say a word, not a whisper, to anyone.

twenty—seven

So the day had begun badly but it was to grow worse. Later that morning the young men who had been on their vision quest returned a day early. They should have stayed four days, fasting and praying to the Above Ones and the spirits in all the directions of the winds for their vision.

It was unusual for them to seek their vision in winter, unusual to go together though nothing forbade it. They had been boyhood friends and were warrior-brothers now, bonded by vows to defend each other. So they had headed up to the sacred bluff in the Pryor Mountains, through which the Big Horn River passed in a deep canyon, there to fast and thirst and beseech their helpers until they should receive that which came out of the mists.

And now Badger Tail and Wolf limped into the village, each carrying the heavy robe that was their sole comfort in the mountains. And even as they entered, a wail rose, for the youths were injured. Both had been bitten around the face, and Badger Tail on his calf and forearm as well.

Skye followed the crowd as it collected around the young men, back early from the sacred mission.

They looked frightened and desolated. Already the women had surmised what had happened, and began a quiet moaning. The men stood silently, absorbing the tooth marks and blood that covered those youths.

Little Horse, powerful and sinewy, approached his son.

"The time of pleading has not passed," he said.

"Father, a wolf came. We thought he was our spirit helper."

"A wolf came so close?"

"He came right up to me and was not afraid. I saw madness in him, but then it was too late. He was not a spirit helper, but a wolf with the madness. Foam and spittle dribbled from his jaws. And then he shook his head back and forth and pounced, biting my cheeks, my jaw, my nose, and for a moment I did nothing for fear of angering him, for this might be a dream and I was waiting for the vision."

Skye listened sadly. Hydrophobia. Rabies. A rabid wolf had bitten the boys, and he was staring at two doomed youths, barely reaching their manhood.

The women keened. Badger Tail's mother rushed to him with a sopping deerskin rag and washed her son's blood away. The tooth marks, especially those of the fangs, remained clear upon his gray flesh.

Wolf, the other boy, seemed less bitten, but bore the marks of his fate as well. Both youths stood there, knowing their fate, frightened and yet brave, their gazes almost defiant. What terrible thoughts were running through their minds now? They had sought manhood and a name and protector, and found only doom.

Skye puzzled over it. Hydrophobic animals usually showed

up in the summer, not winter. But no matter. If these lads had been bitten by a rabid wolf, they would perish in the midst of excruciating pain and thirst. It would take the disease only a short while, a few days, because of the head wounds. If they had been bitten on a limb or foot, they might survive as long as two months. Soon they would face fevers and convulsions and pain in the throat and esophagus that would make them unable to swallow, and no matter how much they craved water, they could not stand to drink it. It was an awful way to die and there was no cure.

Some of the trappers believed in a madstone, a porous stone that was to suck the lethal poisons from the body. Others believed in bloodletting. Cut open each puncture, where the infected tooth had pierced, and let the blood carry away the sickness. But Skye had never heard of a success. Everyone who had been bitten by a rabid animal, wolf or skunk usually, perished.

And here were two boys, the very boys being celebrated by the entire Crow nation, stepping from boyhood into the adult world where they would help the People and keep them safe.

This great and saddened crowd had at last attracted the attention of Long Hair, who made his stately way, his wife carrying the hair chest behind him.

"What is this? What do I hear? Tell me," he said to the young men after inspecting them.

They slowly described the bites of the rabid wolf, which they had thought was only a dream, a vision, the strange initiation of their spirit protector who was testing them.

Now a great circle of villagers surrounded the youths. Chief Long Hair walked slowly around them, two wives dutifully carrying his sacred hair, until at last he stood before the young men.

"This has never happened. Not in all the winters of our

lives. Not in all the stories handed down by the grandfathers. No young man seeking a vision has ever been hurt by anything. Some came back defeated; no vision came to them. Others came back weakened by fasting, but they soon recovered. But this is different. The Other Ones must be displeased with us. Those who inhabit the west winds and the south winds and the other winds have found fault with us. We harbor evil in our midst, and must purify ourselves. The whole People must purify themselves and drive out evil."

Skye suddenly intuited where this was going though Chief Long Hair had not yet gotten down to specifics.

The youths stood somberly, in need of rest and attention but unable to move until they received permission. The chief scarcely noticed their distress or the pallor in their faces.

Long Hair repeated himself several more times, as if he wanted his message ground deep into the heart of every listener, while the poor youths endured in the chill air.

Then suddenly Long Hair paused and faced Skye and pointed.

"He brought evil here. The very horses condemned by the Tobacco Planter, Walks to the Top."

Skye felt the gazes of scores of his friends, his adopted nation, his wife's family and kin, and the somber suspicious study of impressionable children, and all their gazes hammering him like sledgehammer blows.

At that moment the old seer, Red Turkey Wattle, most revered of all the Absaroka medicine men, raised his old hand, palm forward, and such was his authority that even the chief fell silent.

"Our friend Mister Skye, husband of Many Quill Woman, did not bring the horses here. The horses, sacred to him, were taken from him and brought here. I have burned sweetgrass and heard the whispers. The colt, named Jawbone, will live to be a great ally of the People. In the troubles that come, he and his owner, Mister Skye, will be like a hundred warriors fighting for us. The mare has already spared one of us, carrying Many Quill Woman to safety. Do them no harm. That is what I have seen, and what I say."

Contradiction. Skye found himself witnessing a struggle of a sort he had never seen among the Absaroka. There was the word of the elder, Walks to the Top, a Tobacco Planter, considered wise and all-knowing by the People but not necessarily one who communes with the Other World. And there was Red Turkey Wattle, a true medicine man, venerated for his insights, one who did receive gifts from the Other Ones. And now the chief, once a war leader, powerful, whose word was law, following yet another course. And it was the chief's own words that Red Turkey Wattle had challenged. Jawbone and the mare had not been brought into the village by Skye but by the youths who stood miserably at the center of all this. Skye waited uneasily, knowing that whatever happened, his own fate lay in the balance.

The chief took offense, glared at the seer, but did not dare challenge the old man. Instead he whispered to his wives, who withdrew the long hair from its casement and slowly spread it until it trailed behind the chief, an amazing hank that ran perhaps fifteen feet. This was his medicine, and now he was displaying it. He walked slowly, letting that cascade of hair pull along behind him for all to see. He circled the young men once again, so all might see his hair, and then paused before Skye.

"The People will suffer for as long as you and the cursed horses remain among us. Go," he said.

Skye stood there a moment. "It will be as you wish," he said. "I will make it my first business to track down the rabid wolf, and if I find him, I will kill him. The wolf will be glad of it. And the People will be released from danger." He paused, gazing at his many friends, hunting companions, kinfolk by marriage, and others who had shared village life with him. "You are my only nation, and I remain your friend."

He was alone again. Ever since he had been ripped out of London, he had been alone. He walked through the crowd, which parted, and headed for Arrow Giver's lodge, where he gathered his few belongings. He headed for Little Horse's lodge to collect what the boys had taken and found his pack-saddle and tack awaiting him outside the lodge door.

These things he lugged out of the village and into the sheltered bottoms of the Big Horn, until at last he reached the sunlit herd. He spotted Jawbone and the mare and headed their way. Jawbone squealed and raced up to him, butting him and making himself obnoxious.

"Avast!" Skye bellowed. But in truth, he was grateful the little fellow was alive and returned to him, even at the terrible price of his exile from the Crow nation.

Skye settled the packsaddle on the mare, tightening the cinch and tying it. Then he anchored his bedroll on it, along with the few things he still possessed, preferring to carry his Hawken in hand. He had his colt and his mare. He had, in a distant village, his wife, and she had a new lodge, and there were four ponies there awaiting him, the gift of her elder brother. All that was wealth. And he had a Hawken, shot and powder, to make meat and collect hides and protect himself. He was whole again, but once again he was a man without a country: not an Englishman, not a Yank, not a Crow, not a fur company employee, not any damned thing at all.

twenty-eight

*H*e followed the trail into the Pryor Mountains the youths had taken. He didn't know where it would lead. The Crow people didn't say much about the place where their young men pleaded for a vision.

Occasionally he saw the fresh imprint of a moccasin in soft earth or mud. Through the afternoon he ascended into an upland desert and sensed that these mountains were in the rain shadow of the Rockies to the west. Juniper flanked these slopes, but little pine, and some brush in the watercourses. This country was arid, but fine horse pasture and it offered the Crows an almost endless pool of ponies.

Jawbone trailed behind, delighted to be alive and snorting with joy at everything that should have alarmed him, while his patient mother brought up the rear. Skye was looking for the hydrophobic wolf, as he promised he would do. The offer had not been accepted. Long Hair had a different agenda. But Skye felt obliged to find the wolf and kill it before more tragedy struck.

It was a strange story, these youths thinking the wolf came to them in a vision and the biting of their faces and legs was part of a wolf-dream, an ordeal that would lead to the fulfillment of their quest. Not only did they have no weapon to fight it or drive it off, but they were disposed by their innermost belief to welcome the rabid animal. They must have cried out with joy at the sight of it.

In some ways, the Crows puzzled him. Why did they interpret these things as omens, the wrath of spirits, things amiss in the harmony of their lives, rather than simply what this was, a rabid wolf on the loose who happened on two unarmed, vulnerable youths? He had no answers. These were another people with a different way of seeing the world.

Had that wolf wandered into a rendezvous, the trappers would have taken after it, would have hunted it down because it imperiled all of them. Maybe the Crows would too, but he doubted it. Their world was wrapped in mystery and fear of powers that rose like whirlwinds out of the little-known. He sighed. It wasn't only a matter of reality on the one hand and superstition on the other. There were times he thought the tribal seers had something just right, some gift of discernment that seemed to probe the very soul of other life, something that Europeans did not have. But that was balanced by the sort of thing he saw today, the chief acting on a set of invented or imagined beliefs.

Skye knew he'd never understand it so there was little point in wrestling with it. He and Victoria's people lived in different worlds. He hiked up the trail into the Pryors, hardly knowing where to look for the rabid wolf, and growing ever more aware that he hadn't a scrap of food. He was far from the plains and river bottoms where he might find some emergency roots.

He rounded a bend and saw the wolf. It stood directly in

the trail and did not run. It sat on its haunches, unafraid, usually a sign of hydrophobia. It was in terrible shape and looked more dead than alive. It did not slobber but he had seen rabid animals who had not a speck of saliva on their jaws. He would shoot this one, and brought his Hawken up.

Then Jawbone squealed and bolted straight at the wolf.

"No!" Skye roared.

It did no good. The colt raced forward. The wolf stood and snarled, its great murderous jaws snapping. Jawbone whirled, presenting his rump to the wolf, and kicked. The hooves caught the wolf amidships, even as the wolf clawed and snarled and snapped. The kick tossed the wolf into the air, and then it fell in a heap and shuddered. It did not attempt to get up, except for some weak pawing of air.

"No, no, no!" Skye bellowed, and Jawbone pranced aside, for once heeding a command.

Skye saw that the wolf was all but dead and had been even before Jawbone planted two hooves in its side. Skye lifted the heavy Hawken, aimed, and shot. The ball hit the wolf in the chest. It convulsed once and went limp.

Shaking, Skye reloaded at once and turned to Jawbone.

He caught the colt and led him to a rotting snowbank where he scooped up snow and ran it over the colt's forelegs and pasterns and then the rear legs and pasterns, looking for blood. If the snow reddened, Jawbone might well be doomed. The colt stood still, submitting to all this as if it were the most natural thing in the world, though Skye had never before handled his feet and legs.

There was no blood, not a trace of pink or red in the snow. Maybe it would live. Maybe Jawbone was destined by some sort of fate Skye couldn't imagine to survive all manner of troubles. He eyed the strange colt, wondering what fate had given to him.

Skye was done here and it was time to head north. He had killed the wolf, as he said he would try to do. The Crows would read the evidence soon enough. He stared at Jawbone, wondering what sort of horse would run straight at a wolf and not flee it.

Skye took stock. He was high in the Pryor Mountains, which were arid and grassy, almost devoid of forest. To the north lay the Yellowstone and far away, Victoria with her people on the Musselshell. He decided to descend a long coulee, perhaps fifteen miles in length, that would take him to the Yellowstone or one of its tributaries.

It was a good choice. The descent was easy. He was soon out of the snow and into dried-up grassland. An hour later he spotted half a dozen antelope herded up in a swale, enjoying some good grasses. They spotted him, broke for cover, and he swung up his Hawken, gave the rear antelope a good lead, aimed a little high, and squeezed. The recoil slammed his shoulder. All the antelope continued to run, but then the rear one staggered, tumbled, and sprawled on the grass, thrashing. It was trying to get up and run again. He would have to put it out of its misery, and fast.

He hurried to the animal, a young buck that was breathing heavily, and cut its throat with his Green River knife. His shot had pierced the buck's belly, missing the heart-lung area by several inches. It had been a lucky shot at well over two hundred yards.

Jawbone approached the dead antelope and sniffed, and Skye let him. He wanted the little horse to get used to the smell and sight of blood.

Skye was ravenous but there wasn't a stick of wood any-where near. He would have to wait.

He wrestled the buck antelope around, found it was all he could do to handle it, but forced himself to lift it to Jawbone's packsaddle. He thought the colt would go crazy, as most horses do at the scent of blood, but Jawbone accepted the bur-den. After balancing it as best he could, Skye anchored the car-cass on the packsaddle and he continued his long downhill journey through a waning day and twilight. It would have been convenient to find firewood before nightfall, but there was nothing but grassy slope and some occasional low chokecherry brush in watercourses.

Darkness fell, and now Skye saw Orion in the southwest-ern sky, a winter visitor who vanished in the warmer seasons. The horses trailed along through the darkness. It was so black that Skye feared he would tumble into a trench or hollow, so he slowed down. Nothing but faint starlight showed him the path.

He began to feel faint, and knew he must do the thing he had seen his trapper friends do time and again, though it re-pelled him. He halted, slit open the belly of the antelope, tore its guts out, and then probed the bloody interior until he found the liver, resting high under the rib cage. He pulled and cut it free, not even sure in that deep darkness he had what he wanted. His hands were sticky with gore but he ate the raw liver, bit by bit, finding it shockingly tasty.

He sat in the cold grass, feeling icy air eddy down the coulee, and rested awhile. He wiped his sticky hands on dried grasses, with little effect. He had rarely felt so befouled, and yet he had been nourished. His horses nibbled grass nearby. He still had a long way to go to find shelter and some fire-wood. The raw liver worked its peace upon him, and he ached to curl up right there within his robe and blankets, and sleep.

But he didn't like this naked place and somehow didn't trust it either.

He found Jawbone, led the colt to where the antelope lay, and hoisted the carcass to the colt's back. It was noticeably lighter this time, disemboweled. He floundered about but finally caught the mare, and set off down that long dry coulee once again. It was not late, maybe nine in the evening. He was thirsty now, but there was no water anywhere, and no snow here. That, too, would have to wait.

The stars vanished behind a cloud bank and it became much too dark to travel, so Skye stumbled along until he found a level place, pulled the antelope and then his bedroll off of Jawbone's packsaddle, fumbled the packsaddle free and lifted it from the little fellow's back, released the mare, and made a cold bed in utter darkness.

He pulled the blanket and robe over him, grateful for the small nest against a wintry night. Beside him was his loaded Hawken. The nearby carcass might attract coyotes or wolves. But he would deal with that, just as he had dealt with trouble for as long as he could remember. The odd thing was, life was good in spite of every trouble that had befallen him. Soon he would be reunited with Victoria, and she would be strong and well.

twenty-nine

Skye awakened to a winter fog that obscured the whole world in a veil of white. Dew covered the top of his robe as well as the brown grasses nearby.

He sat up, feeling weary after a fitful night. He could not see the horses and knew he might have trouble finding them. There were beads of moisture on the barrel and stock of his rifle. It plainly was above freezing but not by much.

He didn't know where he was, except in the most general way: on the north flanks of the Pryor Mountains. Somewhere above there was blue sky. These winter fogs hung low upon the land. They often didn't burn off until afternoon. He would make his way downhill, that being the sole compass available to him this day.

He would have liked some fire to drive the aches out of him. He would like some water. He noted the beads of moisture covering the stiff carcass of the antelope. He ought to cut it up, carry what he could, rather than try to load that ungainly weight on Jawbone's back. Always assuming he could find the colt.

He had the odd sensation of being the last living person on earth. He had never quite gotten used to being so small a speck of life in this aching wilderness.

There he was, utterly alone, without direction. Surely that was how his life was playing out. Everything he had done had been simply a struggle to survive. He rose, stared at the walls of white that sealed him in this lonely place, and saw his life in it.

In short, his whole life was as fogbound as he was this day, and he ached for some goal, some purpose, some understanding of what he should do with his life. Where was he? He didn't even know that. He felt like roaring so he roared. He howled at the fog, he howled at the white sky. Then he laughed just because he felt like it.

"You bloody horses, fetch your blooming asses here," he yelled into the whiteness.

He scarcely dared move. It would require only a few yards to separate him from his bedroll, his rifle, and the antelope.

He saw and heard nothing.

He walked a small circle, hoping to drive the chill and stiffness from his body, and then he set to work on the antelope, slowly sawing it open, peeling back hide, and severing slabs of meat from bone. It was slow, dirty, mean work.

He sensed the slightest shadow, looked up, and discovered Jawbone studying him and the mare quietly overseeing her wayward son.

That heartened him. He rose, let Jawbone smell his bloodied hands, and then gently stroked the rambunctious fellow.

Soon he had some meat wrapped in green hide. He loaded his few possessions onto Jawbone's packsaddle and started downhill, scarcely knowing what he would run into a hundred feet away. It wasn't particularly cold, but there was something about fog that chilled him and made him crazy. Still, there was nothing he could do. He had discovered long ago that surviving in wilderness required a sense of one's own helplessness. And now he was as helpless as he ever got.

He hiked through what might have been morning, and walked down the coulee through what might have been afternoon, and then discerned naked cottonwoods looming out of the mist. Wood. Maybe if he was lucky he'd find some dry wood somewhere, and have himself a fire and some antelope meat. The land leveled and the woods thickened and he sensed he had reached bottoms, maybe even the Yellowstone River's bottoms. But he still could not see ahead and nothing offered any clues. He found a rotted snowbank under some trees and swallowed some snow, alleviating his terrible thirst.

Now that he was on a flat he had no sense of direction; he could as easily be going in circles as heading north toward the river, which is where he wanted to go. Give him a riverbank and he could follow it somewhere. But the fog swallowed up his immediate past. He could not even tell where he had been two or three minutes earlier. And as he maneuvered around fallen logs, deadwood, and brushy thickets, he knew the chances were that he wasn't traveling in a line at all. He was meandering.

Maybe that was a good description of his life, he thought. It was an odd thing: the fog had started him thinking about who he was, where he was going, whether he was going anywhere at all. And the best he could manage was that he had been going around in circles for years.

Then, to his astonishment, he hit the Yellowstone River. He almost stumbled into it. He could not see to the north bank. He was somewhere upstream from the Big Horn River and north of the Pryor Mountains, but that wasn't helpful knowledge. He cupped his hands in the icy water, lifted water to his parched lips, and drank. And again and again.

Still, though he didn't know where he was, he was gladdened. He turned west and kept the riverbank in sight, working through mist, looking now for a place where he might harvest some firewood, anything that hadn't been soaked by cold droplets all over it. His hunger fevered him now. He needed food. He would eat most of the meat he had carved out of the antelope haunch. Meat! The sizzle of it caught his imagination.

But whenever he stopped to hunt for firewood he found only cold, wet deadwood, soaked and soaked again. He would go on as long as he could, and then try to masticate raw meat if he must, a sliver at a time. He couldn't endure much more.

A mirage ahead stopped him cold. Wavering in the fog was the yellow light of a large fire. He must be demented. Not here. But he continued. Jawbone whickered softly. The mare pushed forward too. Yes, a fire, but he needed to be careful. Not every fire offered friendship and safety. Now he discerned figures, blurs wandering about. He worried that his moisture-soaked Hawken might be useless. He paused. It was time to take careful stock here. He might still escape if this was big trouble. He stood stock-still and squinted into the fog, trying to make sense of the blurs ahead. He held Jawbone back and the mare stopped on her own.

They were talking now and then but he could not make out the tongue. He would have to take his chances. He edged closer. The fire cast eerie orange light, though it was still daytime.

Then: "Hey, Mister Skittles, the horses are staring that way."

"Must be something out there. Better go look, Mister Grosvenor."

Skye yelled. "Hello the camp."

The shadowy figures paused. "Who is it?"

"Mister Skye's my name. I'm alone with a couple of horses."

"Come in, then."

He pushed ahead, almost tripped over a slippery deadwood log, and continued onto a treeless flat beside the river. Now he saw white men, maybe a dozen, waiting for him. Some had weapons in hand. They were taking no chances.

"Gents?" he said. "I'm glad to find some company."

They looked him over, examined his colt and the weary line-backed mare, and at last studied that battered top hat. He saw them relax. One, with a neatly trimmed red beard, hiked over to Skye. "Joshua Skittles here. These are my colleagues. We're pelt and hide dealers. And you?"

"Well, mate, I'm a loner traveling through. Trapper, hunter, fur business trader. All that."

"You Canadian?"

"What you hear, mate, is some London in my voice. I was born there. No, if anything, I'm a man without a country."

"Not a Yank?"

"No, not a Yank. I've a little antelope steak I'd be pleased to roast on that fire if you'd allow me. I'm more than a little past a meal. And there'll be some for you if you want it."

"Help yourself, Skye. We've eaten."

"I prefer Mister Skye, mate. And you're Mister Skittles?"

"Good! I always use the polite form with my men. It's Mister Skye, then."

Skye was amazed. The place seemed safe enough. The men emerging from the fog were outdoor types but with a difference. These men seemed well groomed, in clean clothing, with trimmed beards and hair, and green flannel shirts that showed signs of having been dipped in a river now and then. He studied them all, not recognizing a face. They were young, except for Joshua Skittles. He met a few. Mister Oliver, Mister Parsons, Mister Richter, Mister Balsamwood, Mister Mendelhoff. There were others out there.

Some had heavy dragoon revolvers hanging from their waists, others the new Colt Navy, a sidearm Skye had barely seen.

"Where's a good place to put the horses?" Skye asked.

"Wherever you want, Mister Skye. We've got draft horses here. We're pulling some wagons. Only a couple of saddlers in this outfit."

Skye wandered toward the wagons, curious about them. One was filled with flattened buffalo hides and robes and other peltries. One stood empty and another apparently carried gear, such as tents, mess equipment, and food. One carried little more than medium-sized casks, maybe fifteen or twenty gallons each, carefully packed in rows and wedged tight.

Traders indeed, Skye thought. There would not be a license from the Indian Bureau in this lot. He knew what was in those casks. Pure grain spirits, two hundred proof. Mixed with river water, molasses for taste, a little pepper or paprika for seasoning, and maybe a pinch of strychnine to make the tribesmen crazy, this was the most brutal of all ways to extract pelts and robes from Indians at almost no cost. Get 'em drunk for two-bits, walk away with a hundred dollars of robes.

Skye unpacked and picketed his mare and Jawbone, and returned to the campfire to fry some meat.

There would be some interesting talk soon.

thirty

Skye cooked his antelope steaks at the welcoming fire, aware that these men were watching him, and maybe more: they seemed to be assessing him as well. While he ate, slicing thin bits of meat and masticating them, he observed them as well.

He had never seen such a well-groomed, well-mannered bunch in the American wilderness, and it intrigued him. A few even shaved daily, no small feat in a place like this. Now, in the deepening twilight, they were busily policing the camp, gathering firewood, or attending to their personal toilet. Some washed their green flannel shirts in the river and set them to drying on limbs close to fires, while others aired bedrolls. One man attended to the tin messware, polishing it with river sand, rinsing and stacking it in the Studebaker supply wagon.

As soon as Skye had finished, Skittles approached him.

"You're welcome to stay the night, Mister Skye," he said.

The offer surprised Skye. He thought he was already welcome.

"I'll take you up on it, Mister Skittles."

The boss pulled out a pipe, loaded it, lit it with a lucifer, and settled beside Skye at the fire. He did not offer tobacco to Skye.

"I'm curious about what you do, Mister Skye."

"Well, I'm curious about you, sir. I've been a trapper, a brigade leader, an employee of several fur companies, and I've lived with the Indians."

"That commends you, Mister Skye. We're in the fur business ourselves, as you no doubt noticed when you passed our wagons."

"I did notice."

"We collect hides and furs in the Indian villages, turn them over to the trading posts for delivery in St. Louis, and collect our pay at the end of each season, back in Missouri."

"You turn them over to the posts?"

"American Fur Company, yes. They give us receipts for each hide and pelt, and these are as good as money in St. Louis. We work for a gentleman who prefers to remain anonymous, but who has generously financed our winter expeditions. The men know him only as Mister Quiet, an invented name, of course, but as good as gold."

"And why did he invent it, sir?"

"It is simply his choice."

His choice to ship spirits out, dodge the licensing, and turn over the pelts to licensed fur companies to bring downriver. Skye thought it was clever enough. Ever since the opening of the Oregon and Santa Fe Trails, the Yank government had lost its control of spirits destined for the Indian trade. And here was a simple but effective scheme to circumvent the government.

"We're paid in gold. There's an incentive on each pelt. These incentives are shared equally by my men here back in St. Louis. They contract for one winter season, coming out here in

October and returning in June. We have written agreements, detailing exactly what rights and duties each participant must perform."

"That seems to include grooming, Mister Skittles."

"Indeed it does, sir. We're professionals, and I insist on appropriate dress and conduct and idealism on all occasions. Our goal, sir, is to make money, and lots of it, but there's more: our goal is to liberate the tribes from their ancient bondage upon hunting and gathering, and steer them toward a free and better life, with more personal choices and chances of fulfillment. Let them look at us. They see clean, proud, groomed, disciplined men. In short, sir, we are apostles of liberty and democracy."

"And how's this accomplished?"

"Trading, sir. Our goal is to show them that they can have a more abundant life by becoming animal husbandmen and farmers. We trade sharply, for as many pelts as we can get in exchange for goods they wish to have in exchange, and at the same time, we present ourselves in our dress and demeanor as representatives of a higher nature and calling."

Skye listened, amazed. If his eyes were to be believed, these were cutthroats who despoiled every Indian village they visited, made off with every robe and pelt in the village after soaking the whole village in spirits.

Skittles sucked his meerschaum and surveyed Skye. "I see skepticism written all over you, Mister Skye. Let me say, simply, we are doing the tribes a favor. Only when they see the futility of resisting the modern world will they come to the cast of mind that is open to new things including the blessings of our world. That requires that they know they face a superior race of people, and that their old tribal superstitions will only fail them as time goes by."

Skye laughed softly. He'd heard enough.

"Ah, Mister Skye, think it over. As it happens, I'm short-handed. Every time I send some wagonloads of pelts to a post, I'm shorthanded. I have two wagons out now, carrying pelts to Fort Sarpy, and that occupies four men. I'm a victim of my success. The more pelts I get, the more men I need. I'm prepared to offer you a secure and lucrative position with us for the duration of the season, June thirtieth. Less than six months. That wouldn't be long. You would receive two-thirds of one share in the proceeds because you started late. But it happens that I could use more men, and with your experience you would be most valuable to us. Sometimes new men don't grasp the opportunities and perils of life here. A veteran of the mountains, why, sir, you'd be worth twice a share, and if you prove out, I'll be sure you get a bonus."

"And what are the terms?"

"Why, you can read them anytime. I have several blank contracts which only need to have the blanks filled in. You'll get a copy, of course."

"And my duties?"

"Why, obey my direction always. Assist in the trading. We especially need a man who speaks the court language, or can employ the hand-talk. That's why I'm interested in employing you."

"And obligations?"

"To keep yourself immaculately attired and groomed always. It is a professional statement we make to the tribes. You may shave every other day, or keep a closely trimmed beard. We have a small cache of spare clothing, and will sell you enough to suffice, and you can abandon the buckskins."

"And you mentioned privileges?"

"Of course, of course, Mister Skye. We're not martinets here. We're quite able to enjoy ourselves and I encourage my men to make the best of each trip west. Each man gets a gill of spirits each evening as his due. And Kentucky whiskey, too, not spirits used for the robe trade."

A gill was two good drinks, not bad at all, Skye thought.

"As soon as the men finish their duties, we'll all have a gill, save for our sentries, and that's a task that rotates night by night, Mister Skye."

"And what happens when you approach a village, Mister Skittles?"

"Well, for professional reasons we forgo our evening libations, Mister Skye. Our task then is to encourage trade, inviting men and women of all descriptions to join us for some pleasant conversation. They bring us robes, and we trade for those, and supply them with just enough spirits to make a cold night pleasant."

Skye had seen this sort of thing, but never so veneered over with high talk of liberty and democracy and being a part of modern times. And what he had seen, from rougher and harsher traders, had sickened him. He had seen villagers shivering in their worn blankets or devoid of any cover, children desperate for food and warmth, sickened men and women, their bodies ruined by the debauch, despoiled girls hanging their heads. Some usually died, frozen or choking in their vomit, or ruined in spirit. And in the aftermath of these drunken orgies, the villages remained demoralized. Headmen's warnings went unheeded. No one hunted and so they starved. Skye didn't know why Indians were susceptible to spirits, but he knew the results.

He faced Skittles. "No, Mister Skittles, I'll decline. I am headed toward my family, and the life I know."

Skittles seemed unfazed by that. "Why, that's fine, Mister Skye. I thought I'd inquire. You'd be a valuable asset to me. But in our world, liberty and contract are paramount, and it always takes two or more to make a contract."

Skye nodded. He wasn't sure he should stay the night among these well-dressed, well-disciplined ravishers of a whole way of life. He thought of Victoria and her people, wandering freely over the open prairies, troubled by many things, but always sovereign, always free.

"Well, Mister Skye, the hour's at hand for our gill of spirits. Would you care to join us? The gill's on me this time."

Skye thought of the aches of his body, and his long starvation, and the pleasure of letting some spirits steal into his belly and bring him peace.

"I'll accept with pleasure, Mister Skittles."

A master of revels, of some sort, handed each man a tin cup and filled it exactly half full, working around the circle with a one-gallon cask in hand. Some men sipped their ration neat, but most added some cold river water, and settled around one of the three mess fires for a social hour.

Skye sipped, relaxed, and enjoyed himself while Mister Skittles played the affable host. And when Skye had drained his gill, Skittles added a bit more with a gracious laugh.

" 'Tis a rare night in the wilds of the Northwest when a man can have a drink or two," Skittles said.

Skye found his cup refilled again, and again let the spirits flow through his veins, until at last he had reached oblivion. Lots of talk, lots of amusements. Those Yanks were a peculiar bunch, all right, with an opinion about everything, especially what they knew least about. He would undo his bedroll and plunge into a most pleasant sleep among all these good blokes.

And that was all he remembered.

The next dawn he awakened with a dull ache in his head, and a sense that something about him had changed. Yes, indeed, it had changed. His beard had vanished. He slapped his bare face. His hair, usually shoulder length, had been carefully shorn. His neck was naked. He wore a green flannel shirt he had never before seen. His old Hawken still rested beside him.

"Ready for work, Mister Skye?" asked Mr. Skittles.

thirty-one

S kye bolted to his feet. Skittles was standing there, an amiable smile on his chiseled face, while around the camp, the men were packing up.

"No," Skye said. "I'm not. I'm not working for you."

"Oh, but you are, Mister Skye. You signed the contract last night. Your copy is tucked into your shirt."

"You don't get yourself a man that way, Mister Skittles."

"Oh, now, Mister Skye, that's really not a wise choice. According to the contract, which was carefully explained to you, if you leave—and you are perfectly free to do so—you forfeit all your possessions."

"What contract?" Skye dug around in the flannel shirt, found a folded sheet of foolscap, and opened it. The printed form was actually quite long. There was something at its bottom that might or might not have been his signature. "Sorry, Mister Skittles," he said, and tore it in two.

"Not a good idea, Mister Skye. By your own free will you chose to join us, and you're now committed to service until the thirtieth day of June. Over five months. Two-thirds of a share, which is generous, considering you're working less than two-thirds of a full term of service, as defined in the agreement. Now, I'd suggest that you pack your bedroll and eat the porridge at the mess fire, and then set about learning our ways. You can begin by harnessing the draft horses."

"No. I'll be on my way. I committed myself to nothing."

"Ah, Mister Skye, I'm afraid that would be difficult. There's a dozen men in the company, and they'll hold you to the forfeit. I should tell you, sir, that the language is precise. It says all your possessions. And that is perfectly clear. All is all. Your horses and tack, weapons, bedroll, tools, and of course your clothing, including those excellent moccasins. You may walk away wearing nothing at all, because your possessions are forfeit."

He eyed the rest, knew their attention was on him, knew that a dozen men could swiftly overwhelm him, knew that Skittles meant it: he could walk away stark naked. In the winter. He knew the old trappers lore. How John Colter ran naked from the Blackfeet and survived. How Hugh Glass crawled and hobbled hundreds of miles to safety. But not in winter. Not in January.

He eyed his Hawken. He could grab it, stuff the muzzle at Skittles, hold him hostage until the rest put his outfit together, and then walk out. But he knew better. Under that hammer, the cap would be off the nipple, and they were all waiting for him to do just that, and then give him a little lesson.

Talk, then. Talk until he took the measure of all this.

Skittles watched him intently. "Not a good idea, was it, Mister Skye?"

"A contract isn't a contract when one of the parties is impaired," he said. "You know that."

"Oh, yes, impaired by nature. A contract involving a madman would be a scandal. Contracts must be forged between competent adult people, wouldn't you say? That's the whole future, Mister Skye, and the bedrock of the American Republic. A society forged on contracts between equals, enforced by courts. We've no court here, of course, but a clear contract can be interpreted by our little community here. What a pity your copy lies on the ground. Perhaps you should collect the pieces and read it."

"I was impaired. Unaware of what you were fobbing off on me."

Skittles smiled. "Impaired is a good word. Drunk, you mean. No, Skye, your argument doesn't hold. You are not impaired by nature. In fact, you're the most competent man in the party, which is why I agreed to hire you. My signature's on there too, you know. By your own free choice you chose to have a drink. By your free choice you chose to have another. No one forced you. You were perfectly free to refuse my hospitality and walk away from here this morning. You are a competent man, Mister Skye, and if you chose to sign the contract, it was as a competent and equal man. That's ordinary logic."

"Skittles, a man who doesn't know what he's signing or doesn't remember it is not a man bound by anything."

"It's Mister Skittles, Mister Skye. We are all gentlemen here. This is a company of American gentlemen and capitalists."

"Slavery," said Skye. "You are coercing labor from me against my will."

"That's a quaint interpretation of entering into an agreement, Mister Skye."

"You support black slavery back in the States?"

"Good heavens no, Mister Skye. I'm an abolitionist. I believe in freely negotiated labor, not servitude. No man here believes in servitude, and that includes serfdom or any other form of bondage or semislavery, including debt-slavery. That's what the Republic's all about. What separates us from the rest of the world. Each person is his own master."

"Except when he works for a master who won't release him."

Skittles laughed gently. "You'll find, Mister Skye, that there are other clauses that now bind you. One deals with insubordination. At my discretion it can be punished by flogging. The other deals with laziness, for which there are several remedies, such as being denied meals. But the main one is simply that one's share of the proceeds is forfeit. No work, no reward. Perfectly sensible."

"And of course you make these decisions."

"Who else? A contract is an agreement between a master and employee. If the labor is performed to my satisfaction, you receive your reward. That, Mister Skye, is the law of God. St. Paul said, in essence, let him who doesn't work, not eat." He paused. "Well, sir, enough of this. We must be on our way. Are you going to forfeit your worldly goods or join the company?"

"Why the pretense, Mister Skittles? You knew perfectly well I don't want to work for you and would leave if I were not being coerced. So why do you pretend I'm not being coerced? You're coercing me with my life. You call it forfeit of my possessions, but what you mean is that if I leave I die of exposure. Why not call it what it is? You want me to be a bondsman, a slave."

"You're a card, Mister Skye. All Brits are cards. Here in the States, each man shapes his own destiny, out of his own free will. It is my will to shape your destiny, as long as you don't care to shape your own. It's the fittest who survive and prosper. The dregs are fated to work for masters. Eat the porridge if you want, or don't eat it. And then harness one of the teams. We're leaving."

Skittles smiled cheerfully and walked away. Skye watched him. The man certainly commanded the company. A word from him sent men into feverish preparations. This was a clear, cold winter day and would be a good one for travel.

A slave once again. When he was a boy a press gang had yanked him off the streets of London, and he was a slave in the Royal Navy. They didn't call it slavery, of course. The crown opposed slavery. They paid him a pittance and called it a wage and took it from him for any infraction, and wouldn't release him. He had been a boneheaded youth then, and fought it every way he could, fought it until they all but threw him overboard. Then he came to his senses and began to make himself a reliable seaman, valuable to them, and was watched less and less as he proved himself an able man.

Now, after four decades of hard living, he had absorbed a lesson or two. He wouldn't fight; not yet. He would make himself an able man and trusted man in this company, and as soon as he had his chance, he would be on his way. This was a big land and there would be plenty of chances.

He spooned gruel into a tin mess plate and ate it. It tasted like paste, but it would serve to fuel him. No sooner did he finish than one of the men, Mister someone, snatched his plate, washed it, and stowed it away. Mister this, mister that. Mister master, who pretended this was a company of equals in voluntary alliance with one another.

He rolled up his bedroll, stowed it in the supply wagon, checked his Hawken—which indeed had no cap on its nipple but was otherwise loaded—and slid it into the wagon as well. For the time being, until he was trusted, they would keep weapons from him.

The draft horses were picketed on good grass. He looked for the mare and Jawbone, and found that they had already been tied behind a wagon and loaded with goods not his own. For a moment his temper flared. Skittles had no scruples about commandeering labor as well as property. Skye's horses were simply something to exploit, and what did it matter that Skittles didn't own them? Skye choked back his rage and collected two draft horses, big black geldings, and began harnessing them, remembering from times past how it was done. He dropped the collar over their necks, strapped the surcingle in place, and slowly readied each of the docile well-groomed and muscled horses. This outfit used tugs, and each wagon was teamstered by a man walking beside the paired draft horses.

They were all furtively observing him.

"Mister Skye, we require that the horses be brushed before they're harnessed," Skittles said. "It saves us sores and cankers and trouble."

Skye nodded, unharnessed them, found a currycomb in the supply wagon, and carefully groomed the big, friendly horses, who obviously enjoyed the attention.

This was a disciplined outfit, and it left nothing to expediency. He hated to be among a bunch of easterners, no matter how disciplined, when his own weapon lay useless until they gave him his ball and powder and caps.

Around ten in the morning Skittles pointed, and the wagons rolled along the Yellowstone.

"We'll cross when we find a good ford, Mister Skye," Skittles said. "There's some Crows up on the Musselshell we plan to trade with."

thirty-two

Skye studied his captors. It paid to know who he was dealing with. This outfit was proceeding with military discipline. Each man knew his tasks and did them. The young men functioned as a unit. They knew how to live out of doors. That was it! These were Yank soldiers, either in civilian duds or else recently discharged. He studied their faces, seeing men in their twenties and thirties.

They didn't carry rifles but there were several in the supply wagon, and these were the new Sharps, the very model Skye had coveted. So they could deal with large threats.

These men had teamster skills too. The harnesses were mended. Axles were greased. Draft horses were carefully brushed and doctored and shod.

He studied the wagon carrying the twenty-gallon casks, no doubt of pure grain spirits. Pure alcohol is flammable, and the walls of this wagon box were thick plank able to stop a ball or an arrow. A wooden box at the rear of the wagon probably contained trading trinkets. That wagon was heavier than the others and was in the hands of a veteran teamster, whose task was to preserve the strength of the heavy draft horses dragging the payload.

Ahead, one of the men rode a saddle horse, picking out a trail along the riverbank. He was also obviously looking for a ford, and occasionally wandering out into the river, over rocky shallows, and probing channels with a long pole. He rejected several fords until he found one where the channel itself was spread wide over a gravelly flat. At no point did the water reach the horse's hocks.

Even so, the rider poked and probed with his pole, looking for holes or surprises, and then shouted back to Skittles. They would cross here. There would be a steep rise on the far side, but otherwise a good crossing.

Skittles approached Skye. "Well, how are you faring, Mister Skye?" The question was merely a courtesy. Skittles had come to give instruction. "You'll ride in the supply wagon," he said.

"That brings up a point, Mister Skittles. I would have ridden my mare across, but she seems to be laden with your company's goods. Now where in the contract does it provide that your company can use my stock?"

Skittles's response surprised Skye. "Why, you have a point, sir. There is nothing in the contract that permits it. Mister Grosvenor and Mister Parsons were remiss, commandeering your horses. We'll pay you a small stipend for their use. I'll write it up as an amendment to your agreement with us."

"I'd rather carry my own outfit on my own horses, Mister Skittles."

"As you wish, sir. At the crossing here I'll have your mounts unloaded, and you can put your own goods on them, and we'll proceed without a stock contract."

Skye pondered that. What sort of world did this man Skittles live in, where he was ruthless about commandeering Skye's labor and expertise, but meticulous about the details involving property? What sort of men were these, who would illegally pour whiskey into vulnerable Indians and walk out with every robe and hide in the village? It was almost beyond fathoming.

When they reached Otter's camp on the Musselshell, he would need to signal Victoria. He needed to work up a plan. He had to let her know he was captive, had to let her know what these trim-bearded and well-groomed traders were going to do. His only advantage was that Skittles had no idea Skye had connections there. He thought uneasily of the medicine horse, Jawbone, and the mare, suddenly appearing in the very village where Walks to the Top had told the people these horses would bring evil upon them.

The crossing was done in masterful fashion. Skittles sent two horsemen ahead to look for surprises. Then the teamsters drove the wagons across, never wetting a foot. Skittles brought up the rear, making sure everything was in good order.

On the north bank, Skittles talked briefly to Grosvenor, and then approached Skye.

"Mister Grosvenor will unload your horses, sir, and you may put your outfit on them if you wish."

Skye did so, taking a moment to let Jawbone butt him. The colt had a way of lowering his big ugly head and gently pushing Skye backward. A bad habit, thought Skye, in any colt but this one. He laughed. Skittles watched dourly but said nothing about it. Skye tied the lead lines to the back of the supply wagon rather than letting his horses run free.

"You'll be my relief man, Mister Skye. You'll relieve each of my teamsters in turn, so they can take a break on one of the wagons."

Skye nodded.

They set off to the north, toward what appeared to be a gradual incline out of the Yellowstone Valley, and soon were in jack pine country. The boss man seemed to know where he was going. This route to Victoria's village was as good as any.

He felt melancholic, being a part of a trading outfit that intended to debauch Victoria's people. And yet, maybe he ended up in this place for a purpose. He eyed the wagon carrying the grain spirits, wondering how to set it afire, how to destroy these traders' entire stock of goods. They'd kill him quick if they had any idea what thoughts were teeming in his head: finding some way to spring a leak in a keg. Some way to ignite that pure alcohol. Some way, without being seen.

When it came his turn to relieve the teamster who was guiding the whiskey wagon, Skye began to study how that wagon was put together. This one had steel axles and wheel hubs, well greased. The barrels were wedged in and could not roll around. And around the casks was a wall of wood that would turn a ball or arrow.

"You're admiring my wagon," said Skittles.

"It's stronger than the others," Skye said.

"It has to be. The value of the goods in there can be multiplied between one and two hundred times if we succeed. The wagon is heavy, but armors the goods against disaster."

"Am I hearing right? A hundred dollars of whiskey can be turned into ten to twenty thousand?"

"Minus expenses, Mister Skye. Your pay, your share, the cost of doing business."

"I'm in for five months. What are your plans, sir?"

"To make us all rich, Mister Skye. It takes only half a cask of grain alcohol, properly diluted, to clean out most any village. Ahead is a fortune! Crows! Piegans! Bloods! Kainah! Flatheads! Kootenai! Assiniboine! Gros Ventres! Not to mention Bannocks and Shoshones and assorted mountain tribes."

"What's the procedure, mate?"

"You certainly sound like a man from the sea, Mister Skye. And I prefer to be addressed as Mister."

"Probably Captain unless I miss my bet."

"You missed your bet, Mister Skye."

Skye thought the boss wasn't going to say more, but instead he began instructing Skye. "We stay well outside of the villages, in a spot where we are in absolute control. Then we invite the chiefs in for some gifts. I have a stock of those. Then we open the trading window. One robe, one drink. After we soften them up, two robes for one drink, then three robes for a watered-down drink. Sometimes some politics are involved. An old man starts railing against us, or the young bucks get into a brawl. Shamans complain. Chiefs give orders. That requires some skills I don't have. That's where you'll come in handy. You can talk; you can wiggle your fingers. You can give some out-raged old man or woman a good hunting knife to quiet things down. That's why I hired you, Mister Skye. But sooner or later, we clean 'em out and head for the next village. I cut a wagon loose and send it to a trader, Fort Union, Fort Sarpy, Fort Laramie, Fort Benton, whatever. And we take nothing but a re-ceipt. So many hides, pelts, robes accepted. We head back to St. Louis with empty wagons and not a shilling on our persons. And then, after the reckoning, sir . . ." He smiled broadly.

They toiled up a vague trail toward higher ground. Skye could see that Skittles had outriders keeping an eye on the sur-rounding country.

"I see you observing how we do things, sir. You've been with us a day or so. Tell me, do you see any vulnerability? Things I should do?"

"I'll know better after you make camp tonight, Mister Skittles."

"A good answer, Mister Skye. You are thinking about the horses. Whether we make an adequate defense. How we protect them. Loss of these horses would be a disaster for us, wouldn't it?"

Skye smiled and kept silent.

"This is the season for horse thievery, isn't it, Mister Skye? A mild winter, that's when all the braves are out, seeing what they can harvest. But I doubt that they'd much care for our big draft horses. Slow beasts."

Skittles seemed to be testing him, and he rose to the challenge. "No, sir, they'd prize the big horses above all else. The horses are most valuable to them for hauling. Long ago they carried everything on their backs or the backs of dogs. Horses changed that. Big horses . . . maybe you'll see how hard they'll try for some big horses."

Skittles smiled. "Capital, Mister Skye."

He walked away, and Skye sensed he had passed some major testing. Skittles was no greenhorn and was familiar with the tribes and their special way of making war. Who was he? Who was this Mister Quiet, as he was called, who employed this man and this crew of ex-soldiers? And why were these men so rapacious, planning to ruin one village after another, and despoil one people after another, and yet so obsessed with rules?

Skye planned to find out. The trail had a way of opening men up, forming friendships, and revealing secrets. He needed to know fast. Two days ahead was an unsuspecting Crow village, and there was the woman he loved.

thirty-three

The closer Skittles's trading outfit came to the Crow village on the Musselshell, the more it was observed. Skye noted distant warriors quietly watching from ridges. These were hunters or men from the village policing society, and it was their task to protect the village from surprises.

Later, as they descended a long, gradual prairie slope into the Musselshell River bottoms, several warriors he knew well approached the wagons and waited. They recognized Skye and were soon wreathed in smiles. Skye waved. That was all it took. They broke toward the camp, bearers of news.

Soon The Robber's winter camp would know that traders were coming and Skye, husband of Many Quill Woman, was with them. Skye wondered how they would feel about all that in two or three days, after an orgy had shamed and impoverished the whole village.

He was in a spot so painful to him that he could barely imagine how to deal with it. And he had little choice, at least for the moment.

"They seem to know you, Mister Skye," said Skittles, who had approached the wagon that Skye was teamstering.

"They do," Skye said.

"All to the good. We'll make camp and then go visit them."

Skittles certainly knew the ritual. There would first be a parley with the chiefs and headmen, some gifts, maybe a smoke, and eventually the trading windows would open. The Robber would certainly want to know who had come and how Skye fit in.

Skittles took them across the shallow Musselshell, so dry this time of year that men and horses could cross without getting soaked, and then headed east, along the riverbank, where a thin blue haze just above the horizon suggested the smoke of a large village.

By now, Skye thought, Victoria would know of his presence. He wondered whether the advance guard of village police had spotted Jawbone and the mare, the very horses condemned by Walks to the Top as bad medicine.

Skittles halted his wagons at a good place perhaps a mile from the village, a meadow near firewood, close to the river, and sheltered from wind and weather. The low sun was heating the sandstone bluffs nearby and at night that pleasant heat would radiate back upon the camp.

Almost without direction, his men formed a camp, unharnessed the wagons, picketed the big draft horses and saddle horses, collected wood, and quietly unloaded a single cask of pure grain spirits, along with the paraphernalia to turn that into Indian whiskey.

People collected now. Warriors first, watching benignly, some younger women, children, a couple of headmen Skye knew. They said nothing, smiled, and Skye waved to acknowledge their presence.

"Well, Mister Skye, we appear to be ready for action. Come with me to translate. And ride your mare."

"That's not a good idea, sir. My horses are considered bad medicine in this village."

"Bad medicine? How so?"

"A certain seer proclaimed that their presence was a bad omen and that I must either leave with them or the horses must be killed."

"A marvelous superstition, Skye! All the more reason for you to ride the mare. We'll show them we're not bound by such nonsense."

"Sir, it will affect your trading. And it would endanger my horses."

"You will ride the mare, Mister Skye."

"Sir, my mare and colt are my own property, and not leased or sold to the company, and not available to you without my consent. No contract exists concerning them. So I must decline."

Skittles smiled quirkily at Skye, eyed the mare and Jawbone, and came to a conclusion. "It doesn't matter, Mister Skye. You will ride the mare. And bring the colt. It is exactly the display of powers belonging only to white men that I wish to convey to them."

"Sorry, Mister Skittles. They aren't your property."

Skittles smiled, and Skye saw a flash of menace in his eyes. Skye had him. The man who was so punctilious about contracts had no right to those animals. Skye was not going to risk the lives of his medicine horses.

Skittles didn't waste a moment. "Mister Skye," he said

softly, "according to your employment contract, you can be flogged for insubordination."

There it was.

"Thanks, mate, that answers a lot of questions. Now I know where I stand."

"It's Mister, sir, not mate."

"Sorry, mate, you don't deserve the courtesy."

Skittles's temper leaked from him.

Skye waited quietly. He was in for it. But with half the village watching, whatever happened here would send a message swiftly to The Robber. He glanced quickly through the gathering Crow people, looking for Victoria, and didn't see her.

"Go ahead, mate," he said.

There were a dozen of these men, mostly ex-soldiers if Skye had it right, and they would overwhelm him and it would hurt. But he wasn't without a few resources. Two steps away, on his mare's pack, was his belaying pin. Probably not a one of these Yanks knew what it was. But he thought he'd just show them what a limey tar could do with a piece of polished hickory.

Skittles eyed them, and him, and backed down. "Later, Skye," he said. "I have a long memory and not an ounce of forgiveness."

"Thanks for letting me know."

Skittles collected a small sack filled with gifts, and started toward the village, hiking through rich pasture along the riverbank. Smiling children paraded beside them. Boys staged mock ambushes. The village policing society formed a rank, escorting Skye and Skittles along the river meadows. Skye knew most of them. They walked buoyantly, fulfilling their office of protectors and peacekeepers. Girls smiled and whispered.

The Crow village lay just around a bend. Its tawny buffalo-hide lodges bled smoke from blackened tops. Here were old people, wrinkled and bronzed, warming in the midday sun. A dozen women scraped fresh buffalo hides, while others were tanning and working two other hides. Smoke permeated the air, along with the scent of stews and other less pleasant odors.

Chief Robber's lodge stood at the center of the arc, somewhat larger and more formidable than the others. It was decorated with brown stick figures, each symbolizing an event in the chief's life. He was waiting there, his hair in glossy braids, his expression benign.

Skye searched anxiously for Victoria, and spotted her. She came running, her eyes bright, her cheeks swabbed with vermilion in celebration of his arrival.

"Skye!" she cried, working through the gathering crowd. "Skye!"

She burst through the police guard, threw herself into Skye's arms, and he hugged her mightily, dancing over the ground with her, knocking his top hat to earth. She was laughing.

"God damn," she said.

"A squaw man, Mister Skye," Skittles said. "I should have known. Man like you wanders around out here with a squaw in every village."

Skye drew himself up swiftly. He would not let that pass.

"This is my wife, Victoria, or Many Quill Woman of the Crows," he said. "Victoria, this is a trader, Skittles by name."

She caught whatever was in his voice and stared at Skittles, suddenly reserved.

Skittles laughed. "Then I've brought you your husband," he responded. "All the better."

"Skittles here is a trader, Victoria. He will trade spirits for robes."

"Aiee! We'll have a good time tonight!"

Skittles watched her, amused, perhaps contemptuous. He urged the party forward. Victoria squeezed Skye's hand and then retreated. There would be time for a reunion later—maybe. Skye had a bad feeling eating at him, and didn't like any of this.

When they reached The Robber's great lodge, the blanket-wrapped headmen had gathered, and were cheerfully awaiting their guest.

"All right, Skittles, I'll translate. They don't know much English."

Skittles nodded.

"Chief Robber, I am honored to be among you, and pleased to tell you we will be trading for robes and hides and pelts and all manner of furs," he said. "My name is Mister Skittles, and my company of traders has settled a little way up the river. Tell them that."

Skye did, translating into Crow as best he could.

"We will be trading many things and offering good prices," Skittles said. "We are pleased to be in this camp of the mighty Absarokas."

Skye translated. The Robber asked him a question.

"The chief asks whether you brought gifts for him," Skye said.

"I have gifts! A mighty knife for the chief! Green River knives for these gentlemen!"

The Robber nodded. "Ask the trader if he will trade with our enemies next."

"The chief wants to know whether you'll be trading with the Crows' enemies next."

"Tell him we only trade with our friends the Crows," Skittles said.

Skye paused. It was always a temptation to add or subtract

or comment on what had been said. But a translator has a sacred duty to be exact. Mendacious translators cause more grief than the harshest truth. Skye knew he must honor what was said. In any case, there were some in the village who knew English.

"The trader says he only trades with his friends, the Absaroka," he said.

The Robber nodded, pleased with this pledge.

thirty-four

Chief Robber was a discerning man. He was given to the Indian way of weighing words carefully, often with a silence that white men found disconcerting. He stood there in quiet contemplation, aging but with unlined features, as keen a man as Skye had ever known.

The villagers waited quietly. The Robber gazed at Skye, who stood two or three paces from Skittles, rigid and stern.

"It is said among us that you have in your wagons the spirits that make men mad. Is it so?"

"Oh, yes, Chief," Skittles replied. Skye translated.

"I do not think these things are good for the young men. It makes them bad," The Robber said.

Skittles listened to Skye, and nodded.

"I think these traders are welcome if they agree not to trade the spirits that make men mad for robes. Tell the trader this. Ask him if he agrees."

"Chief Robber says you are welcome to trade if you agree not to trade for spirits. He wants your agreement."

"Why, tell the esteemed chief that we will trade only for those things his people wish to have."

Skye translated and The Robber was not satisfied. "Tell the trader he must agree to serve no spirits. That is my word."

Skittles bowed slightly, smiled, and nodded. "No spirits," he said. "But I can't always control my young men."

Chief Robber's eyes turned merry. "Tell him I can't control my young men either. That is why there will be no spirits."

Skittles smiled easily, enjoying the joke. "Tell the chief we will be ready to trade as soon as I return to the wagons."

"We will see," said The Robber, a sudden smile on his face. Skye sensed the agreement would not be taken seriously by either party.

He followed Skittles back to the wagon. Victoria rushed up to him, alarm in her eyes, but a gesture from Skye quieted her. She sensed trouble.

Skittles's men had set up shop. There was a paltry array of small steel items: awls, knives, fire steels, and arrow points. In addition there was sugar and coffee, hard candy, some one-pound casks of powder, small pigs of lead, caps, vermillion, beads, needles and thread. That was it. But nearby was a great black kettle brimming with firewater, hastily manufactured while Skittles was parleying with the chief. A dozen tin cups and a stack of hollowed gourds were at the ready.

Skittles looked over the array, nodded, and gave his men a thumbs-up.

"Mister Skye, you'll translate. The price list's on that tailgate. One good robe for a drink. If it's mangy or worn, half a drink. No exceptions. The rest, awls, knives, and all that, it's there. Tell 'em, and don't back off."

"No," said Skye.

"What do you mean, no?"

"Didn't you just make a contract with Chief Robber?"

Skittles smiled, dangerously. "No, a little palaver isn't a contract. Now, if you want to stay out of trouble, do as I say."

"No," said Skye.

A flame leaped up in Skittles's eyes. "No? No? You're saying no?" Then he saw the villagers drifting close. Everything was set. "You'll learn the hard way," he said. "If I deal with you now it'd disrupt my business."

"Do that."

Skye had the measure of the man now. For Skittles, a contract was a means to take advantage of others. It wasn't an agreement for mutual gain. If a contract was inconvenient, as far as Skittles believed, it didn't exist. In Skittles's new world, powerful combines would force the weak or the wounded into contracts and use contracts, enforced by courts, to bleed the world's laboring classes white. It all came clear to Skye. He saw enough of that in England. He was seeing even more of it in the Yank republic. A contract was nothing but a serfdom agreement when it was negotiated between a humble man and a rich combination. Slavery, papered over by the notion that both parties going into a contract were on equal footing.

But there was not time to ponder that now.

"What, what?" cried Victoria.

He saw her reaching for him, mystified by all this. He caught her hand and held it. "No time. It's a long story. There's something you must do. These are bad men. I'm their prisoner. I'll explain that later. Tell every woman in the village to hide robes. Take them out of the lodges. Hide them away from the men. Hide them!"

"But, Skye . . ."

"Do it!"

"Who would listen?"

"Try!"

Something steeled within her. "I will."

"Good! Then help me escape. I'll tell you later."

"Escape, Skye?"

He saw wild fear in her now. It matched his own fear. "Save your people from death and grief," he said.

She glanced bleakly, then walked away, her pace urgent.

Behind Skye, the trading had started. Young men were the first. They heaped luxurious buffalo robes, thick with curly hair, onto the back of a wagon, where one of Skittles's smooth-shaven men lifted it, examined it, and then gave the young man a chit. Already there were twenty splendid robes laid flat in the bed of the wagon, and more pouring in.

Skye glanced at the rest. A few of the women were trading pelts for sugar and beads and needles and thread. An old man, wrapped in a blanket, was trading an otter skin for a knife and ten arrow points.

Skittles smiled blandly, glanced maliciously at Skye, and urged people to step right up. The firewater flowed. Tin cups, handed down to grinning youths. One sipped, coughed, whooped, spit, and downed the entire cupful with a gasp. That had cost him a good buffalo robe.

"Oheeee!" he howled.

A toothless old granny dropped a worn and hairless robe on the wagon gate, and waited patiently. "Half a cup, grandma," said Mister Balsamwood, who appeared to be doing most of the evaluating. She nodded. He gave her a chit. She traded it for a tin cup and sipped, sputtered, and then smiled. She sat down and sipped slowly, nodding and smiling at the passing parade.

There went her winter night's warmth, Skye thought.

He saw a headman he admired, Talking Drum, glaring thunderously at all this.

"I wish to talk to you," Skye said.

"My ears are stopped. I will not listen."

"I tried to prevent this."

"You lied to us."

"I translated truly."

"You will never be welcome again among The Robber's people."

"I was brought here as a prisoner."

Talking Drum's scorn laced his face. Then he smiled cruelly, the sort of smile that mocks and destroys. "I will tell The Robber. The Robber will be entertained," he said.

The powerful headman abandoned Skye, walked slowly and massively through the throng, eliciting swift sharp glances. He headed toward a young warrior, Eagle's Claw, and slapped the spirits from the youth's hand.

The boy's temper rose until he saw the massive headman looming over him, ready to deliver ten times more than he got. The youth slipped away.

Talking Drum cut a swath through the crowd, slowing things down, until Skittles approached, with a smile and a gift.

"Here's to the chieftain," he said, handing the headman a good hatchet.

Talking Drum took it, threw it into the soft earth, where its blade sank up to the hilt. In an instant, half a dozen of Skittles's smooth-shaven men surrounded the headman, and handed him a cup of spirits.

Talking Drum poured them into the ground and walked away.

Skye took his chance during the confrontation and hastened out of the trading camp, trotting toward The Robber's village, eliciting stares as he passed scores of people lugging heavy robes and lush fox and weasel and mink and wolf furs, or elk hides, or deerskins.

They greeted him cheerfully. He hurried into the circle of lodges, found it half deserted, headed straight toward the small lodge of the Tobacco Planter, Walks to the Top, collected his breath, and scratched.

No one responded.

He scratched the lodge door again.

"I see no token of your esteem," the old man said.

Skye had nothing. Then he thought of his green flannel shirt, and swiftly stripped it off and laid it before the door. The winter air chilled him at once. After a long wait, the door parted, the seer beckoned him in, and took the shirt.

"Your vision came true," Skye said, preempting the talk and cutting straight to the heart of things. "You said that if the mare and my medicine colt remained here, disaster would strike The Robber's village. That is happening."

The old man stared, swift and sharp and also startled.

"I was brought here as a prisoner by bad men who plan to take away every robe and pelt in the village, and debauch the young men. Now I am trying to prevent it."

"A prisoner, Mister Skye?"

"They gave me the option of leaving them one bitter cold day. Naked."

"What are they doing?"

"They do not have a license, a permission, from the Fathers, and they are ruthless. There will be much weeping."

"What do you want of me?"

"The headmen think I'm one of the traders. They are deaf

to me. I cannot tell them of the trouble, or what has happened to me, or what will fall upon this village. You can. You are an elder. Chief Robber and the headmen can stop this."

Walks to the Top stared into the ashes of his fire, and then into the warm winter day.

"That which I saw in the sweetgrass smoke and the clouds will come to pass," he said. "I will do nothing. Who can resist an ill wind?"

thirty-five

*H*e felt the cold air on his back. He needed a shirt. It was a bright winter's day. If Skittles's men hadn't made off with his buckskin shirt, it would be among his things. But first, find Victoria. She needed to know the whole story.

He hunted through the village. A few women were indeed carrying the heavy robes away. Somehow Victoria had talked them into it. He found her collecting robes in her brother's lodge.

"Oh, Skye!" she cried, and flew to him. They hugged with all the pent-up love that months of separation had built in them.

"Oh, Skye," she cried, touching his face, running her hand through his shorn hair. "What? What?"

He pulled her down to the robes and sat beside her. "Too long to tell now. No time. I'm a captive, or they think I am. These traders are evil. They are not offering a little whiskey and a lot of other goods. They mean to make The Robber's whole village crazy and walk off with every robe and pelt here. The Fathers in Washington don't know about them. The traders think they own me. They said they'd keep my possessions, Jawbone and the mare, even my clothing, if I didn't obey. I'll need your help. My rifle and gear and the horses need to be taken away and hidden. The Hawken's one I got at a trading post.

"We need to let Chief Robber know. And the headmen. Maybe they can stop this. Let them know that evil is here among them. And beware. These man are armed and capable of anything."

"Skye, what first?"

"Talk, Victoria. Tell them. Tell everyone. Warn them away. Hide robes. Stop the young men from drinking the spirits."

"How did you lose your green shirt?"

"Gift to Walks to the Top."

"Did he believe you?"

"Yes, but he says it will all happen just as he dreamed it."

"Sonofabitch!"

Skye laughed suddenly. Victoria was an army.

"Come," she said.

He followed her to their own lodge, which he had never seen. Its new hides shone golden in the bright light, and smoke had not yet blackened the top of the cone. There were half a dozen robes within, but little else. All this had been a gift of her brother and his wives.

She plucked up a buckskin shirt.

"Try this."

"Victoria—"

"I was making it for my brother. Maybe it fits."

The shirt had been sewn of the softest doeskin he had ever

felt in his fingers, fringed and partly quilled. There was a red geometric design over the heart.

He slid it on, feeling its soft silkiness cover him against the winter air.

"Damn! I make good shirts!"

This one had an irregular hem that followed the contour of the hide, dipping low on the left side. It had long sleeves, fringed all the way to draw off water.

"I feel like a chief," he said.

"You're my chief. Ho ho, Skye, let's get those bastards. Now you got medicine. This here shirt, it's big medicine."

He didn't need an invitation. He stepped into the light somehow transformed. Now he was a man of the mountains again, not some interloper in a green shirt, like all the others over there in their green flannels.

"I go talk. Then we see what we can do," she said.

He watched her race toward a knot of angry headmen, who plainly didn't like what was being purveyed over at the trading camp.

He had his own business to attend, and headed along the riverbank to the trading camp. He had to acknowledge there were a lot of happy people on the trail and around the camp. He had never seen so many smiles in a village. Young men swaggered expansively, parading themselves before the maidens. But so were cheerful wives and sisters, old warriors, and scores of older wives, who had bargained for sugar and needles and thread and awls, but also tried a cup of the brew.

In a glance Skye saw that one wagon was nearly filled with robes, carefully laid flat. And that Skittles's men were busy brewing another batch of firewater, this one no doubt thinner and meaner than the first. Less of the spirits but more of the cayenne pepper and maybe now a pinch of the bug powder used by fur outfits to control insect damage to hides and furs.

The camp was perfectly orderly. Young men stood around in circles, sipping out of gourd cups, horn spoons, and sometimes a tin cup. They were at ease, laughing, enjoying the crisp bright afternoon. In small knots old men wrapped blankets tight, folded their arms, and glowered at those who were abandoning the traditional Crow ways.

Skye's plan was simple. Spirit his horses out of there, along with everything in his packs, especially his rifle. Victoria would hide them. Then he was free. Nothing Skittles might throw at him would compel him to stay. After that, somehow, wreck the trade as much as possible, get these people back to their lodges.

And after that . . . he eyed the well-guarded wagon with the casks in it, knowing he would have his hands full. But if he could destroy that pure grain alcohol, trading would come to an abrupt halt.

He headed into the traders' camp only to run into Skittles.

"Where've you been?"

"In the village."

"Why aren't you in your green shirt?"

"I gave it to a powerful man."

"Gave company property away, did you? That's going to cost you. You're out of uniform. That's going to cost you. All my men wear green shirts. That's so the redskins know we're a company. Now what'm I going to do with you?" He eyed the beautifully made shirt. "Put that in the wagon, Skye. You just traded it for the green shirt."

Skye started to walk away, but heard the snick of a revolver being cocked.

"No you don't, Skye. I'm not done with you."

Skye doubted the man would shoot. It would start a riot. But there was no telling about Skittles. He stood quietly, not liking that black bore pointed at his midsection.

"You don't seem to understand, Mister Skye. You're my employee."

"Slave."

"Go to that wagon and start spreading those robes flat. I want every robe just as flat as it gets. We can put a lot more robes into a wagon if they're loaded right."

"Slave," Skye said.

Skittles laughed. "I can read your mind, Mister Skye. You're wondering where your nags are, and your outfit and your rifle. I don't know what you see in that ugly colt and spavined mare, but they make handy hostages, don't they? They're well guarded, Mister Skye, along with your other truck. If you even approach the pen we've put them in, the first bullet goes into them, not you."

"Thank you for warning me, mate."

"And don't suppose you can send your little trollop after them. The guards are well aware of the slut."

"Victoria is my wife."

"Ah! Wife! A squaw in every camp. A sailor has a whore in every port!"

"Wife," said Skye.

He smiled brightly, walked toward the wagon where two other Misters were spreading robes, tossing a little bug powder on them, and coughing. In the other wagon a few uncured hides were being laid flat.

Skye stepped up to the wagon bed and began the labor. Skittles watched, and then slid his dragoon revolver into its nest at his waist.

The trading was going smoothly. An endless stream of

Crows, most of them lugging valuable buffalo robes, or elk hides, or wolf or mink or ermine furs, wound toward the trading area. The Crows were colorfully dressed, as if this were a festival occasion, many in deerskins decorated with bright ribbons. The older ones were wrapped in blankets, and Skye was glad. They, at least, would sleep warm this night.

To the casual observer, it looked more like an idyllic rural fair, with laughing Indians telling their usual bawdy jokes, and orderly lines of people waiting their turn to bargain a robe or a pelt for a cup of brew.

But this was only prelude. He eyed the sun, slowly sinking now, and knew that when dark fell, so would all civility, and before the sun rose again, the ground would be soaked with blood and the wealth of a village would be lost.

He furtively studied the whole scene, looking for ways to do what must be done, and found none. Skittles and his ex-army bunch would not be taken by surprise.

He spotted Victoria wandering in, her eyes bright, her greetings to all around her cheerful. But what set him to worrying was not her presence, but what she carried in her arms. She had a prime robe with her and it would buy her a cup of that brew, and he knew he had to stop her.

He jumped down from the wagon, raced to her.

"No, Victoria!"

"Skye, dammit, I will have a drink."

He clasped his hands about her shoulders. "If ever I need you, I need you now."

She smiled gently and worked free.

"Ah, the little Missus," said Skittles. "Welcome, welcome. I see you've brought us a good robe."

"Her name, to you, is Many Quill Woman, Skittles."

"Why, Many Quill Woman, we have a treat just for you. A

little drink back here, with your mate. A little jug just for the two of you."

Skye knew suddenly how Victoria was gaining access to the traders' camp.

thirty-six

Skittles led them behind the wagons to a quiet spot near the traders' campground. Skye didn't like it. The mob around the trading wagon was safety of a sort, but here, fifty yards away, whatever happened would not be noted. There was plenty of daylight now, but in a couple of hours whatever happened here would be cloaked in night.

"Now, little lady, you just settle yourself and have a drink. If you're Mister Skye's friend, you get all the spirits you want for that robe. We treat our friends just right."

"Hot damn!" she said. "Wooee!"

"Victoria, we'll go back to the lodge now," Skye said.

"Dammit, Skye."

He tried to lift her up, walk away with her, but she fought him off.

"Maybe you'd care to join her, Mister Skye?"

"No thanks, mate."

"I've just decided you'll join her. This is quite perfect. If you were elsewhere, I'd have to keep track of you. An unhappy employee can cause problems. So, have a drink on the house."

Skye grinned and refused to sit down. He was as vulnerable as Victoria. They both could wrap themselves around a jug and enjoy the whole shot. Many a rendezvous, back in the trapping days, they had whooped their way into oblivion. But not now. Not when everything was at stake.

He heard shouts. The party was becoming a little frolicsome around the trading wagon. Someone had brought drums, and now the throbbing beat was hammering the village. One young man in a red blanket was parading himself back and forth before some bright-eyed girls.

"Skittles, I quit."

"I thought you might, Mister Skye. A pity. According to the contract, you surrender your worldly goods to us. The ugly horses you put so much stock in, your outfit, your rifle . . . and the little Missus here. We'll enjoy her."

Skye swung, caught Skittles off guard, knocked him to the turf, but Skittles was an army man and up like a cat, his revolver blooming in his hand.

Skye didn't much care. He swung again. The revolver barked. Skye felt the ball part his hair. He jammed in, wrenched Skittles's arm just as the next shot sailed by. Then half a dozen green shirts landed on him, yanked him back, threw him to the earth, and twisted his arm until he thought it'd break. These were skilled brawlers.

Victoria howled, and dashed her jug over one of them. Then they caught her and pinned her down near Skye.

Skittles rose, dusted himself, smiled blandly. "Why, Mister Skye, you've mussed up my attire," he said. "We don't want to give the redskins the wrong impression."

Skye felt a half a dozen hands and arms pinning him to the cold meadow. Victoria was caught in the same vise. Some

Crows stared. Mostly they kept on sipping, peddling furs at the wagon, and courting each other.

Skittles gazed blandly about until he was satisfied that the uproar behind the wagons had scarcely been noted by the Crows.

"It seems we have the upper hand, Mister Skye. We always do. But you're a little slow to learn."

Skye stared up at him.

"Let him get up," Skittles said.

Skye was lifted to his feet. Arms continued to immobilize him.

"As it happens, I need you, Mister Skye. The traders have trouble with the Crow tongue. You'll come and translate."

Skye started to object but Skittles cut him off.

"Don't say no. Don't ever say no to me, Mister Skye. The only words I plan to hear are, 'Yes, Mister Skittles.' That's what you'll be saying from now on."

"Let her up and let her go," Skye said.

Skittles smiled broadly, revealing those perfect teeth.

"She has a new name, Mister Skye. The name is not Victoria, and not Many Quill Woman. The name is Hostage. We now hold everything you care about hostage. Your ugly colt is a hostage and so is the mare. Your, ah, wife is our hostage. Your miserable possessions, a battered Hawken, a bedroll, a few tools, those are all hostage too. You must be in your forties. That's not much for a lifetime, is it?

"It's all hostage now, Mister Skye, and you will say 'Yes, Mister Skittles' whenever I ask you to do something. If you say 'Yes, Mister Skittles,' maybe your squaw won't get hurt. Maybe you might even get your horses back. And your rifle. Maybe. Only maybe. It will all depend. You are going to be a slave, Mister Skye. You are going to say yessir, yessir, and you are going to smile, and you are going to invite your old friends from this village to the trading wagon, and smile at them. And if you don't, Mister Skye, the things that will happen tonight, once the orgy starts, oh, yes, there's usually an orgy and a few redskins dead by dawn—the things that will happen to your squaw, and your animals, won't even be noticed."

Skye nodded.

They stepped back. He stood free. He could run. He could howl. He could maybe even walk away.

Skittles smiled again. The man worked at smiling, had a smile for every occasion, a bright smile, a condescending smile, a triumphant smile. He flipped open his revolver and ejected the two spent shells and reloaded from a handful that fit into loops on his belt.

"Time's a wasting, Mister Skye." He pointed toward the trading wagon.

Skye watched them steer Victoria toward the traders' camp, and then she disappeared inside a tent. He watched the flap close. She was in there with a couple of green shirts.

He clenched and unclenched his hands.

"Mister Skye?" Skittles asked. He pointed gently toward the trading wagon where two or three green shirts were still raking in pelts and robes and pouring out watered-down spirits. It was not yet evening, but soon would be.

He saw no quick or easy way out. But he would await his chances and break when he could.

"Why, it's Mister Skye, going to help us out," said one of the green shirts, Mister Oliver.

A familiar old woman was approaching. He knew her; he was acquainted with most of the people in Otter's band. This plump old lady was Little Red Fox, a graying widow who made and decorated cradleboards and gave them to young mothers. Her bead and quill designs were famous for warding off dark spirits and bringing luck to the infants in the cradleboards, and she was revered for the goodness she brought to the newborn.

"So it is you, Mister Skye," she said in her own tongue. "I heard it was you. You're a trader now?"

"What's she saying, Skye?"

"She's asking after me."

"I am not a trader, mother. But I will translate."

"That is good, Mister Skye. I brought this good robe, which has served me well for many winters. I want to trade it for some needles and thread, a new awl, a new knife, and many bright beads."

"What's she say, Skye?"

"She wants to trade her robe for needles, thread, beads, an awl, and a knife."

"Tell her to take the robe over there to have it looked at. We're not trading for the hardware now, Skye. We'll trade her for a cup of lightning."

Skye didn't like what he was being forced to do. "Mother, they say to take the robe over there, where the men in green shirts will look at it and offer a price for it. Then they say they'll give you some of the water that makes people crazy. They say they won't trade for the things you want now."

She sighed. "Are they out of these things?"

"She wants to know whether you're out of the things she wants."

A green shirt grinned. "Just tell her we want her robe and we'll give her a treat."

"They want your robe and they'll give you some of the water that makes you crazy."

"I think not, Mister Skye." She smiled and walked away.

"What'd she say? You let her go!"

"She said no."

"You let her go!"

"She makes beautiful cradleboards and decorates them and is famous in the village for the things she makes with her hands. It is very good luck to get one of her cradleboards."

"Go tell her we want that robe."

Skye shrugged, and hastened after her. "They said to tell you they want the robe."

She paused. "I wish you and Many Quill Woman would make a child. I would make the most beautiful cradleboard I have ever made. I would weave powerful signs into it."

"I'll tell them."

He returned. "She said she wishes my wife and I would have a child so she could make a cradleboard for us, and for our baby. She said it would be the most beautiful one she has ever made."

"Damn you, Mister Skye, take this hooch to her and snatch that robe."

Skye stood paralyzed. He thought of Victoria, in that tent. He thought of his medicine colt, and the mare. He thought of Victoria at the utter mercy of those green shirts. He thought of the colt and mare lying dead, their throats slit.

"No," he said. "She doesn't want your spirits. She wants what she wants. And we don't steal robes."

The green shirts laughed but let it go. Skye had won a tiny victory but he was losing the war.

thirty-seven

Chief Robber himself showed up with three of his youngest wives beside him. He paused, rocked on his heels, studied the bacchanal, looped his way around the trading wagons, and then discovered Skye.

"Ah, it is you, Mister Skye," he said. "Are you working for the traders?"

"I am their captive."

"What's the chief want?" asked a green shirt.

"He's inquiring about my employment."

"Tell him, he's got robes to trade, we'll give him some good brew. Nothing but the best for old Robber."

"The traders wish to trade robes, and will give you the best of their water that makes men crazy."

"Why are you their captive?"

"They have taken Many Quill Woman and my horses and my rifle from me."

"That is a good joke."

"What's he say, Skye?"

"He asked me about my employment, and I told him."

The Robber smiled. "It is a good evening," he said. "The young men drum and dance. The girls flirt. Friends sit around the big fires and laugh. It is a good time. I was wrong about spirits."

"Translate," yelled a green shirt.

"He says it's a good evening, and he was wrong about spirits."

The chief studied the cheerful crowd. "I like this. I see no harm in it. I will trade. I want a big jug of crazy-water. Here are my three youngest and prettiest wives. They will make the traders happy. Say this."

The ladies smiled seductively. Skye noticed they were all gotten up in their best, with vermillion on their cheeks, and wearing their finest quilled dresses. Their eyes shone.

Skye didn't want to translate. He coughed and hemmed and settled his top hat on his locks.

"Come on, Skye."

"Chief Robber wishes to trade for a large jug of your best stuff. His payment is to lend you his three youngest and prettiest wives."

That caught their attention. The green shirts suddenly quit grading and loading robes, and rushed to the women, who were delighted with the attention. To be lent out by their husband the chief was a delicious honor.

"No," said Skittles.

The boss appeared out of nowhere and grasped the transaction instantly.

"Mister Balsamwood, go back to work," he said. "Mister Skye, tell Chief Robber we'll be delighted to give him our very best spirits, one cup for one prime robe."

"But, sir," said Grosvenor, "that's a dandy offer."

"Business before pleasure, Mister Grosvenor. After we clean out all the robes, then I'll consider it."

"Yes, sir."

Skittles turned to Skye. "The squaw's enjoying a drink or two. Behave yourself, Mister Skye."

"Same to you, sir."

Skittles clouded briefly, smiled, and wandered off.

Night was falling. The incessant drumming was affecting Skye's heart, making it beat to the rhythm of the drums. Some of the Crows were chanting, their hard voices violating the twilight peace. A few young women crowded about the trading wagon, where they were disposing of ermine and mink pelts, each for a half cup of the hooch, poured into the gourd bowls they brought along.

Green shirts tucked the mink and ermine hides into the corners that no buffalo robes filled. The wagon with cured furs and pelts was full; the other wagon, with raw buffalo hides, was not. The green shirts were making a haul. And this was but one village. The outfit planned to visit several more. It was working north toward Blackfeet, Gros Ventres, and Assiniboine villages. It struck him that the owners and their employees would split upward of twenty thousand dollars from a winter's work.

One by one, the young men slipped away, dug up another robe somewhere, and returned. Now it bought them watered-down spirits, and with a pinch of bug powder to make them crazy. Skye didn't need to translate. They dropped a robe before the traders, who examined it by lamplight, and the warrior walked away with another cup of the rotgut steadily being stirred up by a couple of expert green shirts.

It seemed an idyll. A mild winter's night. Some good

drumming. Stars popping out. A few warming fires. Some flirting, some giggles, some couples meandering away from the light and into their own world. The spirits were dissolving restraints. Men laughed. The girls turned seductive. Even the chief was joining the revels.

Skye thought of Victoria. Was she guarded? Was she bound or constrained? How could he free her? How could he free the mare and Jawbone, corralled in a makeshift pen? How could he get to her? He didn't even know which of the traders' tents she was in. But nighttime was a good cloak.

Chief Robber's women showed up, each bearing two robes, which was all most women could carry. These were prime robes, luxuriant and thick.

One came to Skye. "Jug. He wants a jug."

"The chief wants a jug," he told Mister Oliver.

Skittles materialized out of the dark. He had been prowling, ever alert, ever aware of everything in the camp.

"Six prime robes, Mister Skittles," said Oliver.

"All right, six cups."

"Of this?"

"What else?"

He motioned toward the kettle of watered-down muddy-water stuff, spirits and pepper and whatever else the traders felt like tossing in.

It was Skittles's deliberate act of disrespect for the chief.

Skye watched the green shirts prepare a jug and hand it to one of the wives. She beamed and hurried away with the two other women, and were soon lost in darkness.

He felt bad. Everything about this was bad, and he included his own yearning to settle in a corner with some of that rotgut somewhere and pour it down his gullet.

In an hour or two the sober green shirts would be absolute

masters of this Crow camp. Many of the younger Crows were plainly drunk. But they seemed cheerful enough, and Skye thought maybe the night would pass without tragedy.

But then in a flash of flame everything changed. One young man wrapped a blanket around a young woman, an old courtship ritual, and a rival howled, drew a knife, slashed, and all Skye saw was blood gouting into the old blanket. The girl screamed. She raced into darkness, spilling her blood and covered with her swain's. A young man fell, rolled across cold ground, and lay in a widening black pool. Other young men howled. Firelight glinted off of naked knives.

He didn't know their names. He only knew that brothers and friends were fighting brothers and friends, old men were wrestling with young ones. The beat of the drums stopped cold, but now there were howls and shrieks terrible to hear.

Skye raced into the melee.

"Avast!" he roared, the roar erupting from his belly.

He threw men apart. But drunken warriors howled at him and slashed the air with cold steel.

"Let them brawl, Mister Skye. It's all part of their nature."

Skye turned on Skittles, only to see the man smiling, the revolver casually in hand.

"There now, Mister Skye, you step back and let them destroy themselves. It is destined, you know. The inferior races will fade away. The superior races will triumph and possess the land and its wealth. That's historical reality. There's nothing we can do to change it."

Some few youngsters were still brawling, but now village headmen were pulling people away, clustering around the fallen, stanching blood. And the wailing had begun.

Skye smelled death in the air. Along with vomit, fear, and maybe something like hysteria. He itched to land on Skittles and thrash him into the cold ground, but he knew better. It was a good thing he himself had not been drinking. He would be among the dead.

In time, the Absaroka people, those who could still function, came for the sick and the dead and hauled them away. Chief Robber was not among them. One or two headmen, including his testy old friend Otter, had restored order. Now there was a lonely gulf between the village and the traders' camp, a no-man's-land where no one dared venture. An aching silence.

Death and grief had come. Skye didn't know who had perished. What boys lay wounded. What girls wept into their cold beds, for there were only a few blankets to warm these people this winter's night. They would lie on cold ground where robes had once protected them from the earth. They would shiver, not only from cold, but from the evil unloosed in their camp. They would remember the prediction of Walks to the Top, that Skye's medicine horse Jawbone would bring down the wrath of the spirits upon them.

He thought that in the morning they might come to kill his horses, or even kill him, for had he not assisted in the trading?

And even if he might escape with Victoria and his animals, would he ever be welcome in a Crow village again?

But there was not time to ponder that. The traders were working by the flickering light of two fires as they closed up shop. They had filled one wagon; the other was nearly full. There were no doubt few buffalo robes left in The Robber's village.

"Time to be moving, gentlemen," Skittles said. "We've done all the good we can."

thirty-eight

By the light of the bonfires, green shirts dismantled the trading camp. Two canvas tents had already vanished into the bowels of the supply wagon. All that was left was blood and vomit on the grass.

Skittles obviously planned to make time this night, putting distance between his outfit and the Crow village they had debauched.

"Mister Skye, you'll harness the teams," he said easily.

He had an air of total triumph about him. The outfit had raked in a small fortune, almost without cost.

Skye nodded. If he was going to make a break, it had to be now. But where was Victoria? The tents were packed and the wagons were loaded almost to the bows and canvas tops.

One green shirt stood at guard before the wagons, his rifle at the ready. The rest were packing up. Some lifted the empty booze kettle and stowed it. Others collected tin cups, gourd cups, wooden cups that littered that bloody ground, and piled them into a burlap sack. Others raised the tailgates of the wagons carrying the ill-gotten robes and hides, and levered them tight.

Skye started toward the rope corral that contained the draft horses and the saddlers, as well as his captive colt and mare. The harness would probably be lying there, ready to drop over the big draft animals. He would have trouble in the dark.

His mind seethed. Another guard stood at the horse pen, rifle at the ready, no doubt to prevent theft of the stock. Skittles was not one to let anyone or anything slip through his hands.

Two green shirts were already harnessing. Putting eight draft horses into harness and hooking them to wagons was a tough task, especially at night. Add to that the loading of the packhorses, and you had a half hour of hard labor by several men.

Skye looked toward the dipper, trying to tell the time as it rotated around the north star. The night had turned wintry and dead quiet. He was grateful that no wind stirred, so that his hands wouldn't go numb as he dropped collars over those thick necks and tightened bands under their great hairy bellies.

It was perhaps midnight. An eerie silence lowered over them all, all the louder for the drumming that had shattered the peace only an hour or so earlier. Now not even the wail of the mothers of the bloodied boys caught the tendrils of winter air.

He clambered under the rope fence and found a heap of harness awaiting him.

"Good evening, Mister Skye," said one of the green shirts. "You can start on that big black over there."

Skye thought it was Oliver, or maybe Parsons. Men who were groomed alike were hard to pick out. Jawbone discovered him, trotted up, squealed, and butted him.

"That miserable thing should have its throat cut," said another of the green shirts. "Makes trouble."

Skye nodded. He found the mare now, faint firelight reflecting off her side. She whickered softly and drew close. But there was little Skye could do for the moment. The firelight revealed too much. He needed darkness, real darkness, a cloak of darkness, the kind of night where a man can't see ten feet.

Where was Victoria? How could he make a move without knowing? Had they knocked her in the head and left her in the woods?

And where was his kit? His bedroll, his rifle, his packsaddles, his gear? He hadn't the faintest idea. He found a collar, which felt icy in his hand, and found a halter. These teamsters rarely used bridles with these superb animals. They walked beside their teams, lead rope in hand. The big draft horse stood quietly, letting itself be haltered. Then Skye dropped the collar over its thick neck, and led it to the heap of harness. A belly band would be next.

It was then that he heard the harsh whistle of a magpie. It was a thing unknown in the night, but apparently not a thing that troubled the green shirts anyway.

He felt a surge of joy. She was there.

He finished with the big black's breeching and led it to one of the pelt wagons, backed it into place, and buckled the traces. Skittles was watching him. Skye walked slowly into the darkness again, entered the rope corral, and found another big draft horse. The two green shirts from the rope corral were each leading a harnessed draft horse toward the wagons.

No one was watching him. It was the moment Skye needed.

He collected another halter and belly band and headed for the next draft horse, only to bump into a small person in the moon-shadow side of the horse.

"Dammit, Skye, don't step on my toe," she said.

Skye's heart raced.

"Come."

She led him to the rear of the corral, closest to the naked cottonwoods that lay fifty yards away, and they simply walked through the darkness. Somehow she had discerned that the fire-blinded night guard could not see them. Skye followed silently, his heart banging, not knowing what to think but filled with joy.

They raced into the naked trees, the distant firelight eerie on the web of limbs. And then they reached the sandstone cliffs, and she headed through brush toward the village, well screened from the river.

She paused at a niche in the stone and pulled him down beside her.

"I hide here," she said. "See, a cave. I got that jug. They gave me a jug of the good stuff. They put me in the supply wagon, guard in front so I couldn't get out. But they don't know Absaroka. I got my knife from my moccasin and cut through the canvas at the other end and walk out as soon as it got dark. They never knew. Dammit, Skye, I got a whole jug here, big enough for us to have a good time. But not now."

"You rescued me."

"Hell, yes. Maybe I'm good for something, eh?"

"Can we get my gear? Rifle, bedroll, packsaddles? Do you know where they are?"

She didn't respond. She didn't know. One of the wagons.

"We need to get the mare and the colt."

She pressed a hand over his. "Let them go, Skye. We can't go back. They're hunting for you now."

Without a rifle once again. Without means to make meat. Without weapons. Without horses. All that time at Fort Sarpy lost. But he had escaped.

"We'll head for the village," he said.

"The hell we will, Skye. They're looking for you there. Why do they want you, eh? You never told me."

"At first I thought it was because they wanted my labor. They're shorthanded and don't have a good translator. Now I think it's because I'm a witness. What they're doing is against the laws of the Fathers. Any white man who doesn't go along, he's dead." He turned to her. "Maybe you saved my life."

"Witness?"

"Someone who would talk in St. Louis. Someone who would tell the Indian agency about them. Name some names."

"You people crazy."

"I'm not a Yank, Victoria."

"You want a sip?"

"Yes, soon as it's safe."

"Who died, Skye? I heard the wailing."

"I don't know. One of the young men drumming."

"Sonofabitch," she said.

"Let's work back and see," she said.

He nodded. They left the sheltering sandstone and worked back at the base of the bluff until they were opposite the traders' camp, and then slipped like wraiths through the naked forest until they could peer out onto the meadow.

Nothing. Gone. All the wagons, all the livestock. But for the trampled brown grass that whispered of large events, it was as if the traders had never been there.

"Don't go out there," he whispered. "It would be just like Skittles to leave a man behind, his horse hidden, waiting for us. They know I'll come looking for my kit."

"I won't."

They waited an eternity, it seemed. A cloud canceled the moonlight. The meadow of sorrows lay in deep darkness. A deep predawn cold settled over the meadow, frosting the broken grasses. And still they waited.

Then, soft as the flapping of an owl through night air, the clop of horse hooves. The horse moved upriver, away from the village. Probably the direction the traders went.

He didn't know where they would go next. Skittles would have to send his two loaded wagons to a fur post. But he was expecting two wagons back, and there must have been some agreement about where. If he sent the two full wagons out, that reduced his company by four men.

Skye sighed. His Hawken, powder horn, caps, lead and patches, and all the rest were moving away from him in the cold night. He and Victoria slid onto the meadow, searched it closely. Searched with dread for the bodies of his colt and mare, their throats slit. But they found nothing at all in that sad flat beside the river.

They walked toward the village, knowing it was forlorn and defenseless, that its men slept with vomit on their shirts, that they would wake up sick and listless, that many a lodge was shivering this night, that in some lodges bloodied young men were lying in the vise of death. The village was naked to its enemies. A raiding party could sweep through it. The entire pony herd, pride of the Crow nation, could be swept away.

The Robber's village was a desolate place. Something foul hung in the air. Little smoke ebbed from the blackened cones of the lodges. One drunken man sprawled on the ground. Skye wished he had a blanket or a robe to cover the wretch.

Victoria steered him toward her own small lodge, but when they entered they found nothing at all. No robes, no blanket, no parfleche with her things in it. Nothing but frozen earth.

Victoria scratched on the door of Two Dogs' lodge. No one

answered. She tried again. The smell of vomit eddied from the door.

Skye knew what he had to do. He was going to follow that trading outfit, he was going to do it, and he would do it even if he didn't possess a weapon to his name.

thirty-nine

Something frightful had passed through The Robber's village. Skye and Victoria crawled out of their small lodge in the gray light of a winter's dawn and saw a deadness everywhere. No smoke was eddying from the lodges. A desolation hung over what had been, only hours before, a vibrant and happy place.

Skye and Victoria had survived the cold by building a lodge fire and feeding it all night. She had gone to the sandstone bluffs to recover a robe she had hidden there but it was gone, and so were all the other robes the village women had hidden there. Each had been pawned for a drink of the rotgut. So Skye had dug into his fire pouch at his waist, struck steel to flint, and eventually they had a hot fire in their naked home.

Now he braved the cold, wandering through the forlorn village, wondering who lived and who didn't. Victoria muttered softly, wandering from lodge to lodge, looking for life. They rounded a lodge and saw a girl. Victoria knew her. She lay across the frozen ground, her skirts hiked high, her face staring at the dawn.

Victoria plunged to her knees and shook the girl.

"Get up! Get up!" she cried. "Broken Wing, wake up!"

Victoria shook hard, but the girl did not move.

Victoria and Skye lifted the girl, but the girl did not sit. She was stiff, frozen solid, and life had fled her. A rime of vomit clung to the girl's lips.

"Aiee! Broken Wing!" Victoria cried.

Victoria pressed her hands upon the dead woman, and sobbed softly.

When at last she had wept away her grief, she looked up at Skye, and at the other person who now stood over her. It was the old Tobacco Planter, Walks to the Top, wrapped in a bright thick Hudson's Bay blanket.

"I saw this in the smoke of the sweetgrass," he said. "I warned the people. Now it has been as I saw it."

Skye nodded. Would the old man blame all this on the medicine horse?

"The traders are gone. They left in the night. They have almost every robe and hide that was the wealth of this village," he said.

"This I saw in the smoke."

"And it's not over. There are the sick, the dead, and the ones who fought each other with knives. And the girls who were violated. And the old men sleeping half frozen in their cold lodges."

"I went before The Robber and I told him. Do not let business be done with the traders. This I saw."

"Here is The Robber's oldest daughter," Victoria said. "The one he loved most."

The Robber's lodge rose nearby, as cold and quiet as the rest in the village. Someone would have to tell him that his daughter had perished of spirits and cold.

Tenderly, Skye lifted the frozen girl. She seemed so heavy, but probably didn't weigh a hundred pounds. Then he lowered the girl to the trampled earth before the chief's lodge, and Victoria straightened the girl's soiled skirts. Walks to the Top, wrapped tightly in his red blanket, his face dark with pain and anger, came along.

Skye scratched at the door, but this evoked no response.

Victoria slapped the doorskin hard, repeatedly. They heard a stirring, and finally the chief's old sits-beside-him wife, Stirs the Water, poked her head out.

"Mother, we have bad news," Victoria said.

The woman squinted, caught sight of her daughter's frozen body before the lodge, muttered a cry, and then retreated inside. The lodge's door flap slapped shut.

The village was stirring at last. Skye stood unhappily at The Robber's lodge, noting that old people were heading for the bushes, women were building lodge fires, a few shivering children were solemnly wandering about, some of them in tears.

Some wore spare clothing. A few had blankets. One wore a blanket capote. A few did have some worn or torn buffalo robes, somehow salvaged from the devastation that had whirled through this village.

The Robber poked his head through the door, studied the frozen body of his daughter, and groaned.

"She was over there when we found her," Victoria said, pointing.

The chief nodded and dismissed them with a wave.

He looked ill. Skye thought the chief was barely functioning. Whatever it was, headache, nausea, the aftereffects of indulgence, he wasn't ready to cope with this.

Now a crowd gathered, and Victoria told of finding the chief's daughter frozen to death.

Walks to the Top whirled away, exuding anger and sorrow. Skye followed. There was nothing more he could do for The Robber and his family.

"This is the beginning of the end of my people," the Tobacco Planter said. "I have seen it."

"I'm going to try to stop it."

"How will you stop it?"

"I'm going to go after them."

"More traders will come with this poison water. Nothing in the stories of the People prepare us for this. It is a new evil that white men bring. Look at them! They are dazed. They are sick. They hurt. They lost their manhood. A man is a man when he commands himself. But they swallow this poison and they no longer command themselves. They fight like rutting elk. They stab each other, brothers fight, friends fight. And now the mothers and widows cry. Our chief himself drank the poison, and he is helpless now. They will wait for the next traders to give them more, and they will kill buffalo and tan robes so they can trade them for more and more and more!"

The Tobacco Planter saw the thing Skye dreaded.

"Look at them!" Walks to the Top shouted. "We are naked before our enemies. They still stagger. They cannot put one foot in front of the other. Who cooks the morning meals? Who cares for the horses? Who polices our village?"

The elder stopped suddenly. "What are you going to do?"

"Follow them, stalk them, find some way to destroy their spirits. It's pure grain alcohol. It burns."

"You will take a war party?"

"Many Quill Woman and I will go alone. It is better that way."

"With what?"

"That is a good question."

"We will see," the venerable man said, and walked away as suddenly as he had approached Skye.

The village was stirring now, sullen, hungry, cold, and ashamed. Skye spotted Otter, the headman who had suffered ambush at the hands of the Blackfeet.

"It is true, then. You are the cause of this," Otter said. "That's what is whispered."

"Otter, I was a prisoner. My wife was held hostage, along with all my things. My horses were held hostage. I did not sell any of the spirits. I only translated."

Otter eyed him malevolently. "We will see," he said. "I took none of the spirits. I alone am fit and able this morning. I have chosen my way."

"Then you must put this village together, Otter. Put guards out. Start the village police. Watch over the horses. See about firewood. Start hunters. The village needs a thousand robes and hides."

Otter stood, his arms crossed before him, looking truculent. "It is said you should leave here. You were with them. You are a white man. You brought this upon us."

One could not argue with something like that. Skye knew it, knew he would be wasting his breath. This would soon snowball into an exile.

"I have some business to attend, and then I'll leave the village," he replied. "And if I return, I will have good news for you."

Otter simply glared. A storm was gathering over Skye.

He trotted to his lodge and found Victoria there.

"I'm being blamed. We need to leave. The ponies that Two Dogs gave me; are they still in the herd? Do you know them? Can we borrow a few things?"

"I know them, Skye. I don't want to leave my people. I don't want you to be disgraced."

"We have nothing. Food, robes, weapons. Whatever you can scrounge from your brother . . ."

She nodded.

They didn't even have saddles. He could ride bareback, but only for a while, and when his back split in two he had to dismount. They could get hackamores easily enough, and with luck, a packsaddle. But they would be leaving The Robber's camp with barely enough to survive on in wintertime. And Skye had a mission in mind, no matter that he even lacked a rifle.

Victoria begged all that morning, and somehow put together a small outfit. She and Skye caught the horses in the village herd. They were good sound animals, and that was a start. And on a venerable pack frame they loaded their few things: some parfleches of jerky and pemmican, a worn blanket apiece, a hatchet and spare knife, Victoria's bow and quiver filled with arrows, and the small jug of spirits that Victoria had not sucked dry while she was imprisoned by the green shirts.

They rode out amid dour stares, silent curses, grim glances, and deep silence. For most of the village he had called his home, and the people he had called his own, somehow connected him with the darkness that had fallen over The Robber's band.

Victoria sat bareback, her skirts hiked, tears forming in her eyes. These people were her own, but wherever her man went, so would she.

Skye rode straight upriver from the stricken village, reached the somber meadow where the traders had milked the people of all they had, and then picked up the trail of the wagons, fresh still in the frosted ground. He didn't know how he was going to do it, but he intended to put Skittles out of business.

forty

Skye felt like singing, so he sang.

As I was a-walkin' down Paradise Street,
To me way! Hey! Blow the man down!
A pretty young damsel I chanced for to meet,
Give me some time to blow the man down.

Oh, blow the man down, bullies, blow the man down,
To me way! Hey! Blow the man down,
Oh, blow the man down, bullies, blow him away,
Give me some time to blow the man down . . .

Victoria was cross. "Why are you singing?" she asked.

"What else is there to do?"

"You should be watching for the wagons."

Indeed, the furrows of the wagons ran straight ahead, cutting deeper and deeper in the thawing mud. Skittles might end up mired if this winter day warmed much more. That would suit Skye fine.

"What is that song about?" she asked.

"It's a sea chanty. Paradise Street is in Liverpool."

"Where's that?"

"In the country where I was born."

"We should be crying instead. People dead. My family, everyone, sick."

He lifted his battered top hat and settled it again. There were times so dark that all he could think of was singing, as if melody might kill a little hurt in him. Sometimes it did.

He sang because everything had gone bad and he was worse off than he'd ever been. A man likes to make some progress, but here he was, almost as poor as the moment he jumped ship at Fort Vancouver with little more than the clothing on his back to sustain him.

He thought over the past months: a devastating Blackfoot raid that almost killed Victoria. His good old Hawken stolen. Everything else stolen. His horses stolen. A new colt and mare with strange powers. Distrust in her village and exile. Work for a rotten fur company post to get himself a new outfit, and that got him fired for being fair to the Indians. Then some time spent in the Kicked-in-the-Bellies band of Crows, only to get himself kicked out because of a rabid wolf. Then Skittles's imprisonment of him, loss of his kit again including the replacement rifle, loss of his medicine horses, and distrust once again in The Robber's village. All his fault. It was time to sing!

She hailed me with her flipper, I took her in tow,
To me way! Hey! Blow the man down!

Yardarm to yardarm away we did go
Give me some time to blow the man down.

"What does that mean?" she asked.

"It means the singer's about to be shanghaied."

She sniffed. "Talk about something I know about, dammit."

"Did you bring that jug?"

"Yes."

"We'll drink our dinner tonight."

She grinned.

He got tired of riding bareback. After a couple of hours the spine of the horse sawed his crotch in two. So he stopped, slid down, grabbed the line, and walked. She thought that was a good idea and joined him. They were trailing four horses, all good ponies.

They approached a grassy rise dotted with jack pine, and he handed her the lines and told her to wait. He hiked to the ridge and peered over, studying the country ahead. The prairie was surrendering to rougher country with sandstone outcrops and piney ridges. The ruts of the wagons continued straight, generally northerly. But the warming ground was starting to claw at those iron tires, and Skittles's traders were no doubt slowed, and their big horses would be wearied. It was time to be careful.

Skittles was probably too contemptuous of the Crows he left behind to post a rear guard, but he also was an army man and one could be sure of nothing. So Skye settled into the dry grass, studied the country ahead for a while, spotted nothing but cloud shadows cutting across the aching open country, and finally decided it was safe to proceed.

He didn't know what he would do when he found the traders. He lacked so much as an old rifle. They were well armed with short and long guns, some of them the new fast-loading Sharps. And Skye knew they could use them all to good effect. If he had any success, it would be entirely by stealth.

He thought he heard a distant crack of a rifle, but the wind was tricky, and he heard nothing more. His imagination, then. He studied the empty land one last time, then slid down the rise and joined Victoria.

"Looks all right. They're struggling with mud now. Frost's out of the ground. Maybe they'll hole up before dark to let their plugs rest."

"What the hell is a plug?"

"Horse."

"You white men have ten names for everything. I gotta learn the whole damn business over again."

All that afternoon they pursued Skittles's wagons. Skye was sure from the freshness of the ruts that they were gaining ground, and now he paused at every hill for a long look. But Skittles was driving hard.

They came to a low pass of sorts, with a saddle to the northeast. That's where the ruts parted. Skye studied the place. Two wagons were cutting northeast for the Missouri River. The rest continued northward and would hit the big river somewhere west of the badlands, maybe Fort Benton. The great river wound through impassable canyons for a couple hundred miles. There probably would be a flatboat waiting on the river somewhere to carry those hides and robes to Fort Union.

Skittles was down to two wagons and eight men. But he had two empties and four other men coming his way, and they would rendezvous somewhere and then hit another Indian village. It could be Blackfoot, Gros Ventre, or Assiniboine, but who could say?

Victoria studied the diverging ruts.

"There go the robes," she said. "There go everything they could take from my people. Are you going to follow the robes?"

"No, I'm going to follow the booze."

"Goddamn, Mister Skye, are you sure?"

Skye knew she was seeing those robes and hides as a Crow woman would; hundreds or thousands of hours of patient scraping, softening, tanning, the brutal work of generations of women. He wondered how many hours of miserable bent-over labor was expended for each cup of rotgut hooch the Absaroka people got in return.

It was something he didn't want to think about. There was another reason to go after the kegs. He wanted his outfit back. His rifle, his horses, his packsaddle, his bedroll, his powder and shot. They had it all.

And they had all the odds on their side too. But they could get too cocky in a hurry.

He wondered how Skittles felt right then. The man had made a killing. Did he consider what he had done to the Crow village? That the youths especially might acquire a taste for that booze? That he left the village naked and demoralized? Was he so oblivious to the needs of native people that he didn't know or care? Or was he just another avaricious Yank, making a buck and the hell with scruples?

Skye thought the man did have scruples of a sort, which he heeded when it was convenient to do so. That was the odd thing about Skittles. He was full of ethics.

They followed the wagon ruts into a broad valley hemmed on the north and west by a sandstone ridge. Skittles's bunch were pressing straight down the valley toward what Skye believed were the Snowy Mountains, blue, white-crowned, and distant.

Skye called it quits well before dusk. He didn't want to

walk into an ambush. He wanted plenty of light around him for now. A need for the dark would come later, when it would shroud him, cloak them both, conceal their design.

He found a side canyon in the yellow sandstone and went up it, being careful to keep his horses on hard ground. He didn't want hoofprints to tell tales. There were scores of shallow wind-carved caves in the whole region, many of them dandy shelters. He picked one deep in the side gulch, far below the rimrock capping the bluffs. There he could build a good fire that would not be seen, and its heat would radiate off the cave walls, warming them all night.

There would be plenty of grass for the ponies too. He and Victoria picketed them on buffalo grass and gathered wood for the camp. He found plenty of fallen deadwood and built a fire. He had no weapons at all and intended to whittle a belaying pin from a dead limb.

They settled down to a miserable meal of pemmican, but even so, the fat and ground meat and berries in it filled his belly.

"You have that jug?" he asked.

She laughed. This was the jug Skittles's green shirts had handed to her to keep her quiet while she was a hostage. Now she dug it out of the gear on the pack frame.

"Sonofabitch!" she said, pulled off the cork, and sucked.

She gasped, wheezed, howled, growled, and handed the jug to Skye.

He let that awful, treacherous, vicious stuff slide down his gullet. He whooped, groaned, sucked again, and sighed.

But then she plucked up the ceramic jug and hurled it into the darkness. It shattered.

"The whole damn world is broken," she said, and began to weep.

forty-one

*H*er tears fell into the hollow of his shoulder. Skye pulled her tight with his big hands until she was wrapped into his side. He could not comfort her. She wept softly, sometimes muttering in her Absaroka tongue, her English abandoned now.

But he could follow her every thought. It wasn't just that her world had shattered when the green-shirt traders had debauched her village; it was much more. Her life had changed with the wound in her side. It had shattered when he had left her to put a new outfit together. In all that time they had struggled on alone and apart.

"You have not touched me," she said. "You don't want me."

How could he tell her he had feared to touch her? That the terrible wound in her side might yet torment her? That he had been waiting, almost forever, for some hint that she wanted him? Some little flash of light in her eyes?

"I am ugly now," she said.

He slid his hand to the place where he had pressed a red-hot knife into her almost fatal wound to cauterize it, a place of corduroyed and corded scar tissue under her ribs.

"You are beautiful," he said. "This wound is where life is, not death. Without this wound you wouldn't be here in my arms."

"Oh, Skye."

She wept, her hot tears soaking through his buckskin shirt. She was weeping not only for her village, which she saw in its shame and ruin, but also for herself. She had suffered a loneliness just as terrible as his own.

"I love you more than ever, Victoria." It seemed a lame thing to say to her.

"But you haven't had me."

It had been a long time. Some eternity ago, when she was slowly mending, he had left her in her brother's care, headed out to get a new rifle and outfit, and now, months later, he was with her and still had not touched her and it was tearing her to pieces.

He caressed her softly, and felt her torn spirit quiet within her. He had not let her know how he ached for her. He had been away too long. He kissed her. Her hands found his well-shaved cheek and jaw, and he felt the joy in them as she caressed him.

She nestled herself into him, and he held her until the fire dimmed and the cold began to creep into this perfect hideaway, wind-hollowed and peaceful. Then, softly, he rose, built up the flame so the warmth would again echo off the sandstone, and returned to the old robe and blanket they shared. Now his hand found her and slid over her and possessed her, and her arms found him, and her lips and her heart too.

They made love softly, awakening ancient memories. He

kissed the scar on her torso. It was his way of saying something to her, that he loved her whole, all of her, and she was as beautiful to him as ever.

Her hands found his back and drew him tight and Skye and Victoria renewed the bond that had brought them together long ago. And so they passed the night. From time to time he rose, built up the fire, and then they came together again, scarcely noticing when the flames played out and only embers lit their night.

At last he pulled the old blanket over them, but they didn't sleep. She wept again, her tears watering his bare shoulder. He knew she was thinking of other things now. Something had happened to her people. The proud Crows, able to hold their own against the more numerous and more dangerous Sioux and Blackfeet, had been ruined by a poison brought by the white men. And now she wept.

She had long experience of it. At the trappers' rendezvous she and Skye had bought the spirits and sucked their jug dry. But after those rendezvous everything returned to the way it was and the party was over. It was a weakness in both of them. He knew how hard it was for him to resist a good howl with a bottle, and sometimes that's what he wanted more than anything else.

But she was right. This thing done by Skittles was different. The booze was meaner and was used systematically to ruin her people. There was nothing in their entire history to help them deal with this; it was a new menace for which they had no defense, not even a legend, a story with a moral to it. In the world of white men there were hundreds of mocking stories about drunks, a thousand jokes, a folk wisdom about spirits, and these were an inheritance he had that she didn't. None of her people had heard stories or jokes like that, or listened to the wisdom of their parents or their priests. The Crows were naked before this new thing, but so were all the Indians. Would Blackfeet or Sioux fare any better?

They kept to themselves and hugged through the chill, but then she rose until she was sitting, looked at him in the ember light, and said, "Thank you."

Oddly, he knew what she was thanking him for. It wasn't the union they had shared. So close had they been for so long that he fathomed her thoughts, even as she fathomed his. Her thanks were not for the love they had renewed that soft night, but for his resolve. He would destroy the destroyers of her people. Somehow, powerless as he was without a weapon, he would stop these traders in their tracks.

"There will be a way," he said.

And that was all they had to lift them; a sense that there would be a way. They fell asleep at last in the small hours, when the chill descended on them, and their thin old robes were not enough to keep the cold at bay. But the warmth of their bodies was enough, and so the night passed into faint dawn, and the embers had died away with the dimming of the stars.

They dressed quietly, aware that their lives had changed; that they were mates, that they had a great task before them, one that might kill them both. In a way, they grew aware of the danger they faced and resolved to face it.

There was nothing but more pemmican, cold and cruel on the tongue, and they gnawed at the fatty stuff, knowing it sufficed to sustain life.

The ponies had passed the night grazing. Skye collected them and eased the packsaddle over one. They would need watering soon. Then he lifted Victoria onto one of the ponies and he pulled himself over the other. Riding bareback was never easy. Getting aboard a horse without a saddle was hard and he had never mastered it. But soon they descended the side canyon and picked up the clear trail of Skittles's outfit. The ground stayed frozen and Skittles would be making fine time this morning, but the ground would soften that afternoon and then things would be different. The trail had turned mostly west across rolling land, south of the Snowy Mountains.

So Skittles was heading for the Judith country, the very area where Blackfeet had made off with Crow horses and wounded Victoria. Skye eyed his wife, who was riding with steely determination. She was well aware that they were retracing the route from the buffalo hunting camp to her village many months earlier.

There was no sign of the traders but that didn't mean much. They were ahead. What worried Skye was that they had at least one brass spyglass in the outfit, and an ex-army outfit like that would be using it, studying the country from every rise. The chances were that Skittles already knew someone was following him. That would make it tougher, and also raise the prospect of an ambush. There was little Skye could do about it.

Still, stalking an armed body required more than a tracker's skill. Skye wanted to know where Skittles was going. Once he knew that, he could quit following and circle around. Skittles was heading for a village of the Piegans or Gros Ventres, and probably would take those robes and pelts to Fort Benton, the American Fur post on the Missouri.

But all that was guesswork.

They rode across a vast land, with the noble Snowy Mountains, white-topped, guarding the north. Then, late that day, Victoria pointed.

Skye did not see what she was pointing at, but it was something far west.

"Flash of light," she said.

Light? Sun off brass? "Where?" he asked.

She pointed, but he saw nothing. A chance flash had caught her eye. But it was enough to make Skye wary.

"They're heading for the Piegans," he said.

"Maybe we should let them."

Let this southernmost nation of the Blackfeet suffer the fate her Crow band had suffered. Let them drink themselves into a frenzy, kill one another, disgorge all their robes and pelts for another round of spirits, and end up sick, ashamed, broken, and impoverished.

There was something flinty in her face.

"Each time Skittles succeeds, he'll gain strength. He'll come back time after time and destroy your people."

She nodded.

They would continue, demolish Skittles's wagonload of spirits if they could. Only then would the northern tribes, all of them, be safe from him.

But he was certain Skittles knew someone was behind him. Several times more that day they saw, or at least thought they saw, observers on ridges or peaks. One thing for sure, Skittles was not far ahead. Three, four, five miles. As the day warmed, so had the soil softened, and his big draft horses would have a tough time dragging wagons through the mire.

It would pay to be very careful. In fact, Skye thought he would wait for dark and then work north a few miles, and find shelter in one of the giant coulees issuing from the Snowy Mountains. There would be no safety now; no night of bliss, like the last one.

forty-two

Victoria was yelling at him, but the wind whipped her words away. He slowed the pony, and she caught up with him.

"Stop," she said.

He did. The packhorse behind him bumped into the rear of his pony.

She pointed at a distant ridge to the west. He saw nothing.

"Riders," she said.

He still saw nothing, but employed his old way of scanning one sector of the horizon at a time, piece by piece, until he might see what she saw. Her eyes were often better than his.

Then, he made out two moving dots, slightly blurred. He watched them closely.

"Coming our way?" he asked her.

"Damn right."

"Two. Probably sent by Skittles to see what's on his back trail."

They waited quietly until they could get a clearer picture,

and then a trick of light showed the distant riders clearly. Green shirts. Rifles.

Skye examined the nearby terrain. They had been crossing giant coulees and ridges that stretched like claws from the Snowy Mountains. But the country was naked. It was a bad place to be caught unarmed and defenseless by armed riders.

This was a day of sunlight and shadow, of fast-moving clouds driven by high winds, whose dark shadows plowed coldly across the endless open land. It was a day full of tricks of sunlight that made things appear to be moving, when only shadow and wind were galloping along the earth.

They were atop a ridge. Skye retreated from the riders, and descended a shallow grade into a broad, grass-bottomed coulee that had its origins many miles away, and would carry water in the spring. He turned north, sticking just a little off the bottoms even though the going was slower. The passage of four horses through the dried grasses of the bottoms would give them away.

He desperately needed some little side gulch or a gentle turn in the coulee to hide himself, Victoria, and the ponies. To preserve their lives, he thought. He kicked the pony into a slow trot, the fastest he could travel over a rough and eroded slope. At least they were below the ridge, and maybe had not been seen. That was optimistic, given the spyglasses that outfit owned.

For a time he found no place to hide, but then the coulee's west wall retreated slightly, and he found himself riding around a slight bend, and in a moment he and Victoria were riding into a small, shallow side gulch, not much deeper than a mounted rider. He slid off his mount, and she did too. They pulled the horses farther up, past chokecherry brush that would help hide them, and into a shallow hollow that ran only six or eight feet below the surrounding rolling prairie.

Victoria held two horses, ready to slap her hand over their nostrils if they were about to whicker. Horses, famously gregarious, loved to greet other horses. Skye handed her hackamore loops of the two other ponies, removed his plug hat, and edged upward until he could see.

At first he saw nothing, but then he found them, not half a mile off, drifting up the coulee.

"We may have to run," he told her.

It was an impossible situation. They without a firearm, the riders with rifles. Victoria had her bow and quiver but that would offer no help at all, not here.

More cloud shadows rolled across that vast country. One could watch them come and watch them slide by, mile after mile. The riders were identifiably green shirts and in no hurry. But they were out in the middle of the coulee, not on its western edge, and missing the plain trail. They approached another quarter of a mile, quit, and rode south. Skye watched them shrink back to black dots and then vanish.

It had been close.

He turned and found her just behind him, an arrow nocked in her bow.

"They quit," he said. "But there may be more. Skittles knows someone's behind him."

He retreated into the gulch. A pony yawned, baring yellowed teeth. A heavy cloud rolled over, spitting pea snow from its belly, and then it passed. Skye found himself taut and sweaty, even in that chill.

He was a damn fool, going after Skittles this way. He knew it. What did he think he'd accomplish except to get himself and Victoria shot in some lonely gulch and left for the ravens.

"Don't cuss yourself," she said, reading him.

"I've been stupid."

"What is stupid? I don't know this word."

"Dumb. Crazy."

She walked up to him, touched his cheek, running her fingers gently along his jaw, and said nothing.

He didn't want to move, not yet. Not with two snipers drifting nearby. It was cold in that little gulch. He turned his back to the blustering wind.

"Sometimes we are given to do things," she said. "We must do them. We must try to do them even if the end is bad. Sometimes it leads to bad things. Sometimes we are given to do something and we die. Or fail. I think this is given to you to do. If it is given to you, then we will do it."

He clamped his hat down when a gust threatened to whip it away. The wind was rising, and he sensed warmth in it, warmth that would slow down Skittles's wagons when the frost went out and the iron tires of his wagons cut deep furrows.

"We'll get in front of them," he said. "We'll find a place to camp and wait for the warmth to mire them."

"It is coming," she said. "It's in the air."

Skittles would be slowed, and Skye would get around to the front where maybe with some stealth he could slip into the camp and do what needed doing.

They worked patiently up the coulee to the timber and snow, and then cut along the foothills of the mountains until twilight veiled them and they could carve a camp out of a rocky grotto after brushing the snow away.

About midnight the warm winds eddied in, woke them

both, and Skye didn't hesitate. By the light of a tiny fire they collected their gear, loaded the packsaddle, clambered aboard their ponies, and set off across tumbled country, with nothing to guide them except the looming presence of high country on their right.

The temperature shot upward so fast that suddenly the air was delicious, the breezes almost tropical. Within the passage of an hour Skye felt his pony pulling mud with every step. The ponies labored but kept on. He heard dripping water. He listened to the thud of snow sliding off of pines just above.

"Sonofabitch! It's getting hotter than you in the robes, Skye," she said.

He laughed.

If Skittles had any sense, he wouldn't travel much during the coming day. And if the thaw lasted, Skittles might be rooted to the spot for many days.

Dawn caught them several miles west and in rough country, but now it was their turn to study the surrounding land. The first sunlight poking out of the southeast, horizontal orange light, caught something at once: a column of gray smoke a mile or so away and down the long swales to country where wagons could move.

Skye exulted. He knew where they were. For a while, anyway, they could ride in sun-shadow, invisible to anyone down there. As they came abreast of the camp, he could see but two wagons, and a few men. One wagon held the spirits; the other held the gear. He itched to ride down, throw a lit torch into that wagon full of casks, catch them shaving and squatting and rolling up their bedrolls, and howl his way out.

"I just thought of a good way to kill myself," Skye said.

She smiled.

He took some more long looks, and hurried by, wanting to

get ahead before that horizontal light caught them and turned them into bull's-eyes. They were protected by a long ridge clawing the prairies to the south, but even as they worked west, the rising sun narrowed the shadow they were racing through, and in minutes they would be exposed to its bright and deadly glare.

"We've got to drop," he said.

She nodded.

He turned the pony downslope, ever closer to Skittles's camp, down into timber that was even more dangerous than open country because he could not see ahead. But at least they were still shrouded by dawn shade.

They burst out of timber not half a mile from Skittles's camp and could see it and its men clearly. But Skye and Victoria hurried west, racing past the camp, hoping his ponies wouldn't betray him, and hoping that their big, stolid draft animals wouldn't stir.

He could see the horses in a rope pen.

Jawbone squealed. Skye knew that sound as well as he knew his own voice. They hurried west, needing the safety of the next woods or ridge or whatever might shield them from those prying spyglasses.

Jawbone whirled around and around in the rope enclosure, and then bolted straight through the rope. The old mare, suddenly as wild as the colt, bolted with her colt. They raced straight toward Skye and Victoria, who froze in the deep shadow.

Skye heard a shot and another, and then the faint sound of laughter and annoyance. Jawbone and the blessed old mare kept going, and no one was coming after them.

forty-three

awbone kicked up his heels, bounced and leaped, and danced his way up the long grade, and then quit the sun and plunged into deep shade, the very shade that hid Skye and Victoria and their ponies.

Skye dreaded what would come next. Jawbone and the resolute old mare were racing full tilt toward them and would give them away. He was in more than enough peril from the rising sun, which in minutes would bathe the slope he stood on, leaving him exposed to every eye below.

And now this boneheaded colt was frisking and kicking and squealing his way up the long grade while men watched.

But a sharp command below set the green shirts to work. They had draft horses and their own saddlers to round up. For a moment Skye stood, paralyzed, and then began looking for cover. There wasn't much, copses of naked-limbed trees, a few swales. He would edge toward those.

Jawbone danced and pranced his way uphill, ever higher, ever closer, until he was only a few yards away, squealing his greetings.

"Avast!" Skye bellowed.

The colt bucked, kicked, whirled, and plunged right past them, with the laboring old mare behind. Right past Skye, right past Victoria, right past the ponies, and bucked and kicked his way upslope until suddenly he was caught in the morning's glare again, a bronzed horse bounding along a ridge.

Then the colt headed straight for the pine forest above, and plunged into it, bucking through the heavy snow at its base, while the razor-backed old mare followed. The sun caught them pushing into the forested flank of the mountain, and then they vanished.

It was beyond explaining. Skye stood, shaking, aware that if that colt had paused, had rushed up to Skye and butted him, started his ponies milling, it would all be over. Down below men were collecting the straying stock, but also glancing up the long grade straight at Skye and Victoria, who could not remain hidden in shade for long as the sun began its swift ascent.

Skye collected his animals and walked along the path he had chosen, desperate to find cover. But far above a strange squeal echoed down the mountain, and Skye found himself staring at the tiny figure of the colt, bathed in bright sun, on a small promontory overlooking the vast country below.

Down in Skittles's camp men paused, pointed upward, and then resumed their business. They had stock to harness.

Skye shivered. What possessed that colt? What strange medicine, or luck, sent the little fellow straight up the mountain, far from Skye and Victoria? Were they free and saying good-bye?

They hurried to a place where a slope hid them in trees and soon they were out of sight of the camp. But not safe. They were leaving a plain trail that anyone, even a Yank soldier, could follow. Skye hurried westward, for distance was the sole protection he had.

Victoria followed, her gaze slipping upward, searching the empty mountain above, even as the shadows dropped lower and lower and eventually vanished. They were walking in full daylight now, the dawn was a thing of the past. Victoria paused at a ridge and studied their back trail, but no one followed. Skittles had probably abandoned the ugly colt and scrawny mare. Good riddance.

That suited Skye just fine. Good riddance indeed. Even if he never saw that colt again, his spirits lifted at the thought that the mustangs had found their liberty. Let that feisty creature and that faithful mare escape snares the rest of their days. They had blessed Skye, saved Victoria from death, and deserved whatever goodness nature had in store.

He began at last to relax. He was where he wanted to be, ahead of the Skittles party, riding the flank of the Snowy Mountains. Ahead was the gap, the broad flat between two ranges that permitted travelers to move north or south through country where the mountains ranged east and west. Skittles would enter that gap sometime soon, depending on whether the ground would stay firm under the iron tires of his wagons.

Skye reached a ridge where he could see the gap, which spread below him, naked rolling prairie between the ranges. This was bloody ground. Here, Blackfeet pounced on unsuspecting Absarokas heading north, or Crows ambushed Blackfeet pushing south. Nature had conspired to funnel all manner of life through this hole in the wall of mountains, and war parties took advantage of it.

Victoria squinted at the place.

"Bastards," she said.

Skye grinned.

They descended to prairie country along the flank of the Snowies, and turned north. Skye was looking for the right place to pounce on Skittles, but right places were in short supply. He didn't know where Skittles would go. For that matter, Skye didn't know just how he was going to jump Skittles's company. But it would have to be in the dead of a moonless or cloudy night, when a man could hardly see ten feet. He was going to have to slip through Skittles's defenses and torch that whiskey wagon. And collect his kit if he could. And do it without so much as a revolver to help him. And get Victoria, himself, and his horses away to safety.

He had one advantage. He had been here many times over his long life as a trapper and denizen of the wilds. He doubted that Skittles knew the country.

The more Skye thought about it, the worse his prospects looked to him. The best he could do would be to shadow the trading outfit and wait. Somewhere along the way there would be a chink in Skittles's armor, and it would be up to Skye to find it and exploit it.

No wonder Skittles had recruited former soldiers. Somehow these traders understood that they might need to be a small army. Might have trouble with boozy Indians. Might have trouble with tribal leaders. Might have trouble with rival companies, of which there were several roaming the Northwest hunting for robes.

Skye wondered how he could shadow an outfit like that, especially with his pemmican running low, two more horses than he should have, and a lot of open prairie ahead where a man could see everything for miles, and a man with a spyglass could keep track of movement everywhere the lens could reach.

Nighttime, then.

He paused at an overlook and waited for her.

"I want to catch them here. Once they get through the gap, they could head any direction."

"This is a bad place."

"It will be for them."

"We need a camping place on the flank of the mountain," he said.

She nodded. They moved slowly upslope, studying the land, and finally selected a rocky ledge a couple hundred feet above the valley floor. It would do nicely, and was watered by a runnel from above. They picketed the horses on good grass nearby, made camp, and settled down for a wait. It had turned warm, and Skye didn't doubt that the wagons would roll slowly, if at all this day with the mud so thick.

He settled back to wait, letting the intense sun warm him. He had never seen such a clear day. The air was so transparent it drew everything close. The Belt Mountains, on the other side of the gap, seemed so near he could touch them, though they were six or seven miles distant.

Victoria joined him, sitting cross-legged with her skirts hiked, as she often did. He was glad she was there. The horses grazed contentedly on the slope behind them. The air was warm, and he felt good.

He remembered how, only a few weeks earlier, he had wandered through a winter's fog, not knowing where he was going, and thought that was how his life was playing out. But the important thing was that he kept on going through the fog, through the air filled with ice crystals.

She touched his arm and pointed. Across the southern heaven were sun dogs, bright miniature suns at the exact altitude of the real one, shimmering and sometimes shifting color, a phenomenon he had never before seen.

"It is a sign," she said.

"I know where I am going now," he said.

"I wondered if you ever would."

"When I lived for myself I walked through fog. When I give myself away, I can see to the farthest horizon."

"Damn, you better tell me that in my tongue," she said.

"Your people are my home," he said.

His response was enough for her. She caught his big hand and held it.

They waited through the warm, bright day, but Skittles and his wagons never came.

forty-four

S kye and Victoria sat on their cliffside rock and watched and waited until the sun plunged toward the western rim of the world. Skittles's party should have rounded the flank of the mountains and headed through the gap. Skye didn't know what to make of it.

"We go look," Victoria said.

"Leave the horses," Skye said.

Stiffly, they began back-trailing along the rough foothills, pausing at every promontory or spot that afforded a view. Then she pointed at a distant collection of moving dots. They hiked another half mile eastward until they could get a better look from a ridgetop.

Disaster had struck Skittles's party. They had started their wagons across a shallow coulee, little knowing that the earth beneath its grassy surface was water-charged gumbo the consistency of jelly. The whiskey wagon had gone first and was mired up to its bed, its wheels mostly lost to view. Worse, the noble draft horses hauling that heavy load had mired, fought their fate, and now were bloodstained bodies lying in the muck. They had obviously been shot when it became plain to the green shirts that those big, gentle, hardworking beasts were doomed.

The supply wagon, behind it, was mired too, and its giant draft horses also lay dead. No legs were visible from any horse. They had sunk to their bellies, struggled against their fate, and were put out of their misery.

Skye thought that he had heard no shots, but that was not surprising, given the brisk wind and the distances.

"Dammit," Victoria said. "If we were down there we would have been caught too."

Skye nodded.

Off as far as his eye could see even on that bright day, he could make out the green shirts salvaging what they could. They had pulled the walls off the supply wagon, along with its tailgate, and made a sort of ramp back to safe land on the east side of the grass-topped river of mud. They had salvaged the whiskey barrels, which stood like stumps on safe ground. They had rescued a pile of gear, perhaps including Skye's rifle and his bedroll and packsaddle.

The outfit's saddle horses were safe, picketed on the east side. Skittles would probably build packsaddles and load as much whiskey as he could, leaving his men to carry their own kits. But there weren't enough saddle horses for all that whiskey. He would have to cache most of it.

Unless Skye could destroy it.

"Sonsofbitches got what was coming," she said.

"They're not licked yet. They'll clean the mud out of their revolvers this night. Tomorrow they hunt for more horses. Skittles will send men to look for Jawbone and the mare."

They needed to know what Skittles would do. They sat quietly, watching the rescue efforts. In time, a horseman started off, heading southeast.

"Skittles has two parties out somewhere. One's delivering the robes he got from your village, and the other party's returning empty or maybe with some supplies from a trading post. That means he still has four wagons and four teams. He just has to wait."

As if to confirm Skye's judgment, the green shirts threw packsaddles over the remaining two saddle horses and began shuttling the whiskey kegs toward a copse of cottonwood trees perhaps a quarter of a mile from the disastrous crossing. There would be firewood and shelter there. The men would tote their gear to the cottonwood grove and move the whiskey and wait for help to arrive.

"See that horseman? Skittles is sending for help. He's got wagons coming and going. Looks like that rider is headed for Fort Sarpy."

"He's headed for hell, that's where," she muttered.

"Well, they're stuck in that grove. They might be there for weeks," he said. "They can't do much until they get some wagons and teams."

"And every day they stay in that place, they get stronger," she said. "They wash away the mud, clean their guns, start hunting for meat, and maybe get that whiskey hidden somewhere."

The men were frantically dragging everything to the cottonwood grove. They were obviously tired, yet seemed impelled by something menacing. In the grove, two tents rose. Skye could not fathom what was happening; it was all too far away, but the distant green shirts were obviously in a hurry.

A darkness was descending too early. Skye whirled, discovered behind him a massive gray overcast rolling out of the northwest from behind the Snowy Mountains, galloping across the heavens.

"Trouble," he said. "I should have read the sun dogs. They were telling me something but I wasn't listening."

Victoria's single glance took in the weather. They needed to get their horses and find shelter, and there wasn't much of that. Swiftly overtaking this country was a massive spring storm, the type that could dump feet of snow on the high plains. They abandoned the overlook and hurried back to the rocky ledge to the west, found their horses nervously tugging on their pickets, released them, and headed downhill. They needed to get to woods and find shelter from the wind. They needed firewood and a place to keep a fire going. But there was nothing, only the anonymous rolling foothills on the south flank of the Snowies.

No wonder the green shirts were throwing up tents and heading for the cottonwoods. A cold wind plucked the warmth out of the air, and eddied through the slopes and hollows, brooming away a day's work by the sun. Not bitter yet; that would come later, maybe after snow.

The land descended for miles and Skye had only to find a coulee and it would eventually deposit him in the valley of the Musselshell River where there would be shelter. But that was a ten-mile hike through the night.

They simply could find no place to go to ground.

The massive dark reef of cloud was wiping away light, turning a lively day into an iron-gray twilight. When dark finally fell, it would be pitch-dark, not even starlight, and they would be stumbling through inky night.

They had reached the gumbo-bottomed coulee but on the opposite side from the traders.

He surprised himself: "Let's get into that camp when this storm hits and burn the booze."

She stopped suddenly, laughed, and the gusts whipped her laughter away.

They turned into the wind, into the iron twilight, until they had gained ground and reached the foothills. Then they turned east, cut past the head of that evil coulee, and started their descent on the same side as Skittles's men.

Skye began laughing. They were in peril from a cruel storm, but laughter bloomed through him and she joined him. They laughed as the wind at their backs bullied them south toward the traders' camp. They laughed when the wind plucked Skye's old top hat and sent it sailing. He roared, recovered it, and anchored it to the pack frame perched on one of their ponies.

"Maybe we can save out a jug, Mister Skye?"

"Maybe we can!"

Behind them rose a great commotion. Skye turned to find two equine specters galloping down on them.

"Ah! You've found us at last!" he bellowed.

Jawbone jammed to a halt, butted Skye in the belly, disturbed the ponies, and began pushing Skye backward, while the mare stopped just short of Victoria and bobbed her head up and down in wild greeting.

"Oh, ho! You've come to join the fiesta!" Skye said.

The first blast of icy pellets smacked into them. Not snow, just slivers of frozen moisture that stung their faces. Skye ached for his capote, but the green shirts had it. Maybe he could get it back. Maybe he could get his bedroll, his rifle, his kit, his packsaddle back. Maybe he could grab something for back wages. Maybe he could find a shelter-half or some canvas to crawl under until this storm blew past.

But maybe that was all wishful thinking. The only reality was the blackening heaven, the sting of ice in the air, a wind that probed through his shirt and numbed him, and a skiff of snow on the ground that could swiftly heap up into impassible drifts.

They almost ran into the traders' camp. Off ahead they caught a glimpse of things that didn't fit in nature. They halted. Jawbone had the good sense not to squeal. Skye strained to see, and finally made out a mesh of black limbs. They were on the west edge of those trees. Nearby were heaps on the ground. Off somewhere just beyond the wall of night were the two tents.

Mister Skittles, Mister Grosvenor, and the other misters were huddled within. There would be no fire on a night like this unless they had found some protected hollow out of the claws of snowy air. But there was no sign of light. The gents were rolled up in their bedrolls, safe under canvas, and glad to be halfway warm.

Skye began howling. Victoria joined him. They laughed and the wind whipped their every sound away. He lumbered from one heap to another. The whiskey casks were collected in one place. The company's supplies were stored under a canvas tarpaulin. Somewhere in the woods were the company's saddle horses. And the seven remaining men were locked into their tents.

Snow was beginning to build around every barrier, along the sides of the tents, around the casks, around the supplies anchored under the tarpaulin.

It was time to get to work.

forty-five

Nature helps and nature hinders. Anyone living in the wilds knows that. Skye worked frantically to strap his own packsaddle on his pony before the light failed entirely, while Victoria probed under the tarpaulin to see what was there. By the time he finished buckling the packsaddle, he could no longer see anything. He worried about losing Victoria.

The wind helped. It rattled the cottonwood branches, whispered and yowled across the earth, and flapped the canvas of the traders' tents. There was no silence to expose Skye's activities.

"I found the rifle," she said. "Lotsa stuff."

"You'll have to load in the dark."

"I can do it. I got a bedroll too, maybe yours."

"Good. It has my powder horn and a hatchet in it."

She began loading now, working in full blackness because all light had fled the world. Snow stung Skye's face.

Skye tried to remember where the casks stood. He hardly

dared venture that way. He could move twenty feet from Victoria and lose her entirely.

The barrels were a few yards out from the supplies, about where they had been rescued from the gumbo.

"Talk quietly, Victoria. Just talk," he said.

She took him up on it, cussing steadily, trapper cussing, the oaths rolling out of her like a waterfall. He laughed softly.

He stumbled and fell upon the casks, felt them with his big hands, brushed snow away, and tried lifting one. Oaken staves, iron hoops. It was all he could manage, maybe seventy or eighty pounds. He lifted all he could find, hoping to find a light one. After lifting five, he did lift a light one and he rejoiced. Now he began probing and patting it, and found a bung faucet in it. More good luck.

Victoria was cheerfully cussing away, the oaths peppering the air. He carried the light cask over to her.

"This one's been opened. We'll use it to burn the rest. Unless you can find an axe."

"Dammit, Skye, how am I supposed to find anything?"

"Is there an old blanket I can soak?"

"How am I supposed to know, eh?"

They were fighting nature now. He hardly knew what to do. He didn't even know whether he could start a fire in all this wet wind. He wanted an axe. Maybe a swift blow to each cask would open it. He thought that maybe he could start a fire if he could strike some sparks into a rag soaked with pure spirits. But a fire would bring them all boiling out of their tents, and they would shoot at anything that moved.

This was proving harder than he had wanted. And now he was getting numb. His hands would quit him pretty soon.

He felt his way to the packhorses and found that Victoria

had anchored his Hawken on one. He could tell it by its feel. He found his bedroll, opened it, and pulled out his powder horn. He found his capote in his saddle kit, and gratefully put it on, feeling its welcome warmth at once. He had everything: his rifle, his kit, his horses.

There was only one task left, but it was the reason he came, the reason he was here on a black night in a storm. The only thing was, he didn't know how to destroy those casks.

A light bloomed behind him. He whirled, and found vague yellow light emanating from one of the tents while shadows bobbed on its canvas walls. Someone in there had lit a lamp. He saw Victoria, who was holding the reins of two horses, whirl them around so their eyes would not pick up lamplight. And just in time too. A figure parted canvas and emerged into the night, bearing the lantern in one hand and a revolver in the other. Skye was sure he and Victoria had made too much noise, or disturbed the rhythms of nature too much. A veil of snow, blowing horizontally, obscured the man. Skye knew that the trader was seeing little but the white wall of snow. The man stood before the tent, uncertainly, and then jammed the revolver into its holster and relieved himself.

Skye took the opportunity to orient himself in the lamplight. The casks stood in a cluster, mostly snow-covered now. The supplies remained under the tarp, which was a salvaged wagon sheet. Skye wanted that tarp; it would give them shelter. It wasn't particularly cold, but it would be plenty cold when this storm blew over. A wagon sheet was twice the canvas he wanted, and three times heavier than he wanted. Maybe he could slice it in two.

The trader finished. From the dark tent, two others emerged and relieved themselves. They were talking but Skye could not make out any of it. Then they retreated to their respective tents, and Skye had one last chance to study the layout before they blew out the lantern. He and Victoria were plunged into utter darkness once again.

"You there?" he asked softly.

"Damn right."

"I don't know how to burn this booze."

"I don't either. It's snowing too hard."

"I don't think I can bust these barrels with a hatchet."

"Shoot them, Skye?"

"In the dark?"

"One, maybe?"

"Shoot one and hope it leaks enough spirits to burn the rest?"

"We ain't gonna hang around and let them shoot us, are we?"

"They won't see; they'll be blinded."

He found Victoria holding the ponies. Somewhere out in the dark Jawbone and the old mare were standing.

"The only thing I can think of is to start a fire beside a barrel, get away, and then shoot one barrel and hope for the best."

"So what's gonna happen."

"They'll see fire, come busting out of their tents, maybe shoot into the dark, try to put out the fire. I shoot a barrel. More spirits out, more fire."

"Damned waste of good booze, Skye."

He could feel the snow caking on his capote. It would be caking his horses, caking Victoria's robe. It was a wet warm snow, plastering whatever it touched, including those barrels. That was good, white on white.

He fumbled his way to the casks, began lifting and rocking them to find the light one, and located it. He lifted it easily and was immediately worried. Was there anything in it? He found the brass bung faucet, turned the cock, held his hand under the spout, and felt nothing. Empty.

There went his only plan. Worse, he had been counting on some firelight for a getaway. He knew he was next to a cottonwood grove, and next to a coulee that could mire him. He needed light enough to get away, get out of rifle range, escape those deadly Sharps.

"Nothing in here," he said.

"Sonofabitch!"

"We're in trouble."

He felt her draw close, something intuitive because he could see nothing. They could not even see the white canvas tents a short distance from them.

"We got to wait for the first light and hope we can escape," she said.

He felt the warmth of the horses she was leading, or was it their moist breath? Who could know?

"We got that wagon canvas to keep us warm," she said.

That was a good idea. He didn't know where the heap of supplies was, but she seemed to, and eventually she stumbled, cussed softly, and drew him toward her. They clambered under the canvas. She held the lines of their horses and hoped the others would linger close. In truth, he had no idea what direction he was facing. He couldn't remember a night so black, or being so lost.

The wagon sheet served well to shield them from the pelting snow, though he insisted on keeping his head in the open, relying on the hood of his capote for warmth. If the traders lit a lamp again, he wanted to know it.

It would be a long, long wait. It wasn't far past dusk. And first light wouldn't come until six-thirty or seven. And then they'd run the risk of being seen, and they would leave a plain trail in the snow. Well, that was war, won or lost by weather, or an unshod hoof, or bad luck.

"Victoria . . ." he started to say, but couldn't continue. He just wanted to tell her it had been a good life and she had made it so.

She found his hand and squeezed it.

The minutes dragged. An hour passed by his reckoning, but maybe it was only five minutes. The snow diminished. He couldn't see it but he felt it. The men in the tents had buried themselves in their blankets and Skye heard no talk from that quarter, nor did he see any lamplight.

He was growing stiff, but at least under that sheet he was dry and not cold.

"Sonofabitch, look," she said.

She turned his face with her hand. There was a slit in the sky. Off to the north eerie moonlight shone on the white peaks of the Snowy Mountains.

forty-six

Everything changed. That crack in the sky across the north was his compass, his lantern, his escape. He knew where he was. He could see his way out. The snow glowed eerily.

Such was fate, where the fortunes of war hung on chance.

"Get the horses together. I'll cut my way through a barrel with my knife."

"Wait," she said, touching his arm.

She crawled out of their canvas shelter, hastened to one of the packhorses that stood dimly visible as a silhouette, and returned with something. She stooped, flexed something, and he realized she had gotten her bow and quiver.

Maybe it would work. Her reflex bow, made of yew wood wrapped in sinew, was as strong as she could draw. Her arrows, with iron points, were carefully crafted by Crow artisans and had grooves in the shafts to draw away the blood of animals she pierced, thus killing them faster.

He followed her to the stockpile of whiskey, praying that

they would not be silhouetted by that crack of ghostly light to the north.

She cut around to the side, making sure no arrow, if it careened off a barrel, would pierce the tents. The moonlight from the distant mountains quickened just enough so they could see the barrels, snow-clad on their tops, dark bulks gathered together.

She nocked an arrow, drew and aimed easily, and loosed it into a cask. It hit with a thump, and Skye turned sharply to see whether it had stirred anything in the tents.

She slipped close to the barrel to see the effect. There wasn't enough light to know, but when she slid her hand around the arrow she raised her arm high, to touch sky.

She beckoned, and drew his hand to the arrow, which projected from the cask. Wetness. The grooves were drawing the spirits out.

She danced a little jig in the snow. Then he beckoned her close, so he could whisper.

"We'll get the horses ready first. At the edge of the woods. They'll come out shooting."

She nodded.

They led their horses around the cottonwood grove, just out of sight of the tents. Jawbone and the mare followed. The colt butted Skye, who butted back.

The crack of moonlight to the north widened. The snow-clad peaks of the Snowy Mountains shot white light under the massive storm cloud. Light glistened off the thin snow covering the land.

"How we gonna light it?" she asked.

"Flaming arrow?"

"I can do it."

They hastened back to the casks. Victoria nocked arrows, sped them into the oaken staves. They checked each one, running their hands around the buried shaft, finding wetness as the spirits slowly drained to the snowy earth.

The moonlight brightened. Skye kept a sharp eye on those tents. Snow was now the enemy, bouncing pale light everywhere, wiping away the cloak of blackness. It was only a matter of time, maybe only minutes or seconds, before one of Skittles's men crawled out of a tent.

Still, their luck held. There were seven casks, and Victoria punctured each one. These were slow leaks, and not much of the grain spirits was puddling on the ground, and that worried him. He tried pulling an arrow, but its iron head locked it in. He would just have to trust.

Skye cut a strip of wool from the bottom of his blanket capote, and cut some fringes from his buckskin shirt, and Victoria wrapped the wool around an arrow and tied it tight with the fringe leather. Then they prepared a second arrow, and soaked both in the spirits.

Victoria slid her bow over her shoulder, lifted her hands to the black sky, and supplicated the Other Ones, singing softly. It was a pleading, a soft song of empowerment. Jawbone arrived, sniffed the barrels, and tried to butt her.

Skye grabbed his mane and yanked him away.

They retreated twenty yards in the direction of their horses. Once that flame bloomed, they would be easy targets. It was a risk they had to take.

Skye checked one last time to see whether the barrels were still leaking spirits. They were. Their staves were wet. But he could find no pooling on the soft ground.

No matter. It was now or never.

He retreated to where Victoria stood, her bow ready.

She held the fire arrow.

He slid the curved steel into his hand, and held the flint in his other, and struck, his practiced scrape shooting a constellation of sparks outward, where dozens landed on the soaked wool. It flared instantly.

Swiftly she nocked the arrow, aimed for the mass of casks, and let loose. It dropped short and burned lazily five yards from the casks.

They lit the second and she drew harder, running the flaming tip almost to her bow hand, and let loose. This one struck between two barrels, and for a moment it looked as though nothing would ignite. But then curls of blue flame crawled in two directions, and suddenly scaled two casks.

They watched, transfixed, as the flames captured two barrels and then a third.

Then she pulled the bow over her shoulder and they began the long retreat to the woods, even as the mounting flame began to throw light.

The naked limbs of the cottonwoods hid them. Skye turned, and saw men boil out of the tents, stare at the flame, and study the darkness. He heard Skittles shouting orders. The men returned to their tents for arms, bloomed into the firelight, and deployed to either side, away from the blinding light.

Skye and Victoria reached the horses, grabbed lead lines, and tugged them hard. The ponies, laden with packs, snorted and clopped through a couple inches of snow, gaining speed, putting distance between them and the great blaze.

But then revolvers cracked. A bullet sang through limbs, clipping wood. The traders had seen something through the trees and were firing, perhaps blindly, but with a soldier's discipline. A ball raked past Skye.

Victoria tugged the ponies, hastening them, pulling them until she was running beside them.

The fire retreated as more and more trees blocked its light from Skye and Victoria. But now the moonlight from the Snowies caught them, and Skye felt naked.

The throaty crack of the Sharps rifles spoke, and he knew some of those murderous bullets were probing clear through the woods.

He glanced at his party: Victoria first, tugging the lines of two ponies. He was second, tugging two more ponies. Jawbone was somewhere near Victoria. The mare was somewhere behind. He could see them all, vaguely, ghostly shapes racing toward safety.

A Sharps cracked, and Skye heard something he dreaded, the thump of a slug smacking horseflesh. But nothing changed. They continued to escape. Rifles cracked. No one followed. But one of his horses was wheezing, its breath labored. The sound was loud and agonizing in the night.

"Victoria, slow," he said.

She slowed. They were out of effective range, and the traders had their hands full with the fire.

Now they would just keep on walking, never stop, walk and walk toward the Musselshell.

Then the laboring horse stumbled, and walked another twenty yards, and slowly capsized. Skye raced to it, and knew at once it was the old mare, the very horse that had carried Victoria, sick and wounded, to safety. The horse that had borne Jawbone.

They halted. Skye ran back, found the mare lying in the light snow, her old head on the ground, her neck stretched backward. There was a hole in her chest, seeping blackness into the pale snow.

Skye fell to his knees, drew his thick hand over her neck, under her mane, even as she died, one last cough and a shudder convulsing her.

Jawbone squealed. He danced around her, nudged her, smelled her nostrils, from which no moist breath emerged.

Skye studied the back trail sharply but saw no one. For the moment the traders had enough to keep them busy. But this light snow left a perfect trace of Skye's passage, and it would not be long before experienced soldiers were after them.

They could not wait.

Skye nodded to Victoria, and they moved ahead, leaving the old mare sprawled in the snow. Jawbone wailed. He stood solidly over the mare, unbudging, loyal, his fierce soul guarding his mother.

Skye could not bear to watch. If Jawbone stayed, that was his right. He and Victoria tugged their ponies into action again and raced southward, wishing for the cloud cover that would shroud them once again. He stared at dark shadows, at anything that moved or seemed to move. Once they got their ponies moving, he found his old Hawken, untied it from the packsaddle, pulled his powder horn over his shoulder, hunted for the small vault of caps and wads, slipped a cap over the nipple of the Hawken, but still didn't know if the weapon was charged. It had lain in the traders' wagon for many days and kept from him.

It was all he had to answer those Sharps rifles carried by the traders.

They worked over naked slopes, hour after hour, open country, buffalo country, its dried grasses good fodder even in winter.

He could not stop. Skittles would follow, on horse, on foot, whatever it took, so long as there was a trail to follow, and there was. Skye could do nothing at all about those prints in the snow, his prints, Victoria's moccasin prints.

At least the cloud cover thickened again, and the Snowy Mountains slipped from view. A blackness lowered over them that matched the blackness of his heart.

And then he heard a squeal, the patter of hooves, and Jawbone was walking beside him.

forty-seven

With the dawn came spring. As the golden light quickened, so did the warmth. By the time the sun was a finger's width above the horizon, a tender joy was spreading over the northern lands, wiping away snow as if it hadn't existed.

The whole world seemed ready for the warmth, and the chastened snow retreated into small heaps where there were shadows to protect it, and then sank into the pungent earth.

Skye and Victoria plunged southward, tired but dogged after a sleepless night. Something about this day was touching them both. Skye paused, shed his blanket capote, and tied it to one of the packs. He lifted his top hat and let the tendrils of warm air eddy through his hair.

No one followed, and with each passing minute it would be harder to follow, the trail less visible, especially to traders, former army men not well versed in the lore of the wild.

Below stretched the sleepy valley of the Musselshell, basking in the morning. The whole world was quiet. The lightest zephyrs curled over the dried grasses. Skye glanced back again, not wanting surprises, and saw only the peace of a morning on the high plains. Not even a crow soared, not even a hawk hunted.

He led his entourage down a long grade to the river, where ice jams lined the banks but green grasses were poking up next to the rippling water. Jawbone nipped the grasses, then caught up in little rushes.

A little way east there would be sandstone bluffs, and he welcomed a chance to curl up in one of the innumerable caves wrought in them by wind and rain and frost and sunlight. Victoria was worn, though her step had quickened with the golden light, and he saw joy in her face. Their eyes caught and he knew she was thinking about a rest. It had been a long and perilous night.

They hiked east along the river bottoms until they struck the sandstone bluffs, and Skye pushed them onward a little way more. He saw a good hollow in the south-facing cliff, with green grass below it and a good view in most directions.

He pointed, she nodded, and they struck toward the bluff, climbing slowly, crossing over some talus. The little hollow was like a throne, perched above a wild kingdom. Skye swiftly unloaded the packhorses, turned them loose on grass, picketed one for swift use if needed, and then plucked up his bedroll and stretched it in the warm hollow. He stood there a moment, Victoria beside him, feeling as if he were the lord of all he could see; that this was his dominion and hers, and his kingdom was the most beautiful kingdom ever known.

He was ready for a nap. And when he awoke, he wanted to come to decisions. Victoria lay down on her old robe beside him, curled up, and fell asleep. He sat motionless, feeling the sun heat his buckskins, feeling the warmth caught in the stubble on his cheeks, feeling the sunlight ride his chafed flesh and cleanse it of hurt.

He had his outfit back now: a rifle, a bedroll, some horses, the various tools he needed to survive. It was a poor man's outfit but he believed he was rich. What began in the fall with a surprise Blackfoot raid on a Crow hunting camp had come clear around to this.

He eased back until he was supported by the rear wall of the shallow cave, and he could sit and wait. That struck him as an odd thing, sitting and waiting. Waiting for what? For Mister Skittles and a vengeful pack of traders?

It was quite possible Mister Skittles didn't even know who or what struck him. He and his traders would have seen arrows poking from the whiskey casks, and might well have supposed they had been raided by Indians.

Mister Skittles was a mystery that Skye could not fathom. He and his colleagues had expended enormous energies upon their whiskey trading trip. They had organized and trained a company of men to pillage the plains villages. They had invested heavily in wagons and draft horses, in a uniform of sorts, in weapons, tents, and all the rest. They had welded a deal with the licensed fur and robe companies, the ones more or less abiding by the flat Yank prohibition against the whiskey trade.

Why? So much effort and capital could have won Skittles rewards in any legitimate business. Why this? Skye almost wished the man would show up and submit to questions. Why, sir, have you come a thousand miles from your borders to do this? Why, sir, do you treat the tribes worse than you would treat a mad dog? Why, sir, do you clothe it all in the cloak of civility, courtesy, and your Yank republican virtues, even as you engage in a patently illegal and cruel enterprise?

Skye thought he would never know. That whiskey that burned last night probably cost the company twenty thousand dollars of profit, and meant that their entire enterprise was a failure. They would straggle east, not even covering expenses from the few loads of robes and pelts they had acquired.

Yes, he would like to talk to the Honorable Mister Skittles, for this man had risen out of a young new nation that Skye didn't entirely grasp, and which in some ways repelled him as much as it attracted him. And that reminded him that even now, as his hair was turning gray, he remained a man without a country. More, a man without a people. He felt that old stab of separateness that had tormented him ever since he escaped his virtual imprisonment in the Royal Navy. For he was a man alone and had been alone ever since he set foot in North America.

His mind floated and drifted as he dozed through the middle of the day, his sleep-starved body making what it could of a brief respite halfway up a sandstone bluff.

Then he was awakened. His name was floating upward from below, down in the bottoms of the Musselshell River. Victoria had come alert also, her gaze outward. And yet nothing very threatening loomed. The horses grazed, or stood yawning.

"Mister Skye, sir. May I have a word?"

Skye dared not lift his head for fear that a ball from a rifle trained on him would tear into his skull. But it was clear someone knew he was there, and that someone sounded very like Skittles.

He turned to Victoria. "What can you see?"

"Not a damn thing."

"We're trapped."

"Maybe I can sneak out and get a better look."

Skye shook his head. He found his top hat, stuck it over the barrel of his Hawken, and slowly lifted it until the sun shone plainly on it. He wiggled it a bit. Nothing happened. The half-dozen shots he had anticipated and feared, knowing what a ricochet could do in that cavity, didn't happen.

"Who is it?" Skye asked, making his rifle ready.

"It is Joshua Skittles, sir."

"And what do you want?"

"I wish to talk to you."

"Alone?"

"Entirely alone, Mister Skye. I came alone."

"How did you find us?"

"The horses, sir. They left prints in the mud."

"Why are you here?"

"I'm not sure I know, Mister Skye."

Skye could hardly imagine a conversation with Skittles along these lines, but it was happening.

Skittles picked up where he had left off. "At first we thought Indians had set the whiskey on fire, sir. Arrows. I thought it was Indians until we started out in the melting snow and found your dead mare. So it wasn't Indians, it was Skye. Now this'll surprise you, sir. I sent the men back to camp to wait for help and salvage what they could, and see about getting at least one wagon free. They went back reluctantly and I took our remaining saddle horse and followed you here."

Skye could not imagine it.

"May I come up there and talk? Will you grant me safe passage?"

"While your men do what, Mister Skittles?"

"I am alone, and you have my word and pledge."

Oddly, Skye believed him, and cursed himself for playing the fool.

"Come up with your hands above your head. Leave your horse below."

Victoria found her bow. It was not an easy task to arm a powerful bow while lying down, but soon she achieved her goal, found an arrow, nocked it, and waited.

If ever there was a mystery, Skittles's appearance alone and in a pacific mood was one.

The distance was only fifty yards or so. Skye, lying on his belly, watched Skittles move slowly over talus, his hands held above his head, then up a grassy slope past the horses, and finally large and close.

"Stop," said Skye. "Turn around. Show me your back."

Skittles slowly revolved. There was no weapon, nothing but the back of his shirt. He wore no coat.

"All right, Mister Skittles."

Victoria slid to one side. The trader would have an arrow in him if he tried anything.

But Skittles, his bare hands before him, stepped to the lip of the sandstone cliff cave, and Skye nodded him in.

Skye could not imagine what this was about. "Talk," he barked.

Skittles sat down, carefully staying several feet from Skye, and studied Victoria, who eyed him fiercely.

For a moment the man seemed unable to say anything. He blinked, stared at Skye, and was plainly trying to organize his thoughts, or at least find some way to begin.

"I wish to start my life over," he said.

forty-eight

O f all the things that Skittles might have said, that was the least expected. Skye stared at the man.

Skittles said nothing for a moment, plainly struggling for words. Then he startled Skye again.

"It was the dead mare that did it. You were attached to the mare. I don't know why. A wreck of a horse. But there was some sort of bond, and a bullet destroyed it."

Skye nodded. The loss of the mare was an open wound. Skittles had been unwise to bring it up.

"I'm ruined, you know," Skittles said. "You delivered the coup de grâce, but I was ruined before you burned the spirits. The mired wagons, the dead teams. Worse, we got word from a courier that one of our wagons loaded with hides tipped over when they were fording a creek, Flat Willow Creek, I believe, and we lost the whole load. I can't pay my men. I can't pay my creditors. We thought to make at least ten dollars on the dollar, and now I'm in debt."

Skye sat, annoyed. He didn't want to hear of the man's

troubles. Skittles was a scoundrel, ruining villages with illegal whiskey, demoralizing a whole tribe.

"If I wish to change my life, Mister Skye, it's because you've inspired me." He turned to Victoria. "And you also, madam."

She muttered something under her breath that was an Absaroka version of "Off with his head." Skye smiled slightly.

Skye settled down for an ordeal. It was plain that Skittles would be a bore and the glorious spring day would waste away in a drone of words. He noticed a great disturbance of ravens up the valley a bit, and watched it closely. Something, or someone, was approaching. Victoria noticed it and glanced sharply at Skye.

But Skittles didn't seem to notice. He was caught in his own world. "I started after you at dawn. Of course I had no idea who it was. Arrows stuck from every burning cask. Indians, of course. Indians, burning my spirits. It was a bonfire, all right, Mister Skye. Flames climbed maybe twenty feet at the worst of it, and we couldn't get anywhere near. I told my men to pull our tents back, and pull our supplies away. That was after I ordered them to shoot at any faint movement. I told them not to blind themselves looking at the fire, but to run out to the darkness and then study the world. They did, and they shot your mare."

"You're a military man," Skye said.

"I was. A lieutenant. But there is no future in it."

The horses were alert to whatever was coming down the Musselshell Valley. They all stared, ears forward. Skye was less interested in Skittles than he was in the invader.

"There was no saving those barrels, sir. I ordered my horse saddled. But it was too dark; I couldn't pick up a trace, so I waited until first light, and I started with three men, leaving the rest behind to guard what was left of my outfit."

Skittles had at last settled into a narrative, and was droning along.

Skye saw the cinnamon bear as it worked along the bottoms; no, not cinnamon, but brown, and with the massive hump at its shoulders. A grizzly.

The ravens followed, making a fuss.

Skye pointed. "He's fresh out of his den, hungry, and mean as a man with a sore tooth. There's not much to eat now."

Skittles stared. "I have not seen one," he said.

The bear was pawing at stumps and deadwood, sniffing the earth, paying attention to nothing but himself. The horses were tugging at their pickets. But Skye thought nothing much would happen. The bear was far below, in the bottoms.

Skittles drew a breath and plunged in. "We found your mare a mile from camp. I knew at once who had come. And I knew why. You were destroying something evil. Something that endangered your, ah, lady's people."

"And other native people," Skye said. Suddenly Skittles was more interesting than the grizzly.

"Yes," Skittles said. "Mister Skye, I saw that mare and I realized you had taken great risks, put yourself in harm's way, to destroy a stock of Indian whiskey. I wondered why. Why would a white man do that? You see, it's all about race. You planned an assault on my camp. Was it vengeance? Hardly. You were doing it for your friends the Crows. I had my men inventory my supplies and found that nothing was stolen. You could have made off with all sorts of valuables.

"So, again, I asked myself, what is this man up to? And again it came to me that you were protecting your Crow friends. And that surprised me. Why would any man, any Englishman, do that? And it came to me that you were acting entirely from altruistic motives. Because spirits are evil, or at least evil to people who have no experience with them and know no restraint. And I realized the Crows were more than your friends; they had become your people and you were defending them against . . . predators. At risk of your life. We are well armed and we are all formerly in the services, and we are well trained to deal with trouble. And I was the predator. Like that bear there, working along the river."

Skye could think of nothing to say to this man.

"So, sir, I stared at your dead mare, and I put it all together, what was taken, what was still in our camp, what your assault had accomplished. It stopped us cold, sir. As long as I had the stock of pure grain spirits, I might yet recoup our losses, but once that burned, I had nothing and the whole trading expedition was a disaster."

The grizzly was now directly below the bluff, and the horses were watching itchily, their withers and flanks twitching as if they were being attacked by horseflies. But the big, hump-shouldered beast paid no heed. It was hunting for anything that lived under rocks and deadwood.

"I stopped at the dead mare, and knew you had suffered. I had the measure of you then, Mister Skye. But that wasn't all. I had the measure of myself. I told my men I would go ahead alone on horse; they were to return and put the camp in order, put up the tents, and wait for further instruction. I came along alone and I found you. I came to tell you, sir, that by your example you have set me upon a new chart."

The grizzly paused, raised up on his hind legs, studied the nervous horses, and dropped to fours again. He shuffled upriver, past Skye's aerie, a menace slowly receding.

"So I came here to tell you that you have changed a life, sir. I will never be the same. I'll have to go back and see to my men.

It's my obligation to get them back East unharmed. I can offer them nothing more. The few hides we've gotten to the fur posts won't even cover our expenses, wagons, teams, supplies, all that. But I'm done with this."

Skye listened, a thousand questions whirling through his mind. Who was this man? How did he get involved in a scheme to debauch the Indians of the northern plains? Why was he quitting? Traders routinely suffer disasters; most try again.

"You hungry, Mister Skittles? We have a little pemmican."

"I've been too hungry all my life, sir, so I will decline, with gratitude."

Skye couldn't puzzle that one out, either.

"I'm West Point, 'forty-five. Saw some action in Mexico, stagnated ever since, and resigned my commission last year. There were things afoot. The Indian Bureau's under the army, you know. Some officers, they see the tribes as barriers to western expansion. Some thought that if the buffalo were killed off, the tribes would collapse. They live on buffalo. They need to be turned into farmers. But there's a much simpler way, faster, crueler but more effective, and it fell to me to attempt it on behalf of men who preferred not to be involved, at least openly. But they are not averse to profit.

"It was all for white civilization, sir. Europeans will own the whole world."

Skye sighed. It was coming to this, then. He wondered how Victoria was coping with this.

"Absaroka say we are in the best place in the world," she said. "Not too hot, not too cold. Mountains and lakes for us in the summer, grasslands with lots of buffalo in the winter. But there's too many Piegans and too many Lakota! We have to fight for our place on the breast of the earth."

Skye thought Victoria and Skittles could understand one another.

Skittles smiled thinly. "Madam, perhaps you are right."

Skye wanted to know more. "Who financed this? Who expected a profit?"

"I am not at liberty to say, sir. I am honor bound to keep silent. But I can say this much: this rose out of the army, and required that no active-duty soldier or officer be involved."

Skye hardly knew what to say. "What are your plans, Mister Skittles?"

"I am going east to tell people in power that the Indian Bureau should not be run by the army. I am going to remember your example. You risked your lives, not for any private gain, but for your wife's people. I will bear you in mind as I find my way."

He paused. "Mister Skye. I don't quite know what I'll do. But I have met a man of honor here, a man who sees what must be done for his people, his people of another race but his people, and then he does it at great cost to himself. I don't know how to say that to you. I'll go back to my camp, get my men back East, and then see what I can do to salvage my life. I'm the one who has to look at myself in the looking glass each day. I hope someday I will like what I see. You must like what you see in your glass, sir."

"What I see, Mister Skittles, is a man in need of a shave and improvement."

Skittles stood, eyed the peaceful valley. "I came to tell you this." He turned to Victoria. "I hurt your people. I am sorry. I have no way to repair what was broken, but please convey to Chief Robber my regrets."

Skittles fled.

forty-nine

ictoria was grouchy. She was squinting at Skye as if he were an evil spirit. She was stomping around among the horses, making a hash of a beautiful spring day, yanking girths tight, mauling the animals until they laid back their ears. One tried to kick her.

Skye had a guaranteed cure for Victoria's moods. He slipped up beside her and patted her on the rear.

"Go to hell," she retorted.

This was getting serious.

"What is it?" he asked.

She faced him, hands on her hips. "When a bunch of white men talk I don't understand a damned word."

"When a bunch of redskins talk I don't either," he retorted.

"Skye, dammit, what was that all about?"

He found a sun-warmed yellow rock, dug into a parfleche, and extracted some pemmican wrapped in greasy leather. He cut off a slice and handed the piece to her.

"Skittles was doing something he knew, at bottom, he shouldn't be doing. And we inspired him to quit."

She nibbled at the pemmican, squinting at him as if he were on trial.

"The Yanks back East, you've seen them, think they own the whole world. This land, anyway, from one sea to the other. It belongs to them, not to native people. They keep pushing west. Settlement, they call it. They start farms, plant crops, drive off the Indians, and take over."

"Well, Skye, I'd like to drive the Lakota into the ocean. So I got that, all right."

"It's not the same. The white men, sort of cousins of my English people, think they own this land. And think they're smart and wise and the world belongs to them. But the tribes stand in the way. Especially these tribes, living off buffalo, well armed, with more fighting men than two or three of their bluecoat armies put together. So the officers, the chiefs, have ideas. How can they get rid of the Indians? They could maybe kill the buffalo and make the tribes start planting crops. They talk about that. But there's an easier way. Bring spirits out here, ruin your people, and get rich ruining them, by getting their robes and hides for almost nothing. You following me?"

"Sonsofbitches," she said.

"It's illegal. The Fathers in the capital, Washington, say they can't do that. Treat the tribes right, at least in theory. Give them credit for that."

"Theory?"

"The laws are intended to protect the native people. But they can be evaded."

"Protect us? Why the hell would they do that? Give me a Blackfoot and I'll make a slave out of her. In fact, Skye, I'm tired of doing all your work."

"How about another wife?"

"Hell yes. Three wives. You're a lot of work. Chief Robber, he's got four."

Victoria smiled, her first smile of the hour. She nibbled the fatty pemmican and stared at the serene valley. "I will hold you to it," she said.

"Their army checks the steamboats coming up the river for spirits. No spirits are allowed. They are quite strict about it. But they can't control spirits going out the trails, the Santa Fe Trail, and now the Oregon Trail. That was Skittles's chance. He resigned from the army, made an agreement with the fur companies, and took spirits into the villages. You know the rest."

She stared at him stonily, and he knew she wasn't liking this at all.

"Why did he come here, then?"

Skye knew he had to try. "To thank me. He saw me trying my best to defend the Absarokas, to keep them from destroying themselves."

"Why did he talk like that? Mister this, Mister that?"

"His way of being civilized. His way of saying to the Indians, you're savages."

"Well, sonofabitch! I should put a savage arrow into his civilized ass. I should tie him up and peel a little flesh off him."

"I want to go back to your village and tell The Robber that we burnt the barrels of spirits. And that Skittles won't be back."

"Yeah? Why won't he?"

"He had a change of heart. Here's the thing about that man. He is a man of honor. And he couldn't stand what he was doing."

"You white people are crazy, Skye."

"Let's get going. It's a good day."

She walked in circles, round and round. He had never seen her circle around like that.

"You're one hell of a chief, Skye. You sent them back to where they came from with new ideas."

"Skittles has very old ideas, but now he is listening to them."

She homed in on him, stood before him. "You're one hell of a chief, Skye. You help the Absaroka people. You make Skittles different.

"Let's go back to my people. You don't talk. Maybe they need to listen to me. I'm going to talk. You just stand there and let me tell them."

"I think that is a good idea," he said.

They bounded through a glorious spring afternoon, with the moist earth scenting the air, and a warm sun pummeling their buckskins. They plunged down the valley of the Musselshell, and Skye kept a sharp eye out for Old Ephraim, but the grizzly had vanished, probably for a siesta in the benevolent sunlight.

Jawbone alternated between leading the caravan and sliding to the rear, the tug of his dead mother sometimes capturing his brave heart. But he was doing more; he was acting as a vedette, prowling the country fore and aft and to both sides. The colt was made for war.

Late that day Skye and Victoria approached The Robber's winter camp, but something wasn't right. No one was outside the village. No village police were prowling. No women were collecting firewood. The village stood defenseless. Skye walked uneasily, fearful that some new disaster had befallen Victoria's people. But when they at last rounded a river bend and discovered the village in place, wisps of smoke rising from lodge fires, and people huddled about, there seemed to be some shred of normalcy. Maybe the men were out hunting.

"Damn," Victoria said.

She trotted ahead, dragging her packhorses, heading for her brother's lodge. Skye followed, his eye sharp upon the half-empty village. Victoria reached Two Dogs' lodge and scratched politely. In a moment Parts Her Hair opened. She had a bloody bandage wrapped about her hand, and Skye knew at once what had happened. She had cut off a finger.

He got the whole story later. Two Dogs was dead and buried, along with three others of the village. Chief Robber still lay abed, deathly sick. Something evil in the traders' whiskey had felled them. Instead of getting up the next day, they lay quiet and sweated and cold and sick, and gradually slipped into the spirit place where they might walk the path to the stars.

The village was sick. Its leaders were sick or dead. It lay helpless. No one did the daily work. No village police patrolled the area. In some cottonwoods close to the river, there were four burial scaffolds, each with a blanket-wrapped victim of the traders' whiskey.

Bug powder.

Skye knew of it. Experienced traders added a pinch just to make the Indians crazy. These inexperienced soldier-traders added more than a pinch. And the result was murder. A horrible death. For strychnine produces convulsions, nausea, paroxysms, inability to breathe, wave after wave until the victim gives up and dies. One more crime laid at Skittles's feet. The man might repent, but could never redeem himself.

Victoria fell into the arms of her sisters-in-law and wailed. Skye stood helplessly just inside the lodge door, and finally slipped out into the warm twilight. Knots of people stared. Maybe they were blaming him, or his medicine colt, or all white men for this. He could only stand and wait for what was to come, a stranger in a strange land.

He heard his name, turned, and found Walks to the Top, wrapped in an ancient blanket, summoning him. He followed the proud old Tobacco Planter to the seer's small lodge, and entered, swiftly sitting cross-legged before the dour old man.

"All this I saw," Walks to the Top said. "All this evil. And I saw the rest."

Skye wondered what that might be.

"The whiskey traders are leaving and will not come back. And this is because you destroyed the whiskey. And you did it for my people."

"Yes, sir, that is so."

"Then you will lead us. This I saw too."

fifty

ead this band? Skye recoiled from that. "I am not one of your people," he said to the elder, hoping his limited Crow tongue sufficed to make his views known.

"You must lead us. I have seen it."

"I do not know your customs."

"There is no one else."

Walks to the Top stood before him, flinty, adamant, determined, his gaze boring into Skye.

Skye hesitated. This thing was not unknown. His friend from the trapper days, Jim Beckwourth, had been a subchief. Others had lived with the Crows. Still, it didn't seem right. And he had no honors at war. There were men in this village, the headman Otter, for instance, who had counted many coups, won much praise.

"Many in this band would oppose it," he said.

"What band?" The old seer swept his gnarled hand imperiously. "What do you see? Nothing but ruin."

Skye saw a village that looked half dead. On a vibrant spring day this village should be teeming with life and joy.

But the task of restoring it should not be Skye's.

"I must be with Many Quill Woman now," he said. "She grieves her brother, and so do I."

"And let my people be naked before the world?"

Skye retreated a bit. "I will help put things in good order," he said.

Walks to the Top nodded curtly and walked away.

Skye beheld a mournful place, deep in grief, rudderless, in peril. There were always Blackfeet prowling, especially now that one could move over the land.

He glanced at Two Dogs' lodge, and saw no one. Victoria was within, and so were Two Dogs' wives and family, and the flap was closed to the world.

Many of the lodges were closed to the world. No one hunted. No one patrolled. No one gathered wood. Old people did not sit in the sun and smile.

It could not be right, he becoming a subchief. It was not real. To be sure, he had been adopted long ago by Rotten Belly, and that made him a Crow after a fashion.

He stood in the quiet, and decided the first step was to visit The Robber. He was silently welcomed and invited in by one of the chief's wives, and found the chief sitting in a reed backrest, a blanket about his legs. The chief looked unwell, a grayness just beneath his coppery flesh. Two of his wives lay quietly in their robes, staring at him. Two others were ministering to them all, and seemed well enough.

"The Seer said you would come, Mister Skye. Have a seat beside me. Smoke the pipe if you wish. There's the pouch."

That was bad. The chief was not preparing the tobacco himself.

Skye slowly filled a pipe and lit it with coals. "How can I help you?" he asked, after sucking the fragrant smoke and exhaling it.

"I do not wish to do anything. When the sun is warm, I will sit in front of my lodge and greet the world."

"Are you unwell?"

The chief pursed his lips, and nodded.

"Was it the traders' whiskey?"

"It ate the heart out of me, with little teeth like a mink's that devoured my flesh."

"You'll get better," Skye said. "It will pass."

"I want only to sit in front of my lodge on a warm day and watch the People."

"Who will lead them?"

"You will. The Seer has seen it."

"I am not a warrior. I don't know your ways."

"It is done," the chief said, sharply.

Skye finished his pipe in silence, thanked the chief for his hospitality, and left that unhappy lodge. There was one other thing he must do.

He found Otter, the headman who had suffered so much loss on the hunting trip. Otter was unsmiling. "I knew you would come. The Seer told me."

"Then I need say only one thing: you should lead the band now. It is yours."

"It is not my medicine, Mister Skye."

Skye saw how this would go. "It will be soon. I will try to help this band but only for a little time. Then you will be its chief."

Otter smiled. "You are the right one. I will help. I will hunt. It is in me that we will have a great hunt and soon there will be more robes and plenty of meat."

So it was done.

Skye said, "Come with me. I want the young men to police the village and protect it. I want a night herder to watch over the horses. I want young men out, watching, the eyes and ears of this band."

"They will hear you," Otter said.

"I have one more thing to do. Many Quill Woman must decide."

"Her?"

"She is one of you."

"It is so," Otter said.

Skye found her sitting quietly within her brother's lodge, and beckoned her. She stepped outside, into a somber spring evening.

"They want me to lead them," he said. "Is that right?"

"Goddammit, Skye, if you don't kick them in the ass, no one will!"

Look for

The Canyon of Bones

By Richard S. Wheeler

(0-765-31324-3)

Available April 2007

Read on for a preview of the newest Barnaby Skye

The arrow was unlike any Skye had ever seen. The entire shaft was enameled blood red. Large feathers, maybe hawk or falcon, adorned it. It lacked an arrowhead or iron point. A ceremonial arrow, then, and all the more ominous for it.

"This is big medicine, Mr. Mercer," he said. "See how it's made. No point. All red. This is a medicine arrow, a message arrow."

"Who made it?"

"Damned if I know," said Victoria. "Makes me unhappy, I don't know. Maybe the Spirits made it."

"Spirits?"

"Stuff you and me don't know about."

"Surely you don't . . ." Mercer stopped himself.

Skye smiled. Mercer was dismissing Indian legend but was being polite about it. Victoria studied the arrow, cussing softly. "Owl feathers. Owl feathers! That's what these are. This is very bad, owl feathers."

"And what does it tell you, eh?"

Victoria squinted at him. "We better damn well stay away That's what."

Mercer studied the red arrow, turned it over and over. "A taboo. A message. Oh, this is delightful. I love a taboo! I shall record it on the backside of my robe tonight. This makes the whole trip over here much more promising. Something to scribble about. There's nothing like a good taboo to titillate a Londoner over his morning tea."

Skye was growing restless. "I think maybe we should consider it a threat, Mr. Mercer. Someone might have some rather lethal plans for you."

"Oh, pshaw! This is legend, and legend is my meat! We shall carry on."

"I think not. You should not take this lightly, sir."

"Don't be a tiddlywink, Mr. Skye. This is grand. I haven't seen the like since a human head the size of my fist was set in my path in the Matto Grosso of Brazil." He turned to Mercer. "Have you an opinion on it?"

"It would be more comfortable if we were armed, sir."

"But I am armed in ways unknown to you. I know how to deal with all of this. Why, I've dealt with bushmen, cannibals, Zulus, and Lord Admirals of the Fleet. And never had to draw so much as a pocket knife. Here's the secret. We're big medicine ourselves. I make magic. My magic is bigger than their magic, eh?"

He thumped his head and then his skull as a sort of exclamation point or two. "I am the great Wazoo, Moomumba, Atlatl, Kitchikitchi Bugaboo, Lord of the Universe."

"Wazoo, I ain't going," said Victoria.

Mercer's smile was all teeth again. "Very well, then. The men will carry on."

She glared at Mercer.

The explorer mounted his nag, nodded to Winding, and the pair of them proceeded upriver, past the threshold of warning. Skye knew he could either try to protect his client or turn back. There was no stopping Mercer. Uneasily, he climbed aboard the buffalo runner and followed. The women resolutely started their pack animals upriver too.

The going was peaceful enough. Here there was enough bottomland for a river road. Here and there the Missouri was hemmed by great cliffs, often weathered to odd formations, and at these points the trail climbed to the high plain and then down again to the bottoms.

Skye kept a sharp look for ambush, for a glint of metal along the bluffs, or movement around the crenelated rock, or the startled fight of a bird, or a sudden shadow. But he saw naught but silent bluffs and he was tempted to think the warning wasn't for his party. He knew better. He kept his old Hawken across his lap ready for use. But whatever befell them would be larger than a lone man with a lone rifle could cope with.

The river flowed quietly here, the icy water hurrying on its way to the Gulf of Mexico an impossible distance away. He saw an eagle floating above, an osprey, an otter, and something he couldn't identify. The canyon narrowed but a trail carried them to the plains above. The day was utterly peaceful. Mercer was enjoying himself; the thought of doing something forbidden had transformed the man into a daredevil, but also into a sort of invincible, invulnerable purveyor of magic.

They paused at a place where the trail dived downward into the gloomy valley, where the rock changed from chalky to tan, and then oddly blue. The bones were not far ahead. Victoria squinted at him.

"Maybe we will walk the star-path together," she said.

She was saying she loved him and also saying good-bye.

This plunge into the forbidden was tormenting her far more than she let on to Mercer or anyone else. Skye saw Mary sitting resolutely on her pony. She had kept her feelings to herself and would go wherever he went, be with him wherever and whenever she could be with him. Hers was utter faith.

He turned to Mercer. "The bones are close now. Maybe a mile ahead."

"Good. And no lightning bolts have struck us yet, Mister Skye."

But square on the trail before them was a blue arrow, this one unbroken, erect in the ground, made by the same arrowmaker as the red one. Skye dismounted and pulled it up. Its shaft was a deep blue, a dye not easily found in nature; maybe trading-post dye. It too had been fletched with owl feathers.

Victoria studied the arrow and sagged. "I don't know what the hell it means. It means something bad, but I don't know it."

"Ah! More taboos! More mystery! Skye, old boy, this is getting better and better," Mercer said.

"It's *Mister* Skye."

Mary studied the arrow. "This is an arrow of respect," she said. "We must honor what we see and maybe the spirits will not torment us."

"How do you know that?" Mercer asked.

Mary shrugged and turned silent.

Skye didn't know. He thought he would need to know what blue meant to whoever fashioned the arrow. He liked the color. The Blackfeet used it a great deal on their lodges, in their clothing, beadwork, and quilling. For him, blue was the color of liberty. When he thought of himself as a free man, it was always somehow associated with blue.

"There you have it," Mercer said. "What does blue mean? Anything. We will be respectful." He nudged his horse forward, and suddenly they were all descending a rough path down into the shadowed bottoms of the Missouri, past layers of blue-tinted sandstone, dropping precipitously, so much so that Skye worried that the travois might topple or twist the ponies off the trail. But soon they were at the river and entering a broad flat south of the water, a delta that had been carved from a tributary canyon and deposited there.

This was the place. Skye recollected it now from his sole trip there years earlier. And he had the same eerie feeling now that he had then, a sense that indeed he was trespassing. It was quiet here, perhaps because no wind found its way into this sunken vault far below the high plains. There was blue sandstone layered up the south slopes, topped with tan sandstone streaked with red. He had the sense that this was an ancient place, one where the river itself was a newcomer, slowly sawing its way downward.

They paused. Victoria pulled up her pony, and Mary did too. They were alert for trouble even without having any real reason to be alert. A great and old serenity lay upon the land. Skye felt a sort of sadness in him, and couldn't say why. Maybe it was because he was about to experience the world's darkness, something in these primeval bones that spoke of blood and ferocity and struggle.

Mercer pulled up to, and Winding.

"This is it?" the explorer asked.

Skye nodded. He pointed toward a far blue escarpment.

They rode quietly across the flat, which was sparsely vegetated with a coarse grass, and came at last to the blue sandstone wall.

"I don't see a thing," Mercer said.

"You will."

Skye noted evidence of other visitors. There was a medicine bundled hanging from a stunted cottonwood. On closer examination he found several amulets and totems, each suspended from a limb.

He pointed these out to Mercer. "This is a holy place. This is a place the Indians come to when they are looking for guidance or needing the story of their people."

"Medicine bundles. Why are they here?"

"They are put there in reverence," Skye said. "They are offerings to the spirits that live here."

They dismounted. The horses stood quietly, content to be in this sheltered flat. Skye led them slowly across the flat to the tumble of detritus that had fallen from the blue stone above. The strata were actually layered in stair steps, with the higher strata farther back from the river, and the lower strata closer.

Victoria knew the way better than Skye, and veered left toward a sector where the ancient tributary had cut its own passage through the sandstone.

She began climbing slowly, working past talus that erosion had tumbled from above. She reached a bench that lay at the foot of an overhang that sheltered everything that lay below it, paused, and decided to head right. The rest followed, somehow silent as they approached what amounted to a shrine carved out of a cliff.

Then she stopped, and stretched to the balls of her feet, proudly. The rest caught up and stared at what lay before them. Protruding from the rock was a long skull of unimaginable size, the head of a monster.

It was oddly quiet. No breeze penetrated here. There was nothing to say. They stood side by side, studying an elongated skull that rose only a little out of the sandstone in which it was embedded, revealing perhaps ten percent of its mass. But it was enough. The ancient jaws held monstrous teeth, each larger than a man's hand, and shaped to pierce. The powerful jaw could catch large prey if indeed the beast was a meat eater.

A huge eye socket, the hole larger than a human head, peered up at them. Slabs of humped skull bone formed a lengthy nose. The back of the skull stopped abruptly, almost as if broken off. Behind the skull, the spinal bones lay disordered, half buried in the stone. From the vertebrae rose flat-topped dorsal ribs, with smaller curved ribs below. From there, the fossil vanished into the stone, only to reemerge ten feet further along. There were more vertebrae all in disarray, beyond the imaginings of the most learned doctors of nature. But here were giant ribs, familiar bones now that spoke of the chest cavity. And an array of tiny bones that formed forepaws. These were so small that Skye could not believe they belonged to the same animal. Maybe this was all an ancient boneyard, the grave of all sorts of strange beasts.

There was a pathway that took them farther along, a path worn by countless visitors. A pathway recently used, with faint imprints in the dust. Next was a few square yards of disorder, a great jumble of ribs and vertebrae, and then odd-shaped pelvic bones, broken into several pieces, mostly buried in rock. And then the shocking thing: monstrous leg bones, each taller than a tall man, mostly buried in rock, but the outlines visible. These were impossible bones, larger than wild imagination could fathom. Bones of an animal as tall as a house. And a few yards away, a well-preserved three-toed foot, a bird's foot, delicately formed but still a pedestal that could support this monster. Beyond was a scatter of other bones, smaller and smaller, yard after yard, as if this strange beast had a twenty or thirty-foot tail.

Skye had been here before, and now had the same response as before. Did this come from God?

Now he watched Mercer; watched the man visibly abandon the notion that this was a carved shrine, some religious artistry worked by an ancient sculptor. This beast had perished beside a river or on a beach and had been gradually covered with sand, and over aeons had become a fossil caught in sandstone until some giant upthrust had pushed this rock high, and erosion had worn through the sandstone and bared these unimaginable things.

Mercer took off his hat. He was not smiling this time.

"How old, do you think?" he asked.

Skye shook his head.

"There's more," Victoria said. She led them silently along that worn path that skirted the sandstone outcrop, until they came to another ledge jammed with bones, these disordered so much a mortal could hardly put them together to mean anything. But there they were, a carpet of bones, mostly broken into small pieces, and yet parts of a beast as formidable as the more complete skeleton they had just visited. But no, this was not the same beast, for when they came to the skull, or the fragment left of it, they found a peculiar horn rising from its snout, a blade where no blade should be, an illogical blade that would serve no fathomable purpose. So here was another monster of the deep, another nightmare to float through a man's soul when sleep beckoned.

"How would you like to run into one of these on your path?" Winding asked.

"Why are they here?" Mercer asked.

Who could say? The sandstone overhang protected them; that was all Skye could make of it.

Mary was careful to touch every bone she could reach. She

an her small brown hand over the rock, her fingers into creases and over bulges, as if the bones were there to give her strength, and the more she touched them the stronger and wiser she would be. Victoria frowned. For her, the bones were sacred relics of her own origins, for she was one of the people of this bird. But Mary saw these bones her own way. Skye smiled at her and she smiled back. Touching the bones was giving medicine to her and she was harvesting the strange powers that lay within them.

"Many more," Victoria said, pointing. Indeed, the trail ran another fifty yards through the mortuary of giants somehow trapped here and hidden from air and sun and wind until recent times.

Slowly Mercer hiked to the end of the bone yard and retraced his steps back to the monster that lay almost intact, the very first they had seen.

"So you suppose the earth, the whole universe, is very old?" he asked. "I mean, hundreds of thousand of years. Maybe a million years. Do you imagine that God is recent; the universe is older than God?"

Skye smiled. "That sort of thing is beyond me." He would not speculate on things that seemed forever beyond understanding.

"Well, I've seen the bones," Mercer said. "Now let's measure them. As it happens, the length of my belt is exactly a yard, and I've marked off feet on the belt. It's my wilderness measure."

He pulled the belt from its loops. There indeed, on its interior side, were foot markers, and half-foot markers, and a set of six inches marked in some sort of ink or dye.

"How am I going to record all this when I lack so much as paper and pencil?" he asked.

It was a good question.

"I will bring your robe. We will put the marks on the robe," Mary said. The Shoshone was dealing with the bones a lot more easily than Victoria, who turned tight and silent and maybe angry.

Skye watched Mary head back to the travois. But Mercer was already heading for that giant skull.

"I say, Skye, I owe you an apology. I didn't imagine these bones could be real. Just a mystery or some madman's art. Not something that taxes my limited grasp geology. Not something that turns my world, my theology, my universe inside out. I'm glad you brought me here."

That was the thing about Mercer. He was always redeeming himself. Skye nodded and smiled.

Mercer crawled up on the shelf and began measuring. Victoria looked ready to explode. He ran his belt over the skull and finally pronounced his verdict: "Six feet four inches from the extremities." Then he measured the eye socket. "Over a foot. No make that fifteen inches." And then he measured the largest of the exposed teeth. "Can you imagine it? Eleven inches or so!"

Mary returned with the robe, some reed paintbrushes, and the small sack of ochre grease paint. These she handed to Victoria. "I do not know how to make the marks," she said.

"Don't give it to me," Victoria snarled. The explosion was so dark and pained that Skye and the men paused.

"We'll be leaving directly, Victoria," Skye said. "We will be very respectful and do no harm."

Victoria sullenly turned her back on him. Skye had never seen her in such a state, and it worried him.

"Oh, not quite that fast, Mister Skye," Mercer said. "I'll

want some sketches. Blast it for not having paper. But I'll do what I can on the back of the robe. What else can a man do?"

Mercer laid the robe, hairy side down, directly on the bones and began the slow process of painting line drawings of what he saw. There was little room left on the robe, which now was filled with stick figures and pictographs. Mary cheerfully helped him but Victoria stormed away.

Skye saw the depth of her anguish and headed her direction, catching her at last well out of earshot of the others.

"He will doom us," she said. "He has no respect."

Skye didn't argue.

"That is the Mother of my people. That is the great bird that came out of the heavens and gave birth to my people. That is the bird the ancient ones, the storytellers, speak of. We are the people of the great black bird. And whoever touches those bones will perish."

Skye didn't believe the legend. It was ingrained deeply in her very soul but he could not share it with her.

"You and I have not touched the bones or shown them disrespect," he said.

"But Mary has! And so have the white men."

"What will happen, Victoria? What does the legend of the Absaroka say?"

"We should not even be here. We should not even approach these bones without a purifying. A sweat and the smoke of sweetgrass and gifts to the spirits. You saw the gifts as we came here, bundles given to this spirit. The spirits of these birds are here. They are offended. Now we will perish, all of us, and I am at fault. I brought you here. I am a daughter of the People, a daughter of these ancient ones. They are my fathers and my grandfathers."

Tears filled her eyes.

"I'll fetch Mercer and the rest. We'll leave the grandfathers alone, Victoria."

"It is too late."

Skye left her and went back to the bones, now resting in deep and cool shade under the sandstone ledge. Mercer was busy painting ribs and vertebrae.

"I don't know what half these bones are," he said. "How am I going to persuade anyone I ever saw them? London is a city of skeptics. The Royal Society is a body of squinting old men."

"Time for us to leave, Mister Mercer. This is a holy place."

"Leave! I just got here. I don't have much to dig with, but I'm going to take a tooth. That'll shake a few timbers."